DEVIANT STORM

THE PURGATORY REIGN SERIES
BOOK 2

BY

LM. PRESTON

CONTENTS

COPYRIGHT

Copyright © 2015 by LM Preston
All rights reserved.
ISBN -13: 978-0-9969195-1-7
ISBN-10: 0-9969195-1-1

Cover Design by Emma Michaels. All Rights Reserved.
Front Matter Design and Formatting by Stephany Wallace.
All Rights Reserved.

A Phenomenal One Press publication 2015
www.phenomenalonepress.com

SYPNOSIS

The battle is on. Peter Saints thought he'd killed It. But bad people never stay down. Now the jail of his enemy is weakening. Luck is running out for Peter and the girl he saved by wagering the Earth. Only now, with each second and secret revealed, his enemy gains the answers to destroy Peter and devour the world.

ALSO BY L.M. PRESTON

PURGATORY REIGN SERIES

Purgatory Reign, Book 1

Deviant Storm, Book 2

Fierce Tides, Book 3

THE PACK SERIES

The Pack, Book 1

Retribution, Book 2

THE BANDITS SERIES

Bandits, Book 1

Wastelands, Book 2

DEDICATION

For my children and my husband, who helped me dream the impossible and gave me the support to achieve it. To my husband who wrote a short story for a class that I dug out of a box, and read to be inspired to create this great adventure.

ACKNOWLEDGMENTS

Thanks to God for giving me this anxious energy to create and tenacious spirit of positivity with an active imagination. To my devoted Beta Readers, Jordan, Missy and my daughter, who helped me create a better story. To my husband, who created the basis and inspiration for this story. To my editor, Cindy Davis, who's been my best support in my art. To my kids and my husband, who continue to give me true and honest feedback for all of my work. I thank you.

CHAPTER 1

He screwed up. So bad, he didn't think he could fix it. Peter tossed the ball against the wall once more to out Kyle's words. He'd never admitted everything that had happened to him in the Stronghold to Kyle. Didn't think he could. One thing was for sure, time was up. Peter was through waiting to be told what to do by the Elders of this dump who seemed to have their own agendas. Dealing with the nightmares of what he'd done - possibly killing a man by pulling something beyond evil out of him - plagued Peter every night. Those times when he wasn't careful, it pressed his thoughts, even when awake.

"We'll go get her." Peter's dark brown eyes landed on Kyle's questioning blue ones. A flutter of the pale face and dark hair of the girl he'd lost flickered in his mind like a jumping flame.

Kyle's foot was tapping the floor beneath the bed across from Peter as though he was waiting for something. The dingy room they shared with the kiss-up kid, Gil, was inside a place called a Sanctuary, considered a safe house to the Decretum Venia or The Order Of Grace. Peter didn't feel safe, no matter how much Gil tried to help them adjust by introducing them to kids Peter didn't want to get to know. After what he'd survived, he'd never feel 'safe' again. The place was only a few beats up from as livable as the orphanage he grew up in. The wallpaper was torn. The place smelled like cedar scented mothballs mixed with the musk of too many kids and not enough showers. But he was used to it.

"About time you stopped feeling sorry for yourself and decided to do it our old way." Kyle's voice was deep but joking as he intercepted Peter's ball before it hit the yellowed flowered-print wall. "Being here isn't helping us at all. It's not going to get you and Angel back together either."

Peter got off the bottom bunk he shared with Gil. "Did you tell Gil to find that door?"

"I'm reading your mind." Kyle grinned, tapping the side of his forehead with his middle finger. "He's creating a bit of a diversion to get us out this stink hole." Kyle took a cursory look around. "I can't believe you said this place was better than where you grew up? This place sucks, and I'm not saying that just because I grew up with a silver spoon in my mouth." He sniffed the air. "It really sucks."

"Shut up, diva." Peter reached under the bed, pulled out his backpack and adjusted it.

"I'm not a diva, more like a playa. You know what I mean?" Kyle smoothed his hand over his blond crew cut.

"Man, you confused or what? You ain't even been in the game. All these girls upstairs and you can't convince one of them to give you the time of day." Peter slid his hand under the pillow and pulled out a picture of Angel. He stuffed it in his back pocket.

"Can I ask you something?" Kyle shrugged on his own bag.

Peter slid open the door and peered outside, spotting Gil jogging down the long deserted hallway. "What?"

"What spooked you that last time we went out? After that, you didn't go outside with us anymore." Kyle came up beside him. "Actually you acted like the true bastard I knew you could be by threatening to kick my butt – like you could." Kyle smacked his teeth.

"Because I don't wanna face what I know is waiting for me out there. Not with you two anyway." Peter wouldn't admit to Kyle all that he'd unleashed the day they opened the Stronghold of the Decretum Venia. Saving Angel's life seemed like the right thing to do. But it came with a price. All he knew was the guilt he felt before that fateful day didn't begin to touch what he felt now. Peter also didn't want Kyle to know he'd gone out, many times, without them. Every time, he ran back, afraid of leading what followed him to the only protected place he'd known of in the last few months. He hoped he wasn't too late to fix the damage that loving Angel had caused.

Gil rushed into the room, practically knocking Peter backwards. "I, uh, the diversion might not last too long." He scratched his thick wool-like hair. His afro sat on his head like a hat since he'd let Kyle shave the sides on a dare.

"What the hell is that supposed to mean?" Peter shook his head and pushed Gil out of the way.

Gil's hand jutted out to stop him. "Some big shot is here, checking out the guys on the upper floor. It's bad." Gil scratched harder through his thick hair. "Real bad. They have a guard in front of our getaway exit."

Peter narrowed his gaze at Kyle. "Your idea to bring another fool into our pile of -"

"Shh! Listen, I got an idea," Gil spoke up.

"Naw, I'm not listening to your idea." Peter pointed at Kyle. "Or you. Let's go, before I change my mind and leave both of you behind."

Kyle walked quickly beside him down the long dingy hallway strewn with trash and dust balls. "Gil will be some help, he's got skills."

"Whatever. I hope enough to keep him alive." Peter cut a

glance at Kyle. "You know what we're dealing with and I don't think he'll survive it. I heard he's been here since he was a baby."

"Doesn't mean he wants to stay here," Kyle replied.

Peter shook his head. He'd never learned to just leave people. Some weakness within him secretly wanted Kyle and others to travel the treacherous road ahead. If he was honest about it, being alone to deal with what was to come scared the hell out him. Bringing them could possibly mean their deaths – even his. Funny how he thought opening up that *book* meant he would be saved, that Angel would be protected. Now no one, not one person on Earth, could live through what faced them. And it was all because of his choice.

The labs were up one level. It was their only way out and didn't include them going through the tunnel Gil had planned as their initial getaway. He was done hiding. Something wasn't right in this facility, and they didn't have time to find out what. Peter tapped the wall under a picture of some guy holding a golden scepter, pointing towards the light from the moon. A small key panel flopped down and Peter punched in the code he'd seen one of the teachers use the other night. Most of the kids didn't know about this exit. The only way they'd been transported was on the elevators. A small vibration on the keypad confirmed his entry and a door opened inward, smoothly separating at the creases of the cracked walls. The others' footsteps were light behind him as he took the stairway up several levels. He was glad the other kids in the orphanage were in class, something he and Kyle ditched regularly.

"What are you doing? Why are we going towards the Elders?" Gil whispered urgently. "Don't you want to get out of here?"

"Shut up! I know the way out. The lab has a back entrance. I've been taking stuff from there for the last few weeks since leaving's been on my mind. They lied to us. No one has done anything to move us to the Sanctuary holding Angel. Just follow me and we'll be out of here." Peter frowned.

Elders—that's what the men who ran this facility called themselves. Pastor Finn had never treated him or the kids in the orphanage the way these guys did. He felt like he was in jail. But for some reason, he knew they considered him and Kyle like some anomaly they had to unlock.

The stairway seemed to go on forever. Definitely more than just a few floors. "Listen up...if anything happens, just leave me, run until you get to that place we went to when I snuck out with you." Peter knew they would remember. It was the only time he'd left the premises with them. It was when he realized his nightmare wouldn't go away just because he was in a safe place. As soon as he left this Sanctuary, the monsters that were after him would know it.

Peter stopped. A slight creak from above alerted that there was someone in their path. He put up a hand to still the others, and frowned at Gil who was about to speak in spite of the warning. On softer feet, Peter walked up several steps. A man dressed casually in khaki pants and a shirt was coming down. Peter would've let the guy go, except he had a gun drawn and a holster on his hip. He knew then, the idea of a quick, painless escape was impossible.

Peter rushed up to meet the surprised guy. Before the man could react, Peter grabbed his wrist, then the hand holding the gun. With a yank, and a push to the back of the man's head, Peter knocked the guy out. He snatched the gun and motioned to the others to follow. Stepping over the guy, he expelled an irritated breath at Gil who seemed to be in shock.

Peter grabbed a stunned Gil by the shirt and slit his angry eyes at Kyle. Bringing this kid with them was a bad idea. Peter knew it, but Kyle apparently didn't care. Gil's jaw dropped and he stuck his hand in it to stop from crying out. Kyle just shrugged and kicked at the man's leg that was slumped unconscious on the stairs.

Peter stuffed the gun in his jeans pocket and adjusted the backpack. He never liked doing this. Just thinking back to the days he was at the old orphanage filled him with regret. However, that wasn't the first time he'd had to fight for his life. Them or him. And with all he'd been through, he'd fight to be with Angel again.

Slowly he opened the door at the top of the stairs, it didn't creek but made a slight groan. Peter held his breath and slid a glance into the hallway ahead. It was clear; he released the air he'd held in and waved at the others to follow. After a few steps, a heated conversation echoed from further down the hall. Sweat beaded on his face as he searched around for a spot to lay low. A janitor's closet was just up ahead and Peter quickly made his way to it. Voices deep and stern were arguing, getting closer. Once he slid inside the janitor's closet, Peter waited 'til Kyle and Gil were safely with him before closing it.

"That was close," Kyle whispered next to him.

"Too close. Be quiet, they're coming." Peter leaned into the small crack between the door and the wall. Outside, the two men stopped out of sight. Peter's lips thinned, he wanted to see them. Hoping they weren't heading to the stairwell, he turned slightly, catching the profile of one of the men. Tall, dark hair, glasses, and appearing angry.

"I don't care what the Order says, Decretum Venia has got to look to the future," the man stated with his deep, forceful voice.

"The boys were brought here after the incident. We're supposed to be protecting them! I can't be a part of this," Mr. Boswell, the elder who managed the Sanctuary, seemed to plead.

"I want to meet this Peter Saints. After that, we're moving him to a facility the Order doesn't know about. Testing his blood and what changed in it will give us the power to control the outcome of the prophecy. Saving the world should no longer be our concern. Doing so has cost all of us the lives of our loved ones, and I'm not willing to risk another person I care about for the cause of the

Decretum Venia's Elders, who want to run and hide. I want mankind to suffer the wrath they begged for centuries ago. Why should we protect them?"

"It is our calling," Mr. Boswell emphatically defended.

"It was never mine. I'd bet this Peter kid would agree with me. He's the one they speak of, the one who's warned the Decretum Venia about the evil one who's been killing our members to a pitiful number."

"Yes he is, but what you're asking me to do will hurt so many people. Even though initially I agreed to let you take him, I see now I made a mistake. I c-can't be a part of this, Dr. Phillips. It's wrong. I made a promise to the boy's former keeper." The shorter man pivoted away.

"It is your choice," Dr. Phillips whispered, and in an instant snapped the neck of the shorter guy.

Peter shuddered as the man searched around the hallway then lifted the other man over his shoulder. With a final adjustment of the limp body, the guy hurried into the room across from them.

"Let's go! Don't stop until we get to the exit door at the end of the hall." Peter rushed them out of the door. He made his way down the hall and slipped into the lab office. "Duck down." He motioned for them to walk low on the outer side of the half wall framing the large glass observation area of the lab. The place was used to carbon date old doctrines found by the Decretum Venia. His hand burned, the palm that was imprinted with a scar left from a girl named Hanna. It throbbed as a warning he'd grown used to ignoring.

Footsteps fell in the outer hall. Peter willed his hand to stop shaking as he entered the password to open the exit door to another service elevator. Pressing in the combination, he forced himself to stay calm. He had no choice but to get them out of there. The elevator opened. Still crouching, he entered, waiting for the others to follow. When the door finally closed, he stood up.

"What the hell was that about?" Kyle leaned on the back wall of the elevator, breathing heavily.

"I don't know, but Gil was right. It's bad, real bad. And I'm not stickin' around to find out. When this door opens, run into the trees. Then we'll figure out how to get to Pastor Finn. He'll know where Angelica is, and I hope have some answers on what the screw-up is with the Decretum Venia and where I fit in this." Peter pushed the Lock button on the elevator...to hold the door open, he guessed, when they were bringing in large items. The hallway with cement walls had a little light from the exit sign at the end. He sprinted to the ladder that led to a ceiling trap door.

"When did you find this place?" Kyle followed Peter up the ladder.

"The times you and Gil snuck out, I investigated every part of this place I could because whether the Decretum Venia wanted me to leave or not, I knew one day I would." Peter pushed open the ceiling door. The smell of fresh air mixed with dirt assaulted him. It brought him some pleasure and a bit of apprehension. This was it, no turning back. He climbed out of the hole and was glad for the cover of darkness that met them. They'd gotten away —this time.

CHAPTER 2

G avin Steele felt the warmth, stickiness, and ripples in the blood, but it did nothing to soothe him, to feed the addiction to pain he'd experienced for what had seemed like an eternity. The emptiness was overwhelming; the Master had left him. There would be a price to pay for this and Peter Saints would pay it. Gavin Steele only hoped his weakling of a brother was able to do what needed to be done to place the Master's essence back within him. Without it, he would never rise out of that horrid, deathlike coma that had held him prisoner for months on end. He'd forever remember the dark skin and glowing eyes of the one who'd caused that frozen death-state. When Peter Saints dislodged the master's demon form from Gavin's body, it almost ripped the only sliver of sanity and peace from him too.

He suspected his brother and the leaders of the Order of the Dragon had covered his mouth, but they'd kept him alive for the duration of the rather dangerous ritual. The air he breathed came through a tube that slithered forward and back again, pumping oxygen into his lungs. He didn't know for sure all they'd done to keep him alive, but the tube and the blood were part of it. He tried to mentally focus on that, for it was the only way of finding any peace. His mind grabbed for any sound, movement, or repetition in an attempt to self-hypnotize, to find some relief from the constant mental numbness, the utter helplessness that had consumed his mind, body, and soul.

Muffled voices grew louder, clearer with each passing second. Soon, Gavin recognized one: Lucien had taken over the gift intended for Gavin. The master, having nowhere else to hide, had been placed close to Lucien. It was a weaker version of itself but still a strong enough resemblance to influence its human slaves. The master didn't belong there though; it belonged within Gavin. Gavin had been born for it. He'd killed their father for it, and the dreams had come to him first.

"The Master wants Gavin!" Lucien screamed. "Do whatever it takes to get this thing back in him or Gavin will never wake up. I w-want it out of my head. Th-the whispering, the voices, they don't stop," a sob escaped Lucien's lips, "ever. Ever stop. Gavin is the only one who has the strength to control its army. I c-can't... he's tearing me apart." Lucien sounded exhausted and a bit crazed. Gavin knew it was because Lucien was never strong enough to control the power to decipher the Master's voices building around him. Nor was he conditioned to tolerate the amount of physical torture holding the being captive required. Lucien was made to serve Gavin, not the Master.

"I will do my best. I've already cocooned him in the blood of innocence. Now there will have to be a final sacrifice to make it so. The pool of blood he's in will lose its potency if we aren't successful this time," a woman responded.

Gavin suspected it was Mara, the queen witch of the Order of the Dragon, known as the Extraho of Obscurum. She, and only she, had enough power to control the demons—foul and powerful entities that were strong enough to be seen or inhabit a human host.

In the next second, Gavin heard wrestling and screams coming from a young boy. He assumed the child had the gift of second sight or that he was slightly psychic, as such were useful when it came to tying demons and humans together. When held in a psychic trance and killed, their blood was a most potent channel for the evil ones to travel to the plane of Earth that was usually inhabited my mere mortals. *Finally*, Gavin thought. *This will work, and I will finally, finally be free.*

"I was happy to deliver the gift that will reunite the chosen one with the demon master, Balaal," a deep and sure voice stated.

Gavin knew that voice, it belonged to one of his leaders—Jack. Like him, Jack had been groomed by his parents to lead the Extraho of Obscurum to power, but Gavin was the one who received the dreams first. The dreams of a powerful creation, one that would allow his demon master and his warriors to cross the planes of time and space to take war to the heavens while draped in the souls of their human host. Because of his early connection to the demonic ones, the witches of the order gifted him with the connection.

"The boy struggles too much!" the witch yelled, frustrated.

"Should I silence him?" Jack asked softly.

"No, he must be awake, in a trance, and experience the terror of the sacrificial knife. Come closer, place him on the pedestal."

"I've got him," Jack assured.

"Good. Shh now. This is a great honor to your family. Look at me, small one, into my eyes, and find your peace there," Mara repeated in a singsong, almost hypnotic way.

Finally, the boy's fighting subsided.

"You did it. He's there now, tranced." Jack sounded almost greedy.

"Now, lift the knife, and I'll bring him slowly to the surface of reality," she snapped.

Within minutes, a bloodcurdling scream resounded through

the room. The ground shook and the warm vat of blood Gavin was submerged in shifted, bubbled, and then heated. Excruciating fire traveled up his legs to his groin and chest. His body lifted up, up, out of the warmth of the blood, the oxygen mask ripped away and some invisible force pried open his mouth.

Flashes of all of his past victims, the countless women who'd been sacrificed and mutilated by his hand, all in the name of the master, pleasured him. The nightmarish torture he'd sustained in his hellish prison, while the master completely controlled his body, beckoned to him like a siren's song, but Gavin fought it. When the master entered his body this time, Gavin was determined to stay there too. He was stronger now, much stronger than he'd been before he tasted the blood of Peter Saints—far mightier than the dimmed essence of the master that Peter Saints had left behind. Now, Gavin would rule the power Peter's blood revealed, along with his master.

Gavin fought the pleasure and pain of being burned alive, of skin ripping, tearing, and being cut and bitten. Bones appeared to break and reset while the sensation of hooks piercing his most sensitive body parts kept him fighting. His anger boiled and built as one face loomed constantly in his mind, the face of Peter Saints. He reveled in thoughts of the things he would do to the boy when given the chance.

A huge weight pressed on his skin, through his ribs, into Gavin's mouth. "Ahhh!" The yell burst forth. He held back the gag, the vomit, of being consumed by the slippery cutting force of the demon master, Balaal.

"It's working! It's working!" Lucien cried, relief flooding his voice. "He's left me! I'm no longer...haunted."

Gavin heard Lucien's cry. The disgust Balaal felt filled him at the same time his body was being sliced from the inside out. No place was untouched from the stabbing of the claws Balaal used to secure himself within Gavin's body. Pleasure, satisfaction, and harmony of a satisfied addiction had returned. At that moment, that very moment, Gavin knew he and Balaal had become one.

While Gavin's body still levitated with the dampness of the blood of innocence, he screamed, "Peter...Peter Saints is mine!"

CHAPTER 3

Peter's chest throbbed. His side was aching and his arms hurt, but he kept running. The footfalls behind him didn't relent; the others trailed him as if their lives depended on it. After witnessing what he had, back at the sanctuary, he didn't blame them. What happened there went beyond all he thought about the Order of Grace or the Decretum Venia. *Murder isn't supposed to happen at a sanctuary...or is it?* The heinous things he'd experienced as a child, living at Pastor Finn's orphanage, had kept him from feeling safe around the other kids, products of parents involved within the Order. So why wasn't he surprised? Maybe because after he'd learned about the origins of the Decretum Venia and its purpose, he expected the angels to pick a more faithful race to protect their secrets.

The soft cushion of grass padded his pounding feet 'til they made it through the thicket of trees that bordered the acres of property they'd run through to get to the city. They eventually made it to the woods that bordered the highway. Virginia was where they'd taken him after he and Angel had gone to Pastor Finn's suggested meeting place to discuss what they'd witnessed with the Decretum Venia. At the so-called sanctuary, Angel had been snatched right out of his arms. They said they wanted to talk to her alone, and only later did he discover she'd been taken to another facility where she would presumably be protected from the Order of the Dragon. Now, he had his doubts about that; for all he knew, it was all just part of some plan to separate them from one another. For some reason, they didn't think Kyle was of any use, but that gave Kyle plenty of cover to move about and hide without being suspected of anything. They had lied to Peter, told him he was being kept there for his own protection, but it felt like they were just holding him there until they figured out what he'd done, how he'd done it, and what impact it would ultimately have on the Decretum Venia.

"The subway station! Up about a mile." Kyle sprinted past Peter. "Follow me."

Ahead, a girl was sprinting towards them, coming from the break in the trees. "Where'd the hell she come from?" Peter slowed.

Gil appeared guilty. "I told Chloe I'd give her a way out if she helped me divert the guys who paid us a visit."

Peter shook his head. Chloe was the quiet type, and she didn't say much to anyone. Under other circumstances, he didn't mind her being around, hanging out in their room to play cards to pass the time. Nevertheless, he was angry at Gil for making promises. Peter had no intention of leading Chloe to safety, as the place where they were going was much worse than the one they'd just left. His jaw clenched at the thought, and he slowed to a gait behind Kyle just as the girl caught up to them.

"You made it!" Chloe ran into Gil's arms, her tan skin glistening against his darker complexion.

"Seriously? You've got to be kidding me, man? Why didn't you tell them what we're up against?" Peter tapped Kyle's arm with his fist.

"I didn't know Gil had help. We needed him to get out. I'm

good, but not that good." Kyle's cocky grin was a cover-up from the brief glimmer of worry captured in his features.

Peter stepped forward, breaking the couple apart by slicing his hand in between them. "What is she doing here?" His eyes slanted to Chloe.

"Like I said, I needed her help. When I went upstairs to get the other kids hyped up over some stupid bet I made to create the diversion you asked for, a bunch of men and guards came through the door with Mr. Maxwell. They ordered all the kids to go to the lunchroom and line up. Something didn't feel right, so I grabbed Chloe and told her to get out, to meet us here, at the break in the trees, where we come to be alone sometimes."

Kyle frowned. "This is your girlfriend? You never told me. I would've let you bring her."

Peter cleared his throat. "I would *not* have." He pivoted towards Gil. "Did Kyle clue you in on why we were there at that Sanctuary in the first place?" Peter stepped forward, face-to-face with Gil. "Well, I killed a girl," he whispered clearly.

Gil gulped. "Y-you what?" His eyes widened.

"Not with my hands, but by my actions. And she gave me a... gift." Peter shuddered, thinking back to the day he'd tried to ditch Hanna by running across the street—the girl followed only to get hit by a car and die in his arms. "The gift she gave me released something in my blood that can unlock the secrets of the Decretum Venia and how they came to be. But with exposing it, I've given our enemy the power and knowledge to destroy us." His eyes fell on Chloe. "All of us." The right hand that had the mark— red and slightly raised—that was left by Hanna—throbbed, heated, and felt as if a worm of electricity moved within it.

Chloe's hand went to her mouth. "You mean you're the one they were talking about? The boy who caused the Decretum Venia to go into lockdown? Before Gil came into the room, we were told we all were in greater danger, more than ever before. He said that one of us—a special child—had been used by evil forces to reveal our hiding places. That all the work done to keep the few surviving children of the Decretum Venia could be lost." Her hand shook as Gil grasped it. "My parents placed me there. They told me I'd be safe, but I never believed them after my brother had been abducted on his way home from school."

Kyle crossed his arms in front of him. "Did they bother to tell you that the Order of the Dragon has been taking kids for the last few decades?"

"Not exactly," her eyes appeared haunted, "but I'd been studying and researching every missing kid story since my brother was taken five years ago."

"Let's move." The hairs on Peter's neck rose for no apparent reason. He darted his eyes around but saw no sign of anyone. It was late, and the only sounds he heard were the sleepy chirps of crickets and the occasional whisper of the wind. There was a definite autumn chill in the air, but that couldn't explain the coldness he suddenly felt.

Peter led them through the trees and to the deserted sidewalk leading to the subway station he and Kyle had memorized when they were taken to this last Sanctuary.

"So, wait." Chloe touched Peter's shoulder.

Peter didn't slow down; he couldn't, not until he got to Angel. He had to find her. The last six months had been unbearable, but his fear and hope for help had held him at the Sanctuary much longer than he'd planned.

Chloe's grip tightened. "Do you know about the missing kids? Why they were taken—is it because of you?"

Peter shrugged her dainty hand off his shoulder. "Yeah...no...maybe," he grunted. "Hell, I don't know."

Kyle chimed in, "The Order of the Dragon was stealing kids,

taking them and draining their blood, to find out what we've been hiding. The Decretum Venia had secrets, many of them, and they protected the locations of all the sanctuaries—not only the ones where we were, but others, special ones, elite hiding places for the Decretum Venia history..." Kyle's voice wandered off, almost giving away the secret he was keeping, the one he and Peter had promised to tell no one. "Secrets that Gavin Steele of Steele Industries wants to have. The problem is, he has to drain our blood to get them."

"You mean it's possible the people who kidnapped my brother may be saving him to drain his blood?" Chloe asked, her voice trembling and her eyes wide with horror.

Peter's eyes shuttered closed a moment, thinking back to the fear and helplessness that gripped him when Gavin had stolen Angel. "Doubtful they saved him. Gavin and his brother—they like to kill. And even though saving the kids' lives until they're eighteen would benefit them, they have this...homicidal urge to seldom let them live that long."

Chloe grabbed at Peter's shirt and pulled him around to face her tear-filled eyes. "And you? What did you do?"

"I ticked them off by fighting back and taking something out of Gavin." Peter's muscles underneath her fingers tightened. He stood over two feet taller than the girl, but her will was strong, her eyes nailed his.

"What? What could you take out of someone's body without stabbing them? Or killing them?"

"A demon." Peter blurted and there was shocked silence from Chloe and Gil.

Chloe and Gil looked at him in stunned silence for a moment before she stepped back from him. "Uh..." she said.

"Look, I know you want to come with us, but I can't promise you'll survive or that any of us will. You have a choice. You can go back to the sanctuary we just left or be ready for whatever comes, but right now, I'm done talking. We've gotta move." With that, Peter pivoted away from her stricken features, straightened his shoulders, and started walking down the street.

The wind picked up, and one streetlight flickered on and off. The deserted office buildings seemed to rattle as leaves and small rocks smacked against their windows in the gusts and chilly drafts, but Peter paid them no mind. All he could see, all he could think of, was Angel. Finding her was the only way to heal his heart, to feel whole again. He had to know that he'd kept his promise, that he had kept her safe, and no one would get in the way of that again.

They'd made it to the subway station just in time for the last train. Peter sat a few seats up from the others. He just watched the lights pass as the train flew down the underground tracks. He couldn't shake that feeling—the vibe he'd been carrying with him for as long as he could remember: guilt. So much of the rotting ache that didn't seem to be going away no matter how hard he tried to bury it. On top of that—he was pissed off to be in this position. Most of it nothing he could've controlled, it just was the mess of a life he'd been dropped in. Now he just had to deal with it. His throbbing palm drew his attention. It always did, even though he tried to ignore it. He studied it like he had a million times before. And it didn't change the piercing in his heart when Peter remembered how he felt when he held Hanna's broken body in his arms. He'd felt like scum.

Death. So much death, and all because of me. Peter thought the worst thing he'd ever experienced was watching his father's body float away in the car his mother dragged him out of. It paled in comparison to seeing his mother shot down as she tried to protect him, placing herself as a barricade between him and some of the hitmen the Order Of the Dragon had sent to kidnap him. Still, even with all the death he'd seen in his first seven years of life, Hanna's was the beginning of something much worse.

"Stop, dude." Kyle smacked the back of Peter's head. "The tortured moping is killing me, all this emo bullshit. Snap out of it, would ya? We survived, remember."

"Yeah, but at what price?" Peter raked a brown hand through his curly black hair. "The Decretum Venia was supposed to have answers for us. They were supposed to help us bring down that machine Steele Industries is building. Instead, they kept us in hiding, interrogated us, blamed us for putting everyone in danger." Peter didn't try to hide the disgust from his voice. It vibrated through him. His disappointment in the Decretum Venia and in himself boiled over.

"Hey, it seems like hiding is what they do. They've been doing it for centuries. They never were supposed to reveal themselves or their secrets." Kyle placed his hand on Peter's shoulder. "But you, my friend, shed the light on some bull-crap they weren't prepared for. Now we have to fix it. We'll get Angel, then end it like we started it, just the three of us."

Peter shrugged Kyle's hand off him. "The *three* of us? You were never supposed to be part of the plan, you or her, but I haven't been able to get rid of you. Now you wanna act like the freaking Three Musketeers and save the world from demonic destruction and the heavens from a demon invasion?" Peter snorted. "You've been sneaking the wine from the cellar, haven't you?"

Kyle chuckled. "Nope. You know I gave up that stuff after watching you die and come back to life as a badass, demon-killing fool." Kyle came around and plopped down beside Peter. "It made a believer out of me. A believer in good. In evil. And the Decretum Venia."

"What's to believe? I haven't been impressed."

"I have. You've done for me what my father never could. Surviving with you and Angel showed me that we do hold the power. And that I don't have to be a full-blooded descendant of the Decretum Venia to make a difference. To save myself."

Peter knew what Kyle was up to, just feeding him the line of hero crap to rile him up and get him over the vegetative funk he'd been in since Angel had been taken. He wiped his throbbing hand down his face. "I don't think we can do this. Gavin was... Man, he was just the beginning. That machine is still there. His brother and all of them in that house had a purpose. Even killing Gavin wouldn't stop them."

Kyle nodded. "True, but we can. And we don't have to go in like gang-bangers to do it. We have to do what we do best."

"And what's that?"

"Sneak in."

Peter smiled. "Yeah, we're good at that. But Gil and Chloe, what's up with bringing them? They'll die with us out here. They, at least, had a chance at the Sanctuary."

"Maybe, but all those prayers and herbs they use to keep the Extraho of Obscurum bastards away don't do much good for those sickos in the Decretum Venia. Just because a person supports a cause or is born to protect the world, that doesn't mean they aren't a bit loony. That guy killed Mr. Boswell , the head of the sanctuary. That's proof that the face of good isn't always the way it seems."

"Whoa! Words of wisdom coming from a former pot-head and drug dealer, I'm speechless," Peter chided.

"Why do you always have to throw my past in my face? Are you just trying to make yourself feel better?" Kyle laughed. "But whatever, man. As long as it gets you out of this pity party and puts your big head back in the game."

"You coachin' me now?" Peter rolled his eyes. "I should've left your ass behind at that carnival, you've been a pain ever since."

"Not a chance! I wasn't letting you leave me in that stink hole."

A voice came over the intercom, "Last stop. Everyone off the train."

Peter cracked his neck. "And so it begins," he said with a smirk.

CHAPTER 4

Peter led them up the halted escalator, taking two steps at a time. The chilly night air hit his face as the bright yellow moon cast a glow on the semi-deserted parking lot of the subway station. There were no buses, cabs, or bikes, no sign of travelers or pedestrians, other than a few parked cars scattered about.

Peter figured they could walk the streets in the direction of the orphanage but it was on the other side of town. There was no way to get to Pastor Finn's Orphanage this late.

His eyes wandered over the others and noticed their fatigue. Peter was tired too, and the truth was, part of him was too wary to continue tonight. "We'll sleep in the subway station until daylight." Peter turned back towards the entrance.

Wheels screeched.

"Damn! Someone's on us." Kyle grabbed his backpack off the ground.

"Split up!" Peter sidestepped the black car that sped up alongside him. Looking at it was a mistake.

The driver was pointing a gun out the window. "Get in and I'll let you and your friends live."

The instant Peter slowed down, his eyes caught the glimmer of something climbing out of the car and onto the hood. The black, ashy demon hissed at him, revealing jagged, pointed teeth and glaring at him with sunken eyes filled with fire.

Peter stepped back. The mark on his palm throbbed and warmed. Stumbling a bit, he dodged the car as it spun around him. Blocking him, here and then there. Toying with him, the guy tapped him with the front of the car, then spun circles around him.

He released a hideous laugh, and the sneer on his face matched the one the demon was wearing. "We waited here, got a tip that you and some others would come out to play," he taunted, waving the gun back and forth as he slowed the car to do lazy circles around Peter to trap him.

"A tip? What are you talking about? You don't know me." Peter hoped the guy really didn't know him. But from the looks of it, his demon puppet master did.

"Funny. Real funny." The guy squinted at him. "You're Peter Saints, of course."

A snake of electrical power burst from Peter's marked hand and course through his entire body, an awakening of the change that had taken place when he'd unleashed the unthinkable secret, the reason why Gavin Steele wanted him.

Standing still, Peter calmly replied, "I don't know who you're talking about. I'm just some black kid on my way home from a party, hoofin' it 'cause I missed my bus. There are lots of us, and I'm not your guy."

The demon on top of the car opened its mouth to four times the width.

"Stop lying!" the driver screamed, skidding the car to a halt. "I'll shoot you right here and take your bleeding body back with me!"

Before Peter could react, the guy pulled the trigger.

In an instant, Kyle's face popped up in the window from the other side of the car. He shot at the guy's head. It snapped to the side, knocking the guy unconscious. Blood slid down his face. The demon on the roof disappeared.

Angry and shaken, Peter stood there.

"Trying to live here! Let's go. Fast...before they call backup or something. Or the guy wakes up."

Shaking the daze out of his head, Peter wiped his trembling palm on his jeans, and willed the energy within him to retract back to where it came from. "Yeah, where are the others?"

"Around the corner, I think." Kyle glanced at the unconscious guy and snatched the weapon from the seat.

Peter nodded and they ran in the direction of some shouting. Within minutes they slid to a stop in front of a chaotic scene. Gil lay flat on the ground being beaten by a slender man, while Chloe was kicking and screaming at another who was trying to stuff her in the trunk of a black car.

Peter knocked the guy off of Chloe, but the familiar burning sensation on his palm distracted him long enough for the man to elbow him in the face. Peter stumbled back, glancing up at two ash-bodied demons. They resembled human men with ashen tipped horns and glowing yellow eye sockets. The man, flanked by the demons on either side, was kneeling down, as if preparing to run. The larger of the two demons grabbed the man by the hair and yanked him up, and he glared at Peter with loathing.

Before Peter could react, Kyle shot the guy in the stomach. But the man didn't flinch. Instead, his demon puppet master mouthed a silent command, as if he was speaking to a trained dog.

The fire in Peter's palm burst through his veins. Peter shouted then waved his hand. Spikes resembling lightning burst forth from his palm. With a single swing he sliced through one of the ashen demons.

Kyle jumped the guy from behind, but part of his arm passed through the remaining demon.

Peter didn't falter as he wielded the spiked lasso of power once more to cut the remaining demon through the back as it attempted to dissipate.

Gil's scream echoed through the empty lot as the car sped off. "They got her!" he said, pointing.

The car sped off with Chloe attempting to get out of the trunk. The car's momentum slammed the lid closed with her inside.

Gil and Kyle chased after the car. Peter shook his head to erase the daze and ran after them. By the time he'd caught up to the others, the car was out of sight. Gil swore, crying out with tortured expression on his face.

"She's gone," he coughed, then slumped to the ground on his knees. Tears ran down his face. "Gone."

Peter's chest hurt. *Dammit,* he silently raged. *I knew this would happen, that Gavin's guys would be on to us and that demons would come.* Still, selfishly and weakly, he had allowed Gil and Chloe to come with him. "I'm sorry."

"We have to go after her. We have to!" Gil lamented. "We have to save her!"

Kyle wiped a hand down his face. "We will."

Peter's jaw clenched. "Yeah, but not yet. I know where he's taking her, and we aren't ready to go there yet. I need to get someone first...and some information."

"But they'll kill her!" Gil's sobs vibrated through the air.

"Not right away. They need her blood. She'll live as long as I do," Peter said, though he wasn't sure if it was true. He didn't know what Gavin and the Extraho of Obscurum had planned for their captives. All he knew was that the blood of the Decretum Venia children was useful. He only hoped their patience would hold out until he figured out how to fight them.

"We'd better go." Kyle pivoted and started walking in the opposite direction from where the car had sped off.

As soon as they retrieved their backpacks from the place where they'd dropped them, the three ran, trying to get as far away from the station as possible.

Peter's arms ached, but he kept running, leading the others away from the disaster he'd caused. Gavin's guys would come after him, and it wasn't that difficult for them to sniff him out. Peter wasn't sure if that was because the demon he'd snatched out of Gavin had tasted his blood, or if it was because he'd opened the book that revealed the secrets about the 1,000-year war fought in a slice of time that had been hidden from humanity for centuries. For all Peter knew, it was a little of both. Gavin wanted him because Peter's blood held another secret, and there were still two more books to be found. Peter hated to admit it, but he needed the information in those ancient pages; only those books held the answer to how his angelic ancestors had won the war and what weapons they had used to come out victorious against the demons.

"How much farther?" Gil asked, wheezing again.

"Not much. See that truck at the gas station up there?" Peter pointed. "We'll hitch a ride with him."

"Haven't you seen all those movies about psychotic, homicidal truck drivers, man?" Kyle asked.

Peter just rolled his eyes and walked faster. "Just c'mon. He won't even see us."

At the gas station, Peter cast a glance into the convenience store, where the flannel-clad truck driver was busy buying coffee, Twinkies, and a newspaper. Peter hopped into the back of the truck and slid beneath a large tarp that covered the floor. The other two glanced around nervously, then made their way into the truck and quietly lay beside Peter.

A few minutes later, they heard noise outside the truck. Peter cautiously lifted a corner of the tarp and watched the driver place the gas nozzle back in place. When the man in the John Deere hat climbed in and shut the door, Peter released the breath he'd been holding. He wiped a hand down his face in relief when the truck finally took off, taking them at least a few miles closer to safety and away from Gavin's hunting dogs.

CHAPTER 5

I t was a bumpy ride in the back of the truck, but no one made a sound.

The street signs blurred by and Peter realized they'd have to get out before the guy made another turn. "Hey, when I give the go-ahead, follow me. We're not far." He slipped back the tarp, glad daylight hadn't made an appearance yet.

"Where are we going?" Gil asked, his voice husky and tired.

"To someone I know can help me find Angel, Pastor Finn."

At least he hoped Pastor Finn could help. He had been a father figure to Peter, and he trusted him with his life. The only trouble was that he hadn't heard from the pastor for months. Peter didn't know if the pastor and the other orphans were still at the beat-up old parish he'd practically grown up in. When it came to Angel, Peter's heart had a hole in it, one that was burned open when she was stolen from him. Nevertheless, if he was being honest with himself, he had to admit that their relationship was already falling apart even then. He'd saved her from Gavin – the sick bastard who started this mess, but she had changed during the ordeal. It was subtle at first, but as the days went by, she began to cover her body in her boyish clothes again. Then Angel stopped talking to Peter, stopped seeking him out, and sneaking into his bed the way she had before to get through the nightmares they both shared.

As the street signs blew by, Peter read every one of them, relying on his memory to help determine the best place to jump off. He tried to concentrate on the present, but a flash of a nightmare caused him to flinch, the memory of seeing Angel tied to an altar, with a rag stuffed in her mouth. He recalled Gavin standing over her, and thoughts of the blond maniac sickened him. Now, Chloe had been lost, and Peter had to wonder if the cloak of guilt and regret would ever leave him. He hated Gavin, and if it was in his power to destroy something so evil, so sinister, he had to try. Luke, his angelic ancestor who'd altered his family's DNA as a safety measure against the Order of the Dragon, had promised he would one day see victory over the evil forces, but Peter wasn't sure he would survive to claim it; in fact, he didn't have a clue how. He was determined, though, to find Angel. He had to, for what he'd unleashed, what he'd empowered by opening the first *Book of Truth*, had haunted him every single moment, and he had to do all he could to make it right.

Kyle elbowed him. "How much farther?"

"Two blocks, if he doesn't make a turn. At the next block, we're outta here," Peter answered, glad Kyle jarred his morbid thoughts.

Peter and the others waited until the truck came to a stop, and then they slid out, completely unnoticed by the coffee-slurping driver who was busy bopping his head to some outdated eighties rock tune blaring from the radio. Peter stuffed his hands in his torn jacket pocket and took off, hoping the other guys could keep up with him.

Grateful that no one was still on the street, Peter walked briskly until he came to an alleyway. "We've got a few hours before daylight." He pointed to an abandoned house with a brick-framed garage that protruded into the back yard. "We can rest there."

Peter made his way through the alley and walked through the

unkempt yard, stepping over broken bottles, drug needles, and piles of dog poop.

There was a hole in the bottom of the battered wooden garage door. Peter kicked it, making it large enough for them to crawl into. Leaving the stench of garbage and the city outside, to be replaced by the musky innards of the abandoned building, which Peter suspected had at one time been a drug house.

"This place reeks," Kyle muttered.

"Yeah, smells like something died in here," Gil said.

"Stop complaining and deal with it." Peter glanced at the floor. It was covered in layers of dirt, but it was still cleaner than the yard outside. He tossed down his backpack, summoning clouds of dust, then lay down on the floor and rested his head on the bumpy bag.

"I'm not complaining," Gil said, scrunching his nose. "It was merely an observation. It's gonna take some time to adjust to the foul stank in here."

Kyle laughed. "You oughtta be used to it. You do share a room with Mr. Grouch over there. He's too busy moping to even take a shower." He plopped down on the floor a small distance from Peter.

"Whatever," Peter said with a grunt. "I've got a lot on my mind. You act like this is all a damn joke, but there's nothing funny about any of it. Nothin'."

Gil sat down on the floor, weary but unable to calm down. "What about Chloe? Do you think we can save her?"

"We'll try. But I can't make no promises. I told you when you came that bad things just follow me. I can't even say that I'll finish this alive. But I will fight for every freakin' breath before I let that bastard Gavin Steele and his followers be satisfied," Peter spat out.

"What do you know about him? I mean, I heard on the news that he hasn't been heard from in over eight months and that his brother was running his company. There was even a rumor that his brother might've killed him," Gil said.

"In the news? Damn, you have been locked up too long." Kyle laughed. "Well yeah, I did hear that story in the lunchroom a few months ago. But Peter and I were there, and we know the truth."

"How exactly would you know that?" Gil twisted his body towards Kyle.

"We were there," Peter answered. "He dropped to the ground unconscious when I pulled that...demon from him."

"Wait. A demon? You really think you pulled a man-eating demon from a human being? What, like an exorcist or something?" Gil snorted. "God, this little fairytale just gets better and better. You two are delusional."

"Hardly," Kyle argued.

"So you saw this demon too?" Gil interrogated.

"Not like that," Kyle answered. "Only Peter is able to see all the demons. But when I was with him at Gavin's place, I swear I saw one. It couldn't have been a hallucination like I tried to believe at first. Anyway, it still gives me nightmares."

"The demons are real, Gil," Peter said, his throat growing scratchy as he thought about it. "I was fighting them off when Chloe was stolen. They were weak though, only ash and fire. Most people can't see them, but they recognized me."

"Recognized you?" Kyle frowned. "I didn't see them, but I did see your hand glowing, like last time, at Gavin's."

"Well, when we first went to Gavin's, the weak demons, called feeders, the ones who manipulate humans and treat them as pets... They didn't even see me unless I looked directly at them. Things have changed now, and these were different. It's like they're hunting me, like Gavin put a hit on me or something. It's crazy, but I felt it when I left the sanctuary with you before. When I went out again, alone, I felt them. It was just...wicked. I ran back to the sanctuary for safety. It was like I had some cloak of protection or something, like they couldn't get past a barrier there, even though the place resembled a dump. One tried to follow me and was burned up outside the parameter of the sanctuary."

"Damn." Gil exhaled. "That's insane. Man, it can't true. I mean, we were never taught that when we learned about the history of the Decretum Venia."

"That's only because you weren't allowed to read the ancient books yourself. They only feed the kids a watered-down version of the truth. The Order of the Dragon is real, a demonic order of warriors determined to enslave humans and destroy all angels."

"It's an age-old story," Kyle said, tossing a rock across the filthy floor, "but it's based in truth. I know, because I saw it myself."

"Hmm," Gil said, almost in a whisper. "I guess I did feel something when we came out of the subway station. It felt like a heaviness, like we were being watched by a wolf or something. I shook it off, figuring it was just because we were out in the dark, but I've never felt that way before."

Kyle snorted. "That's because you've always been safe inside the sanctuary. I've felt that way plenty of times, every day when I was in that boarding school, surrounded by kids from the Order of the Dragon. I may not be a pure-blooded Decretum Venia knock-off like you, but I feel evil when it's lurking around. Those kids there were bred to be a sick, twisted lot. I'm all for getting over your issues and stuff, but there's no way they were gonna get out of it—not alive anyway," he said with a shiver.

"I still don't know how you did it, man," looking at his friend with admiration. "There's no way I could have faked that I liked being in a place like that. You said there were other kids from the Decretum Venia at that school at one time?" Peter asked, now recalling Kyle's broken, distorted story from his past.

"Yeah, but when things started to get bad, they mysteriously withdrew. Only half-breeds or quarter-bloods like me were left behind. Our parents were disowned for marrying ordinary humans, so we didn't receive the get-the-hell-out-of-here memo.

Only the kids of pure breeds, the ones they'd sent in as spies for their families and the Decretum Venia, were safely removed. I, on the other hand, had to run for my life after those bastards butchered my parents."

"Who did that? Why didn't you tell the Decretum Venia when you came to the sanctuary?" Gil asked.

"The teenagers I considered fren-emies did it. They thought I was cool, dealing drugs at school, and they wanted to recruit me, but I wasn't about to split my profits or lose my freedom to those sickos. Their initiation alone wouldn't guarantee me life. I had to get out," Kyle said, his eyes growing stormy.

"Okay, but are you sure you weren't just hallucinating when you saw the demons? I mean, stressful situations can make people, uh...see things." Gil scratched his thick mane of hair vigorously, as he always did when he was trying to figure things out.

Frustrated, Peter cut in, "No hallucination. It's real. I understand that now, and if you stick around for a while, you'll probably see them too. After what I did, they've gotten stronger, much stronger."

Kyle shot up. "Great," he said. "Just what we need, demons on steroids."

"Well, there's nothing you can do. This is something I have to fix. I need Angel's help though."

"What's she got to do with it?" Gil asked.

"I met someone on the other side who looks like her." Peter deduced that the angel was her ancestor, and she was a master in weapons for their war. Peter hoped his hunch was right. He felt it in his bones, but he couldn't capture the memory from his time in the *Book of Truth.*

Gil exhaled. "The other side? Oh crap. You're crazy, aren't you? Why did I leave that place?" he muttered. "I was safe there." He groaned.

"Well, not really the other side, but..." Peter frowned, trying to figure out a way to explain things to Gil and even to Kyle. He hadn't spoken much about it, but he felt it was time to share more about what had happened to give them all a better shot at surviving. "Okay, look, I opened a book...sort of. My DNA, my blood, unlocks it, because of some 1,000-year war between the demons from the Order of Dragons and the angels from the Decretum Venia's descendants. They protected it with the blood of innocent humans that were loyal to the Angels' cause. I unleashed that secret because I didn't know any other way to save my girlfriend, Angel. I didn't know until it was too late that opening the book or unlocking the secret was exactly what Gavin wanted me to do."

"The bastard," Kyle interjected.

"Thanks for the backup, man." Peter couldn't help the smile on his face; Kyle always had to put his two cents in. "Anyway, in order to return from that time or place suspended in the book, that alternate plane of reality, you have to—"

"Die," Kyle concluded. "He died, right there in front of my eyes. But then he healed. He started glowing and was suspended in some freaky formation in the air for a few minutes before he dropped to the floor. Get this. Afterward, Peter jumped up like he had unnatural strength, like he was the Incredible Hulk or something, only his clothes weren't torn and he wasn't green. I almost crapped my pants."

"The Incredible Hulk? Pssh. Can you stop with the dramatics? You're making my head hurt." Peter groaned.

"Mine already hurts," Gil said, his voice cracking, "and I'm scared shitless right now. Still, I can't believe any of this unless I see it. I think you two are just trying to scare me off, but it won't work. I'm sticking with you till we save Chloe. I'm in love with her, and she helped me. I owe her that much."

"If you loved her, you woulda stayed back there with her and heeded my warning." Peter twisted around and punched his backpack. "No one seems to wanna listen to me, even when it's for their own damn good."

"That's because we know, under that hard attitude, the growl and all that brawn, you're just a...pussycat." Kyle said, then purred at him.

Peter picked up a rock and threw it at him. "Just shut up and go to sleep," Peter said, though he couldn't peel the grin off his face. Kyle always made him smile, in spite of all the crud that was bringing him down. Unfortunately, even Kyle's stupid jokes couldn't erase the doubts Peter had about Kyle's jacked-up story about his past, and he wasn't sure where his friend's alliances truly lay. As much as he liked the guy, that still bugged him.

Peter heard voices. He was dreaming at first, then snoring, then feeling pain. The palm of his hand throbbed. Peter would never forget the sensation of Hanna drawing that circle with ancient writing within it. It burned then, and it was burning now.

Crack!

Peter's slit his eyes opened, just as a foot clashed with his face. "Ugh!" Disoriented, he rolled away from the blow, right into another foot that hit him square in the stomach. "What the...?" Peter spat.

Another punch landed on the side of his mouth as echoes of Kyle's and Gil's beating reverberated around the garage. Blinking his eyes for clarity, Peter lifted his fist to the sides of his face, awaiting the next blow. When another kick came at him, he deflected it and jabbed his punch upward, right into the guy's family jewels. He twisted his hip to land a blow to the kid's face. Peter wrapped his arm around the intruder's neck, making the boy take the blow of the bat that was aimed at his head. He jumped up on his feet with catlike precision and crouched in a fighting stance.

"Oh, you think you can take us?" asked a tall, tan kid with ink-black hair, thick eyebrows, and a crooked grin.

"I *know* I will." Peter faked a punch, then landed a side kick to the guy's knee. He made a quick search to see if any demons were attached to the attackers, but he saw none. He caught the flash of a descending plumbing pipe out the corner of his eye and deftly defended: *block, duck, kick, knee him, punch that one...* The adrenaline rushed through him as he handled all three of the attackers with ease. Finally, with his breathing in rapid succession, he pushed his foot down on one of the three unconscious boys around him.

Kyle's gun was pointed at the chest of another, who was standing in front of him. "Don't make me hurt you, buddy. I've got an unstable side to me."

Peter glanced over and noticed a wild, frightened expression in Gil's eyes.

Gil stammered, "L-let's get outta here!"

"Yeah," Peter affirmed, but the kid facing off with Kyle didn't appear to be compliant; his hand was slowly inching toward his pocket. "Knock 'im out, Kyle."

"My pleasure." Kyle stepped forward quickly and hit the kid in the head with the butt of his gun. He bent down and yanked back the kid's collar. "He's one of 'em, those kids from the Extraho of Obscurum."

"What does that mean?" Gil grabbed his backpack and flung it over his shoulders.

"Order of the Dragon. Either someone sent them after us, or this is their hideout. I'd know the brand anywhere. Tons of bastards at my private school had them." Kyle stuffed the gun in the back of his pants and snatched up his bag. He kicked the leg of the unconscious kid.

"It doesn't matter. We'll run the rest of the way. It's daylight, and the streets will be busy, with lots of witnesses. They'd be stupid to try anything out there." Peter exhaled. Time was running out. If Gavin was sending everything he had in search of Peter and the others from the Decretum Venia, something was off, and it was probably worse than Peter had predicted.

With a sigh, Peter led them out of the garage, darting his eyes in every direction to make sure no one else was waiting to ambush them. It was early morning, and dampness still hung in the air. He made his way out of the alley and onto the bustling street of the city. It was an upscale part of town, which came as some relief, but they still had a few miles to go before they'd reach the orphanage.

They weaved in and out of swarms of people. It was a weekday, and most were dressed for work or school. Kids carrying backpacks and adults in suits littered the streets, ignoring Peter and the others, and that was just the way he liked it.

"Where are we going again?" Gil asked, his head moving side to side as he tried to get comfortable with all the people on the street.

"Dude, you've gotta act natural, or someone's gonna think you're touched in the head," Kyle chided.

"We're going to my old orphanage. Pastor Finn practically raised me there. He's an ex-cop, and I'm sure he'll know where Angel is. The old man knows a lot about what goes down in the Decretum Venia, but he doesn't spill much. He'd been involved with the Order since he was a kid. When his brother was murdered, he took over the sanctuary I grew up in."

Peter remembered the place like it was yesterday. He had hated living there and had felt trapped. But when he confessed his involvement in Hanna's death, showed Pastor Finn the mark on his hand and was forced to leave, he found himself wishing he could go back. Regretfully, that wasn't an option; Pastor Finn made it clear that keeping the other kids at his sanctuary safe was all that mattered and that Peter had to deal with the choices he'd made.

"Is the guy safe?" Gil asked. "Remember the nutso we left at the other place? He wanted you, right? Don't you think he'll look for you at your old spot?"

"I doubt it. Only a fool would go to a place they know anyone can find, and he knows I'm not a fool." Peter snorted and side-stepped a man in a pinstriped suit. As he did, his eye caught a glimpse of a girl with a purple streak in her hair. It seemed she was trailing them, but he hoped she was simply walking in the same direction.

"If I'm following a fool, that makes me one." Gil shook his head. "God, I'm so stupid. I shoulda stayed behind, kept Chloe safe, but if going with you means getting her back, I've got no other choice. Can you just promise that this guy's all right, that he'll help us?"

"I know he will." Peter walked to the bus stop on the corner, hoping they would ditch the girl if they rode the bus.

"A bus?" Kyle asked, confused.

"We need to borrow somebody's cell phone so I can call Pastor Finn. Besides, I'm trying to see if someone's following us," Peter whispered as another kid walked up beside them.

"Yeah, okay. If you say so." Kyle's eyebrows rose in suspicion, as if he thought Peter was being too paranoid.

Peter ignored him and turned to the other kid. "Hey, can I use your phone? I lost mine, and I need to call my father."

The younger kid eyed him suspiciously. "Sure. Just give it back when we get on the bus." He slid the phone out of his back pocket and gave it to Peter.

Peter smiled. "Thanks, kid." He pivoted away from the others and kept an eye out for the purple-haired girl as he dialed Pastor Finn's private line. He spotted her half a block away, pretending to look in a store window. The nervous hopping she did on the balls of her feet gave her away.

The phone rang a few times before the pastor picked up. "Finn here," he said, his voice deep and serious.

"It's me, Peter. I can't talk long, but I need to meet you. I have to find Angel. It's important, real important." Peter's eyes followed the girl as she slowly made her way closer to them.

"Meet me at the gatehouse, back of the property...and ditch that phone, kid." Pastor Finn hung up.

Peter erased the number from the call log and handed the phone back to its owner. "Thanks again," he said.

The bus pulled up, and Peter hung back while everyone else climbed aboard. He stared down the block at the girl, who was still a short distance away, then climbed the three steps to move into the bus. Peter sat in the back and shrugged out of his backpack, relieved they weren't being followed after all. He silently berated himself for being so paranoid as the bus started to pull off.

"Wait! Somebody's coming!" a woman called from up front.

Peter adjusted himself in his seat as his eyes collided with the almond-shaped eyes of the purple-haired girl from the street. She quickly took her seat and gave him a sideways glance. In that moment, he knew she wasn't with the gang of kids they'd beaten and left in the garage. *She's different, like Hanna.* A nervous shiver traveled up his spine. The same lost, slightly unbalanced gaze was hidden within the depths of her eyes. The hairs on Peter's neck rose, and he knew for sure that things were about to turn from bad to worse.

CHAPTER 6

Peter pushed his way off the bus, making sure to take the back door in hopes the girl wouldn't get off to follow them. She didn't.

Breathing easier, Peter swung on his backpack and glanced down at the brand on his hand.

"Where'd you get that?" Gil grabbed Peter's wrist.

"Doesn't matter now." Peter snatched his hand away.

Hanna wasn't on his mind anymore; instead, his thoughts lingered on the girl from the bus. He'd been on the run for a long time, and his paranoia was beginning to get the best of him. The kids who'd attacked them in the garage didn't have any demons hanging around, so there was no way to know if they were working with the Extraho of Obscurum or up to their own devices.

"Which way now?" Kyle watched the bus pull off.

Peter waited to make sure no one got off, and exhaled when it rounded the corner. "This way. We're close." Peter led them through the park, which was dense with trees and silent except for the sound of rushing water in the distance. Rocks, scattered leaves, and spots of grass within dried earth protected them from potential pursuers. Peter wracked his brain, trying to remember the passageway to the protected orphanage he'd grown up in. There were several ways in and out, but he'd never used any of them excessively when he lived there, since he didn't want to get caught coming and going.

"How do you remember this place?" Gil asked, a bit out of breath as he tried to keep up to Peter's pace.

"I'll never forget it. It sucked when I had to leave. Even now, I don't think I'll ever see my old room again."

"Why not, I thought dude was letting us crash here?" Kyle asked.

"Not really. We'll be on safe ground, it's sacred. The place was prayed over and protected, so none of Gavin's people can come here, but Pastor Finn's not meeting us at the orphanage. He told me to meet him at the gatehouse. It's like...the place people go to get clearance before they can have access to the rest of the place," Peter said, rubbing his palm on his pants, trying to soothe the itchiness from his scar.

"How much further?" Gil questioned. "My feet are killing me."

"Not far." Peter searched the trees, then the dead leaves on the ground, packed between sparse patches of grass. They were at the right spot, but he needed a clue to find the entrance somewhere beneath the trees, tall and short, that provided them with thick cover. "I think it's, uh..." Peter peered in every direction, till his eyes landed on a hollow tree trunk straight ahead. The leaves flattened against it were a bit neater than the patches of dead leaves between the other trees, as if someone other than Mother Nature had placed them there. "There!"

"Uh...where? All I see is leaves, dirt, and a maggot-infested stump that oughtta be burned out of its misery," Kyle said with a snort.

"He's right. There are no paths, trails, signs, or anything out here." Gil dropped his backpack. "And I'm out of breath. I gotta take a breather and sit for a minute."

Peter stepped to the trunk that appeared to be attached to a large tree, one that stood a bit taller than the rest. This was one of the ways out of the orphanage.

He tilted his chin towards the others. "If I don't come out, follow me."

Gil's eyebrows lifted as though he considered Peter's request a bit unbalanced.

Kyle sighed and lifted his backpack off the ground. "Fine. I get it. Just like the last time, you somehow know there's a hidden way into these places. Get up, Gil, he's probably right."

Peter ignored their doubt and crawled inside the hollow trunk. He stopped in front of a wooden barrier, like a slice of another tree, tiled oddly from the top to the bottom of the enclosed space. Peter ran his hand over, up, and down the bumpy wooden wall and found a protruding chunk. He pressed down on it.

Click! Snap!

The plank fell flat, revealing a circular trapdoor in the ground ahead.

"No shit! This is wicked." Gil laughed, excited. "I'd never would've believed this if you'd told me."

"I barely remembered this way because I only came this way once. I had to go back the way I left, or I woulda been caught sneaking out."

"At least this place doesn't call for blood-letting," Kyle snickered.

"Shut up!" Peter snapped, glancing back at him. It was supposed to be a secret that the most protected sanctuaries and strongholds required blood for entry. Not many people in the Decretum Venia knew about it, and they hadn't taught the kids about it at the orphanage.

"Sorry, stupid slip," Kyle whispered.

Peter turned the rounded lock embedded in the square trapdoor until the lock gave. He opened it and tossed the door to the side, then climbed in. Peter made quick time descending the ladder, motioning for the others to hurry. Small lights, within the walls, lit one by one as he climbed down. He jumped off the final rung, then pivoted and opened the metal door ahead. A large Exit sign above the door cast a dim red glow within the cement space.

"I thought you said you climbed out a cellar the last time you left this place?" Kyle asked while helping Peter push open the door.

"I did, but that's only one way out of this place. I found dozens." Peter stepped through the door, which opened to a cement tunnel with the light of the day seeping through the top on the other side.

"Why aren't we going to the orphanage?" Kyle inquired.

"Pastor Finn taught us to shoot there. I'm not sure why he doesn't want me back at the orphanage yet, but for now, I have to do it his way if I want him to help me." Peter felt a small stab in his chest. Part of him did know: It was because of what had happened with Hanna. He wasn't supposed to leave the sanctuary grounds, and as soon as Pastor Finn laid eyes on the mark Hanna left on his palm, he'd sent Peter away.

"Even if he knows where Angel is, will he know how we can get her back?" Gil asked, "I still don't understand why we have to get her first, before we go save Chloe. She's obviously safe and at some other sanctuary."

Peter shook his head as they came to the end of the tunnel. He climbed up the ladder. "I need to find her." *Because, I love her, and she's the only girl who loved me back.* "And we can't save anyone if she's not with me."

Peter pulled himself out of the hole in the ground and smiled at the wide expanse of thick, neatly trimmed grass. In the distance was a small, rundown house. Its blue, beaten exterior, wraparound porch with broken spindled framing, and rotted wood steps, never appeared so inviting. He smiled.

"This is it?" Kyle asked. "Is the Decretum Venia poor?"

"I don't think so, they had a lot of expensive stuff at the other facility," Gil added.

I think they want to make people believe they are, Peter thought, and walked with the others to the porch. "At least we can sleep. It might take him a while to get here."

"Great, another hard-ass floor to lay my head on. Can't wait." Kyle sighed. "Is the Decretum Venia on Section 8 housing or something? It looks like something from a horror movie, man."

"Shut up." Peter popped Kyle on the back of the head before sidestepping a hole in the steps and hopping onto the porch. He reached in the rusted black mail pocket next to the door and pulled out a string with the key on it. Opening the door, the fresh smell of pine hit him. He was struck by the uncanny difference between the outside appearance of the house and the inside.

The floors were covered with plush, tan carpet, and the walls were painted in a soft yellow hue. Oddly, while the windows appeared cracked and broken on the outside, they were smooth and decorated in stained glass on the inside. Ornate drapes hung around them, and large, antique couches and chairs were positioned perfectly throughout the front room. Large pictures of angels and Decretum Venia elders decorated the walls, portraits of men and women of all nationalities, giving the place an eclectic yet formal air.

Kyle's jaw dropped. "Dayum!"

"Wow!" Gil spun around in disbelief.

Peter laughed. "I got you!" He tossed his bag into one of the chairs and led them to the hall. "Kitchen's in there, help yourself to anything you want to eat. And trust me, you want to eat since I don't know when we'll eat again after we leave here."

Kyle jumped up and down. "Whoa! I just died and went to heaven. I don't remember the last time we were actually in a house that had food—fresh food. Or beds!" Kyle ran through the hallway and into each room, coming out hooting and hollering.

Gil just stood there stunned. "I-I don't know what to do. Eat first? Sleep. We can sleep here right?"

"Yeah, pick one of the two rooms there. I'm taking the one in the back." Peter went into the galley style kitchen and made himself a sandwich.

"Who stocks this place with food? Does someone live here?" Gil asked.

Peter studied him. It was clear the kid was a bit skeptical. Peter figured Gil was afraid to believe they were actually in such a nice place, where he'd have a room of his own and could eat anything he wanted. "This place is Pastor Finn's, and the people who help him out stay in it. He's got another house like this on the far end of the property, and on the other edge is his garage."

Gil still just stood there, staring at him. "I wish I'd been sent here."

"That so? Well, we had some pretty rough kids in this place. The orphanage itself isn't nice like this. It's pretty bad, but not quite as bad as your Sanctuary. It's cleaner here. The kids though, much meaner. Harder. Pissed off." Peter stuffed several pieces of ham in his mouth while piling the rest high on the bread.

"Oh." Gil went to the refrigerator and grabbed a soda and a few packs of pre-made burritos. "I guess you're right. All the kids where I was were real young when they got there. The nanny we had died last year, then Mr. Boswell came in and changed the staff. We got dorm monitors after that."

Peter sat down and started in on his first ham sandwich, oozing with yellow mustard. "When did you meet Chloe?" The girl's haunted, frightened face was etched in his mind, and Peter had to close his eyes against the tingle of remorse he had for her.

"She came there when she was twelve. Real quiet, but beautiful." Gil grabbed his burritos out of the microwave. "We've been seeing each other in secret for about a year."

"Um, impressed you were able to pull that off," Peter mumbled through bites.

Gil sat across from him at the small two-person table. "So what about you and this girl Angel? You didn't talk much about her after she left. And I didn't see you much at all when she was there."

Peter's food got caught in his throat. He tilted the soda to his lips and took a slow swallow. "She's more than just a girlfriend. We've been through a lot together, more than anybody would know."

Gil raised an eyebrow. "More than being on the run, almost getting killed and her getting abducted?"

Peter smirked at that. "You're right, we went that deep and more."

Gil started to eat, but eyed Peter as if waiting to hear more. "So, you two hit it off? I noticed you didn't try to hook up with any of the other girls at the place that were coming on strong to you."

Peter shook his head. "I've been there, done that. Getting a girl to have sex was all I did before Angel. I stopped wanting just that long ago. Being with Angel makes the other girls seem like distractions when all I want is to see her again."

"Was she hot?" Gil asked, jokingly. "Her name sure is."

Peter grinned. "Hell yeah. Her real name is, Angelica Ramirez. I teased her by calling her my spicy Angel. When I first met her though, I didn't know she was beautiful. She was dressed like a boy and tried to steal my stuff. But underneath all that, she had long black hair, dimples, green eyes, and pale skin that made me feel like she was a fragile—someone I had to take care of."

"She was fragile? Weak?" Gil's lips pursed to the side.

Peter belted out a laugh. "No way. She had a fire—you know, the kind that let you know she was a survivor. I wanted that, needed someone who felt it like I did. And, Angel could kick ass. A trained martial artist, but you'd never know it. She didn't have that edge on her shoulders then. She was still…innocent, something I hadn't seen in a while—a long while."

"So why'd you let her go? You could've left right after they took her. I would've." Gil nailed Peter with a wry smile. "That's what I want to do for Chloe."

"Yeah, I know. I wanted to, but—" Peter stopped, unwilling to tell that part of the story. The truth was that he was too scared to go after her at the time, something he hated admitting, even to himself. Fear, loathing, and shame had taken up residence in him long ago, and he certainly didn't want to discuss that with Gil.

"Hey, where's mine, you selfish asses?" Kyle asked, popping his head into the kitchen.

"You may have had servants growing up, but you don't anymore!" Peter threw a balled-up paper towel.

Kyle ducked before it hit him. "And I will again." He laughed.

Peter stood and tossed his stuff in the trash. He ignored the guys' joking and laughing and headed to the back bedroom. Just as he entered the door to the masculine designed plush bedroom, the cell phone on the nightstand rang. Taking a cursory glance back, he kicked the door closed and answered the phone.

"Hello? Pastor Finn?" Peter answered.

"Yes, son. I can't make it right over. Get a few hours rest. Then meet me near the garage, leave your company behind for now. I have something important to discuss with you."

"What about Angel? I came to find out where she is." Peter's voice came out in a gruff crackle. Just thinking about how close he was to finding Angel again got him anxious.

"I have that information for you. Meet me in four hours." His voice sounded heavy, regretful. "I miss you, son."

When the phone went dead, Peter was hit with fatigue. Still, he wasn't sure he could sleep. He needed to, because he knew they couldn't hide there for long. Too many days had passed since he held Angel in his arms, since he'd been able to get past the nightmares he'd revealed in the *Book of Truth*.

Peter slipped the picture of her out of his pocket and propped himself against the headboard of the soft, comfortable bed, on top of the blue corduroy comforter. He stared at the photo, the only one he had of her, a snapshot Peter had snatched out of the discards pile for the ID cards they made for newly admitted students. She was smiling in the photo, though her grin was tiny compared to the ones she used to wear before she was taken by Gavin and the Extraho of Obscurum.

Peter traced her lips with his finger. "I'm sorry, Angel. I never shoulda let you leave the hotel room to get your ID. They wouldn't have gotten you if..." Peter let the silent tears fall from his eyes and felt the coolness of them sliding down his face. "If Kyle hadn't saved me, we'd all be dead."

Inside, though, Peter already felt dead. Death was hunting him with a vengeance, and that death was named—Gavin Steele.

CHAPTER 7

Peter waited patiently at the double-decker garage for Pastor
Finn. He trailed his burning palm along the cool hood of
Pastor Finn's sports car. His baby, he'd called it. Pastor Finn had
the car before he'd taken up full duty at the Decretum Venia.
Before then, he was Officer or Sergeant Finn on some New York
police force.

"Peter," Pastor Finn's deep voice called.

At that moment Peter felt peace. He pivoted around and ran
into the open arms of the man who had impacted his life in more
ways than one, "Pastor Finn," he choked, almost sobbing. "Feels
good to be back. So good."

Pastor Finn pushed Peter slightly away, and he grasped the
boy's shoulders with his firm hands. "God, son, you've grown.
You're taller than me...and thicker too!" His eagle eyes slanted,
observing Peter closer. "Yes, you have changed much since I last
saw you."

"Too much, if you ask me," Peter muttered, instantly becoming
the kid he'd once been. As bad as things were when he was
younger, they had never been that bad, but Pastor Finn had always

protected him for as long as he could. "I never shoulda left this place," he confessed. "I screwed up."

Pastor Finn patted Peter on the shoulder. "Maybe you weren't meant to. Ever think about that? People who are born and created to do great things are fighters. They take risks and even though things might spook them, they carry on. You'll do that, Peter. I know it. I know you."

"That's funny. I don't even know myself anymore." He glanced down at the brand on his hand, which was glowing red and puckering. "Thanks for burying Hanna for me. I didn't want her to get hurt." He turned away. "I didn't want to leave you with another mess of mine to clean up. The brand she gave me, it sure doesn't feel like a gift."

Pastor Finn tugged on Peter's shoulder, getting him to turn around. "It is a gift. I researched it after I sent you away. Hanna gave you the warrior's brand. It's never been given before. It's like a prophecy of sorts. Only the Elders in the golden levels of the Decretum Venia have access to the scrolls regarding this. But Rosa knew it when I contacted her. That woman remembers all the scrolls she's taught and translated."

"I know the prophecy, I've haven't told anybody this, except the kid Kyle who's with me." Peter cleared his throat, trying to figure out how to tell Pastor Finn what happened without sounding crazy. "I found a sacred book, one that told about a thousand year war, fought by the ancestors of the Decretum Venia. Our ancestors were human...and," Peter scratched at the palm of his hand nervously, "altered genetically with the DNA of the Angels that were fighting the war. A man, a human man named Jakaan, used a method and device to transport himself to the heavens. The angels there were jealous because they thought he was more favored than them. So they were cast out of the heavenly realm, with the sole purpose of protecting Jakaan and to understand that human life wasn't easy, and that humans had to earn their way into the life of eternity the Angels took for granted."

"Hmm," the pastor said, appearing disturbed. "I knew the Decretum Venia protects the secrets of the beliefs in the Creator of All, which encompasses all religions, but I didn't know all this. Rosa didn't even fill me in on so many details," he said, scratching his chin. "Anyway, boy, I believe you. Do go on. What happened?"

"Well, Jakaan was captured by the demons, and every angelic warrior who tried to save him disappeared and was damned to be tortured by their enemy." Peter wiped his warm palm down his face. "The angels altered their most trusted humans with their own empowered DNA, specifically targeting certain characteristics they knew would meld well with humans, recessive traits, undetectable by most modern scientific methods. It can only be activated during certain times and in specific ways."

"So Hanna knew how to activate this in you?" Pastor Finn rubbed his chin. "But why would she do it?"

"Because Gavin Steele, and the Order of the Dragon, drove her near insane. Something about her gave her the ability to be manipulated by them. But because she was dying when she gave it to me, and was considered 'blessed,' her blood made the alterations in mine become aware. At least that's what Gavin told me when we...uh, met."

Pastor Finn inhaled a shocked breath. "No! Oh no! Don't tell me..." He ran his hand through his thick, gray crew-cut and rubbed the top of his head several times, something he only did when he was very aggravated. "This is terrible."

"I know. Gavin Steele and the Order of the Dragon found out the secret is held in our blood, in the blood of the children. That's why kids from the Decretum Venia have been going missing. The bastard's been stealing and torturing them in ways beyond your worst nightmare. Not just for the sake of finding our sanctuaries, but for their sadistic pleasure. He wants one thing from me, but I won't give it up without a fight." Peter's jaw clenched, and he flexed his hands into fists.

"What does he want? I'll kill him myself. He'll never get it," Pastor Finn spoke in a low menacing tone, the edge of his former life as a police officer apparent in his stance.

"My blood. It's different than the others now that Hanna's changed me. It unlocks the secret to getting his machine to work."

"His machine?"

"Yeah. He's rebuilding the machine Jakaan created. It was the reason the demons kidnapped him during that thousand year war the Angels hoped to keep hidden. They'd kidnapped Jakaan to find a way to enclose themselves in the bodies of human hosts, and to take the war to the heavens."

Pastor Finn cursed. "This isn't good. There are some major problems and infighting going on within the Decretum Venia. I guess it all makes sense now, but it isn't good at all."

"Oh, and one more thing."

"What?"

"When we left the other place, there was this guy named Dr. Phillips looking for me, I think."

Pastor Finn handed Peter a bag. "Take this, son. You'll need it," he said with a serious look on his face. He released a deep sigh. "I've heard of Dr. Phillips. What little I know about him, I don't like at all. He's one of the radicals, those who think the Decretum Venia should try to come to some truce with the Extraho of Obscurum, since our numbers are depleting and theirs are growing."

"What!? We don't need to strike a deal with them. They are evil, and the angels won't be able to fight alongside us. It's some kind of agreement they made with the Creator of All." Peter shook his head. "But the Order of the Dragon, their demon puppet masters, are around them all the time—and in Gavin Steele's case, even inside them. It's stupid to think they'd wanna do anything good for anybody but themselves."

"I have to do something about this. Rosa had to go into hiding. Ever since she traveled to Europe to confer with the Elder Council about how she tried to destroy every piece of the evidence of the Decretum Venia at the last property the Order of the Dragon was able to steal from us, she's been on the run."

"Why? What happened there?" Peter leaned against the car.

"Mayhem, to put it lightly. It wasn't well received, and supporters from both sides were there. I know where she is. I put it on the map inside that bag I gave you. Make sure you find her first. She'll tell you how to get into the sanctuary where they've hidden secrets to fight for your girl, Angelique Ramirez. No one else has been able to get in, not even Rosa, but maybe you can. Also, when you speak to Rosa, I need you to give her a message for me. Tell her I have to move my kids from here soon. I will need her help."

"What? Why?" Peter felt horrible. This was his fault; their protection had gotten weaker because of what he'd done.

"Someone's trying to buy this place. I don't know how they ever found out about it, the land and all is supposed to be protected by the state as historical, and cut up into pieces to give the appearance that nothing special is here except a bunch of grass and trees. I don't want to leave anything behind for them to find."

Peter frowned. "Like what? There are just the grounds and the kids, right?"

Pastor Finn grinned. "It is a sanctuary, Peter. Every sanctuary holds a secret, a key. That's why we need so much security, and it is why it has been so safe for the kids, at least till now. If you search around the house, you'll find a seemingly unmovable door. Get to it before I destroy this place in Rosa fashion," he said with a chuckle.

Peter understood his hidden meaning, that there was a place

similar to the hidden alcove he'd found at Rosa's. Not only that, at the barn where he'd first met Rosa, she'd warned that she would destroy it. Peter shook his head, remembering the blazing blast Rosa had left behind. "Thanks. I will."

Pastor Finn's eyes travelled to the brand on Peter's hand. "I put some gloves in there too. Hide your hand. Anyone in the Decretum Venia will recognize that symbol. Don't tell anyone but Rosa what's happened. She's the only one now that I trust. You'll find her with an underground group network of Decretum Venia bailouts. Find her. She will know what to do."

Peter exhaled, giving Pastor Finn one last hug. "I hope so."

"I'll meet you and Rosa after you save your girl. Your safety from the Order of the Dragon is just one concern. I've contacted all the other watchers. They'll protect the full-blooded Decretum Venia children. We made a pact, and we all agreed to keep you kids in hiding, even away from the Decretum Venia. It's part of our underground training and oath, that we protect you, even if it goes against the organization itself." He looked intently into Peter's eyes and grabbed hold of his shoulders again. "One more thing, son."

"Anything." Peter felt safe for the first time in months as Pastor Finn pulled him in for another tight hug for that brief moment.

"I love you like you were my own. You can do this. Don't forget that I'll do everything in my power to keep you safe. I've taught you well, and I'm..." tears formed on the corners of his eyes, "proud of you."

"Thanks Pastor Finn, I needed to hear that. You're that best dad I could've ever ask for," his voice cracked, "I love you, too."

A wry grin formed on his face. Peter pivoted away and jogged toward the gatehouse. With every step, he felt his heart strengthen, and he began to leave some of his regret behind. To him, Pastor Finn was a father, and he'd finally had the chance to thank him for taking the job. He only hoped he wouldn't let the pastor down again.

CHAPTER 8

Gavin Steele felt invigorated and whole. It was good to be back in his old office. The brown, red, and gold décor was a perfect contrast to his vast collection of weaponry, ancient texts, and family paintings of a long line of leaders within the Order of Dragon. Leaders in his family were known to be unmerciful, and they killed, fought, manipulated, then devoured anyone who got in their way. All of it now rested upon Gavin's shoulders. He'd known it would, ever since he was a young boy, but as far as he was concerned, the vision and connections he'd gained through the many painful, torturous trainings, perfected by his fathers and the elders of the Extraho of Obscurum to find the next generation's leaders, was worth it.

This office was his favorite, specifically built to support his work for the Extraho of Obscurum. His life's work included years of pursuing a bond between him and his demon master, Balaal, and that journey had exposed to him the key to having it all: Peter Saints. So many psychics and people had been sacrificed to reveal that name to him, the name of the one person who could make or break his powerful role in the master's plan. If everything worked out the way he wanted, Gavin would have control not only of

Earth but also of the heavens. Now, victory was so close that Gavin could almost taste it. He sat down in the plush leather chair and rolled out the plans to one of his greatest creations, the Transfero of Lux Lucis.

"Gavin..." Lucien's cautious voice floated in from the open doorway. "You have a moment?"

Gavin smiled and waved his brother in. "For you, of course, brother." The sickly cordial greeting tasted bitter on Gavin's tongue, but it was purposeful. He needed to groom his brother, his servant, for one day he would be the perfect victim in the master's final victory.

"Is it, uh...he...Balaal, there? Inside, like before?" Lucien trembled as he sat down in the chair across from his intimidating brother.

Gavin studied his sibling's handsome blond form, which would have been considered pleasing to most. To Gavin, the weak, pitiable creature before him was disgusting and would be a less-than-stellar final sacrifice to Balaal, but he would have to do. "Yes, brother, Balaal is within me, but he is resting, allowing me to have reign of my body for the time being."

Lucien visibly relaxed. "It's good to see you again, brother. To have you back. When you were..." Lucien's eyes wandered as if he was trying to find his words. "When Balaal inhabited your body before, I worried about the state of your soul. Where it resided and if he treated you with the care we'd been taught."

Gavin smiled, though the expression didn't reach his eyes. "While Balaal had control, I resided in a place of such pleasurable pain that I have no words for it, brother. It was not even a taste of the pain I've given to you to prepare you for the inhabitance of your demon master."

"I see," Lucien added cautiously. "About that... While you were gone, Balaal wasn't able to reside in my body. He was too weak and had already bonded with you, but he gave me your dreams, the ones about your machine, the Transfero of Lux Lucis."

"I noticed." Gavin recalled Lucien's impassioned plea for Balaal to leave him alone. "You heard his voice, understood what needed to be done to start building this?"

"Y-yes. I understood the plans. And although I was able to get the materials, and start construction at our site in the Outer Banks, I don't know how we will gain enough blood to mask the army of demon hosts that we plan to use. The numbers of the Decretum Venia have dwindled to a pitiful few and those who are left—the children we need—are all in hiding."

"The blood of those children is imperative to this plan. Doing the transfusions of each host will allow them to be transported to the heaven realm, otherwise they will die instantly and their demon host will be revealed. It was your job as my second in command, and my brother to do this for the master." Gavin reached in his drawer, pulled out the gold knife laced with a silver blade and the handle of a dragon.

Lucien's eyes widened a bit as Gavin caressed the blade. "I know Gavin, but I didn't have the time. Balaal asked that I start the building of the Transfero of Lux Lucis and acquiring some of the materials was damn near impossible," Lucien argued.

"Building the Transfero of Lux Lucis includes the latter ingredient, the blood of the chosen from the Decretum Venia. Do you know how many centuries our families have searched for this information? I delivered it to you on a platter, and all you had to do was find those damn children. You do love them, don't you? Torturing the children, as I have, gives you great pleasure, does it not?"

Lucien dared not look Gavin in the eyes. "It did...d-does."

"Then why can't you get the job done? Your men haven't been successful in finding them. According to my records, Jake Eagle-horn has been doing your job, brother. His family is next in line to receive the gifts, but I will never let that happen. Because of the last sacrificial boy he found, I was able to reunite with Balaal. It was your job to see to that, but you only reaped the reward. You, Lucien, are a disgrace and an embarrassment!" Gavin's cool accusation hung heavy in the room.

Lucien's stricken expression stared back at him, and Lucien sank to the floor, ripped his shirt open and put his head downward. "P-Punish me."

Gavin stood and raised the knife. "With great pleasure, brother. It's been a long time coming."

Lucien's screams were music to Gavin's ears. It seemed like years had passed since he had the pleasure of bringing another to such pain. If all went according to plan, bringing Peter Saints to such depths of despair would taste all the sweeter.

CHAPTER 9

Leaving Pastor Finn, for the second time in just over a year, felt like a re-opened wound. Peter hastily wiped away a stray tear, hating himself for such weakness. He was tired. *Way too freakin' tired to keep this up, all this hiding, searching, fighting. What will it lead to anyway? My life ending—again?* The funny thing was that when he died after opening the stronghold of secrets left by his ancestor, he came back not feeling any different inside. His soul still hung heavy in his skin, and he felt as though he was being forced down a rapid river of failures. That was why he hid. He just played the sucker, the punk, the scared wimp, and he'd stayed in that last sanctuary for way too long.

Peter was also sorry about Kyle, that he'd stuck with him for all that time. *If he was smarter, he woulda left me alone,* Peter thought, especially because Kyle, more than anyone, had experienced the muffed-up road Peter had traveled. "What's with him anyway?" Peter mumbled. "No one in their right mind would continue to subject himself to that kind of crap." Peter never had a choice. It was starting to feel like he was a puppet in some horrific plan. As bad as his past had been, it still didn't seem as dark as the path he was now on. Everything about his life felt totally destroyed and riddled with so much death that he got physically ill just dreaming about it.

He snatched the picture of Angel out of his pocket; her fair skin seemed to shine outward from the veil of her black hair. Kissing it, he tried to capture some of the soothing love he'd felt whenever he was with her. She'd always been hopeful and happy in spite of all the things she'd dealt with. Even when Peter, himself, should've been the cause of her pain—she'd forgiven him. He considered himself so unworthy of it.

"I'm sorry Angel. I'll fix this. I will." He sighed then stuffed the picture back into his jacket pocket. His feet pounded on the thick grass toward the shabby home. He stopped and took a moment to study the house from the back. The cellar door jutted out just under the bedroom door that held his stuff. A chipped red wood door led from the hallway just outside the bedroom door and to the grassy backyard that he'd run through to meet Pastor Finn.

He decided to search there before going into the house. He'd only been able to find the strongholds by accessing the maps from a sanctuary. The sanctuaries were usually heavily guarded and rigged with booby traps and explosives, so he knew Pastor Finn's tip would reveal a secret, something that could help him. Although, from what Peter understood, none of the keepers of the sanctuaries could access the hidden rooms, they knew of the possible existence of the rooms. That was why most were protected by some type of guardian. Peter remembered a dog at the first sanctuary, instead of a human keeper.

Peter walked to the cellar door, dropped the bag Pastor Finn gave him and wiped a hand through his curly mass of hair.

He blew out some air and searched around for where a key would be kept. Peter knelt and pressed his hands down and around the frame of the flat trapdoor. Nothing. "Just my luck the door would be locked."

Exasperated, he hopped up and studied the frame around the

house that jutted from the room. His eyes traveled back and forth several times before landing on a flat area that appeared a bit smoother than the rest of the trim. He counted the connected patchwork of wood pieces that appeared as if it had been fixed and re-patched several times. But one spot just shy of the window above the cellar appeared to be even.

Peter pivoted and spotted a shed nearby. Gingerly, he grabbed the ladder leaning against it. He couldn't deny his excitement and trepidation about what he might find when he revealed the maps, but it had to be done. He took a few long strides to get back to the house and placed the ladder against it. He climbed to the point just under the flat metal square piece between the door and the window. Peter trailed his fingers across the overhang of the roof, then back toward the soffit. He scratched away some of the white paint that had been slathered on in a poor attempt to conceal the piece, then felt a small, round button in the corner. With a smile on his face, he pressed it.

Click.

Peter released the breath he'd been holding. He opened his palm just before the little compartment door opened, just in time to catch the small key. He gripped it in his hand, pressed the compartment door closed, and jumped off the ladder.

Peter stood in front of the trapdoor again, turning the key over and over in his hand. The palm of his hand heated and seemed to have an eerie red glow about it. Clearly, something within him knew that place, knew something wanted to connect with him there. Part of him was engineered by angels—not the gentle ones he remembered from bedtime stories but warriors, mighty angels with technology, historical knowledge, and unknown powers most humans could never fathom. Why they'd chosen him, he was sure he'd never know. Maybe it was because he was just in the wrong place at the right time.

Stalling a bit, he kicked his foot against the lock. "Stop bailing out," he muttered.

Peter bent, grabbed the lock as if admitting to an angry defeat, and cracked the door. The smell hit him first. Warm air, putrid, like rotting paper, dust and staleness, furled outward in a cloud of dust. Darkness. No ladder. No light. Nothing.

"There's gotta be one." Peter's angry whisper echoed. He felt around the rim of the door until his hand landed on a small switch. Flicking it, he couldn't help but grin when light flooded the room. Several clicks later, a metal frame peeked from the other side of the door and pushed out a thick rope ladder, framed with metal pieces, which fell to the floor.

Peter shimmied down the ladder, holding firm to it when it swayed back and forth. With one final jump, he hopped off to pivot around. The room was square, with smooth cement walls covered halfway up by worn boxes, trunks, and bins in no particular order or fashion.

"Pastor Finn's work." He chuckled, remembering Pastor Finn's one personality flaw: The man was sloppy when it came to packing, even though his clothes, his car, and his private apartment above his massive garage were always impeccably neat. When it came to storing stuff, he hated it, and he was a bit of a closet hoarder.

"Where would it be?" Peter walked through the small aisles between the boxes, which were stacked as high as the ceiling in some places and only two or three boxes deep in others. There were statues of angels here and there, men dressed in robes and women carrying what appeared to be small trunks carved with ancient letters Peter recognized from some of the Decretum Venia tablets and studies, scattered rugs, paintings, and tapestries, dusty from years of neglect. Methodically, he walked through each section of the room, carefully squeezing between stacks of boxes that appeared to be caving in on each other.

Frustration built in his chest. "I'm getting nowhere." Peter kicked a box in the last corner, what appeared to be a dead end. He leaned his head on one of the protruding boxes. "This blows," he said as the seemingly empty box he was banging his head on went tumbling backward.

"What the...?" Peter grinned. "Why empty boxes? Why here? Aha! Camouflage!" The weight lifted off his chest for the moment, and his palm heated up. His heart beat rapidly within him as he pulled box after empty box from the corner. Haphazardly, he tossed them aside and kept moving them until he'd cleared all of them out of the way, revealing a tapestry in the corner. Its ornate colors of gold, silver, and bronze, with three circles intertwined together, marked the symbol of the Decretum Venia.

"Yes!" Peter rubbed his hand on the thick rug before putting it aside. He gulped. "This is it." His palm itched at the symbol of the three intertwined circles. Inhaling, Peter knew what had to be done to open it. The hairs raised on his neck as he placed the palm of his hand in the center of the circle on the floor.

"Blood...mine." He waited for the pinch of the prick. "Take it."

Finally, it came. Needles extended from the floor and drew blood from within the symbol on his hand. Peter flinched as the needles retracted and a crimson dribble traced through the indentations within the symbol.

Tap. Tap. Click.

A crack formed in the floor, slowly as if being cut out from the inside out. A sizzling sound teased the ground where the perfect design in the shape of a circle unfolded.

"Whoa!"

Peter stumbled back, his large form crawling out of the way of the growing circle within the cement floor. His breath caught in his throat when the circle stopped growing. The engraved center collapsed and disappeared. Peter hunched up on his hands and knees and peered over the side of the round hole in the floor. The cylinder that had been cut seemed to lead to a bottomless pit, dropping forever.

When it finally stopped, a grinding sound echoed in the room as it appeared to sink. Then it illuminated and become one with a floor below. A soft glow rested on the walls of the tunnel leading to the room below.

"This is it? But how do I..." Peter's mouth dropped open slightly as metal bars popped out of the surface of the tunnel to form a ladder. "Figures they wouldn't make it easy."

Peter slid into the channel, grabbed one of the metal rods, and scaled his way down. He released the last rod and jumped about four feet down, into a burrowed alcove. The mark on his palm pulsated, heated and glowing. The jagged walls of the niche were covered with carved figures, artistic representations of huge men who appeared to be giants. Their armor was transparent, revealing their forms and clothing; it was as if the designer had purposely left the shields and swords uncolored.

"Whoa, just like I remembered it? But..." Peter traced one of the weapons. He didn't see the necklace that was worn on many of the angel warriors he'd encountered when he absorbed the book of Truth in the Stronghold almost a year ago.

The symbol replicated on the floor above was in the center of the cryptic designs. Peter placed his hand flat on it. Within seconds, needles pricked his skin, and a sliver of thick smoke, like ghostly lines, slivered through his fingers to reveal a map. Small triangles represented sanctuaries similar to the one he was in now, but only two other strongholds were revealed. Those were the only places where Peter knew he could access the other two *Books of Truth*.

"If the first Stronghold showed the secret of the thousand year war, what does this 2nd book hold?" His eyes narrowed and followed each figure, now aglow, as the suspended map in fine ghostly form floated in front of him. The weapons were illuminated. In a flash it dissipated.

"Peter! Peter! Where are you?" Kyle's voice echoed faintly.

The floor shook.

"Crap. That dummy's gonna get us all killed." Peter jumped up to the ladder. He held his breath as the floor beneath him rumbled, cracked, shook, and crumbled. "Gotta get outta here," he said.

Peter shuffled up the ladder. With each step, one by one the metal bars holding him disappeared within the rock, and the wall receded. Experience taught him that sacred places of the Decretum Venia didn't like being disturbed by others who didn't or couldn't give it blood. Also, he found that when it had shared information about a Stronghold, it destroyed itself. It made Peter wondered how long it had been since someone—another like him —had accessed these places.

He snorted at that thought. "No one else would be this stupid."

With one final pull, he lifted himself out of the hole, just before the cement cylinder closed and locked back in place with a loud click. Peter then jerked around at the sound of someone cursing.

Click.

It locked back in place.

Peter jerked around at the sound of someone cursing.

"I'm going to break my neck!" Kyle fussed from the other side of the wall of boxes.

"Shut up and get back outside. I'm coming," Peter yelled, impatient and ticked at Kyle for searching him out.

"You better hurry, man. We're already packed. Gil wants to get outta here and find Chloe. He won't shut up about it."

Peter squeezed through the wall of boxes to stand in front of Kyle. He wiped his now-tepid palm on his jeans. "We have to get Angel first, and then we'll find our answers as to how to beat them.

There's no freakin' way we can just walk into Gavin Steele's territory and fight him. I know what we left behind is nothing compared to what's waiting for us now." Peter wiped a hand down his face, trying to stop the slight trembling.

Kyle frowned and folded his arms in front of him. "What do you mean?"

"Tell me, Kyle. Tell me what you remember. Ya know, the things you saw when we were saving Angel from Gavin's house in Florida," Peter demanded, though he almost didn't want to know. He was pretty sure of what he'd seen and experienced, but if Kyle saw it all, too, that would confirm his worst fears, his worst nightmares.

Kyle shivered. "At first, when we went to the beach house, I only saw you and Lucien fighting while I was beating up one of their goons. When I knocked the guy out, Lucien was on the floor," he swallowed, "but it looked like you were fighting something invisible. Lights were flashing from your hand, your eyes, and you...dude." Kyle's eyes wandered away from Peter as if he was uncomfortable. "Even your veins glowed blue."

Peter nodded. "What about when I started fighting Gavin. Did you see anything?"

Kyle's stricken gaze met Peter. "Yeah, but don't make me say it out loud. I s-still," Kyle stumbled back, his body shook and he hit one of the boxes behind him. Bracing his hands on the box, his head rested on it, Kyle whispered, "A monster. Evil. You pulled that thing out of Gavin and I literally peed my freakin' pants." A broken sob escaped him. "But I did it, I got Angel out of there for you. I never thought I'd see you again."

Peter walked to him. He put his hand on Kyle's trembling shoulder. "Thanks. I thought only I could see them. That I was going insane. Man..." Peter pressed his eyes closed to combat the dread enveloping him. "It's going to be worse. I screwed up.

Opening that book, it gave him more power. The nightmares I've been having…"

"Are they like mine?" Kyle turned around. "More of those things, walking, and eating us?"

"Something like that. When we go to where Gavin is, we're going to see more of them. He, or the demon he had inside him, controls them. The stronger ones can make themselves come into the physical world. Here on earth. Others, the weak ones, can feed off of humans to seduce or influence them to do what they want."

Kyle tilted his head to the ceiling. "Those I can't see. But you can. That's why you were freaking out when we left the place where you found that book. After that, you saw them—and they knew you."

"I know. And now, they'll know you too."

CHAPTER 10

Peter leaned against the flimsy wall of the shelter at the bus stop. The fall breeze kicked up, sending leaves and scattered trash swirling up into the air around them. As vulnerable as he felt there in the dark, he had purposefully waited till nightfall to leave the orphanage. He didn't want to leave again, and it felt as if someone had ripped his heart out of his chest. That thought of someone destroying the orphanage meant he could never return – there would be nothing left. Nearly drowning with his father, around the age of ten, had done something to Peter, but seeing his mother shot down in front of him still made him want to vomit. He carried so much pain from losing them, and he wasn't sure he could ever truly get past it. But he'd been able to deal with it, except when he had time to think. The guys were quiet, and Peter was glad for the silence. The street around them was vacant, with the exception of a bum or two.

Peter moved away from Kyle and adjusted the bag Pastor Finn gave him. Kyle had been with him in some of the darkest places of this horrible hell he now called his life. But still, Kyle's former lies sat in the back of his mind like a beacon, warning him to be cautious when dealing with the half-breed kid that was mixed with some pure blood from the Decretum Venia but who dabbled with friendships from kids in the Order of the Dragon. Although, he'd have to admit, with Kyle saving his life more than once, maybe the guy wasn't all bad.

The bus pulled up, and they climbed aboard. Peter stuffed cash into the receptacle for all of them and smiled silently at the bus driver. The bus was quiet, even though there were quite a few people sitting in the seats.

As he sat in the last seat on the bus, Peter felt his hand throb. It was a constant, nagging reminder that the crap wasn't over. He squeezed his hand tightly around the pole while the other two took separate seats just in front of him.

Just as the bus started to pull out, it stopped abruptly. Peter's eyes narrowed as he lifted his gaze. He was shocked to see the girl with the purple hair, the one he'd seen earlier. "Damn," Peter said, slouching back in his seat. His eyes never left hers.

"What?" Gil asked.

The girl hesitated and nervously slid into a seat near the front.

"That girl, the one with the purple hair, she's following us," Peter replied.

An uneasy feeling settled in his stomach. The girl reminded him of Hanna. But something about her seemed off. Not in her looks but in the unique way she held her head—to the side as if she was listening to voices unseen. But he'd always considered Hanna a bit touched in the head. Not unintelligent, but distracted, out of place or just plain weird.

"Why would she wanna follow us? Think she wants to steal something?" Kyle asked, leaning over to get a closer look at the purple-haired stranger.

"No. She's...different. She reminds me of the girl who gave me the mark." Peter looked at Kyle as his jaw dropped, and he almost felt the same. Saying it out loud gave him an uneasy feeling, and all the guilt of what had happened to Hanna, the memory that he had inadvertently caused her death, came rushing back.

"I could go talk to her." Gil started to stand.

Peter stayed him with a hand on his shoulder. "Don't do it. Wait and see if she gets off with us. This bus will take us within a few city blocks of where they have Angel. If she follows us to a Sanctuary and she's not supposed to be there, we won't have to worry about her."

"Yeah, you're right. Sanctuaries are protected by the prayers and herbs passed down through the Order for centuries. If she doesn't have some Decretum Venia, she'll get sick when she tries to pass through the barrier." Kyle relaxed when he saw that the girl was acting normal, turning her attention to a book she was reading.

"How do you even remember all that when you were always skipping class?" Gil asked, elbowing Kyle.

"My father's stash. They didn't teach that stuff in the school I went to, but I ate up all the scrolls, books, notes, and historical diaries my father stole from his family."

"Why would he have to steal it? Most kids' parents teach them that stuff. That's why so many kids in the Decretum Venia were schooled at home or in underground private schools that pretended to be prep schools. The only reason I never got to go to one was because my parents abandoned me and went on the run." Gil's longing and discomfort with his past flashed in his eyes.

"Consider yourself lucky. Not too long ago, those schools were destroyed. Set on fire or blown up. It was in the news everywhere —some terrorist act. But we all know who did it." Kyle nodded at Peter.

"Dang. The more I learn, the more I wished I would've left that place years ago. But Chloe was there, and she made me happy. Even though all she talked about was being free." Gil's voice choked. "I tried to give her that, but..." He covered his face with his hand and laid his head back. "I messed up."

Peter pushed his shoulder. "We all did. I made my girl a promise, too, but I didn't realize I didn't have what it took to make it come true. I'm sorry. Really sorry this happened. I'll help you get Chloe back," Peter said, wearing a half-smile. He didn't have the nerve to admit to the kid that Chloe's condition was questionable at best.

The brakes on the bus squealed, and the driver called out the name of the street from the map.

"This is our stop." Peter put on his backpack and made his way through the nearly empty bus. He glanced down. The purple-haired girl was reading. Her hands trembled while turning the pages.

Kyle pushed past Peter. "Hurry up."

Relieved she didn't seemed to be inclined to move, Peter got off the bus. They walked a few feet, but the bus didn't leave. He narrowed his eyes and hesitated, but Kyle tugged him by the shirt.

"I don't know if you realize it, but this side of town isn't the best. We better move on." Kyle dragged Peter by the arm.

Peter pivoted away from the bus and started to jog. "C'mon, it's this way." After a few blocks of brisk walking Peter heard it: a faint voice.

"Wait! Wait! You there!" a girl's silent plea carried through the wind.

"No," Peter mumbled. "It's her. Damn. I told you she was following us!"

"Let's just ditch her, man. It can't be too hard to outrun a girl. Well, maybe for Gil, but still," Kyle chided. "C'mon. We can go through that abandoned building." Kyle pointed and nudged Peter along with his elbow.

"No!" Peter shook his head. He refused to do it again, to treat her the way he'd treated Hanna. Running from Hanna hadn't deterred her from following him, and because he'd refused to stop, she'd gotten run over. Peter couldn't let that happen again, as he knew he would never be able to forgive himself. "We wait and see what she wants."

Gil grimaced. "After what happened earlier, do you think she's safe? I mean, they could have sent her after us."

Kyle looked at Gil like he was crazy. "That girl? She doesn't look like she's had a meal in weeks."

"True. I don't think she's working for the other team." Peter placed his hands on his hips and waited for her to approach. She dropped her book and hastily picked it up to run towards them. Her purple and black streaked hair framed her pale face in a severe bob.

She stopped in front of Peter. Trying to catch her breath, she rested a delicate hand on her neck. Huge almond-shaped eyes, draped in long lashes, blinked up at him. "Thank you for waiting."

"What do you want?" Peter didn't want to know, but he asked anyway. He felt obligated to at least do the one thing he hadn't for Hanna...listen.

"Someone to stay with. I...uh...ran away from home. It was really bad there, and you look familiar or ah, nice. And you're kids like me so I hope you can...that I can maybe hang out with you." She twisted the hem of her raggedy plaid skirt. Her holey white stockings were dirty and she smoothed a timid hand down on her skirt trying to cover one of them.

"That's not a good idea." Peter kept his eyes on hers. His heart sped up when he noticed it: another similarity this girl had with Hanna, recognition. She knew him, or something about him, that made her comfortable. The girl never looked at the other guys, only at Peter.

"My name is Argia." She put a tentative hand out to him. "I'm fifteen. How old are you?"

"Older." Peter didn't reach for her hand. His last memory of

Hanna was of her grabbing his wrist and branding him with her blood. No way, he was touching this girl.

"He's seventeen and a prick when he doesn't know anyone." Kyle extended his hand and shook Argia's. "I'm Kyle, the same age. Gil there is fifteen too."

Peter rolled his eyes at Kyle. "Can you back off?" Peter elbowed Kyle.

"Nope, I'm saving this girl from you. C'mon, we've got someplace to..." Kyle frowned as he looked away from Argia, "go."

Peter's eyes followed his, and realized the wind was picking up behind her, making a small wind devil. The few prostitutes that had been walking the streets scurried in the opposite direction. Peter's skin tingled.

"What is it? Did I do something wrong?" At Kyle's stricken expression, Argia's hand dropped to her side. She stepped backward.

Peter felt it, the rising in him, the snake of power emulating from his hand. It slithered through his veins and his eyes captured a shadowed figure of darkness contained in the small free-standing tornado. Wind whipped around them, getting stronger. In the distance Peter felt someone pulling on his shirt. It felt surreal as if every cell in him needed to focus on the small vortex of wind, smoke, and debris in front of him.

"Let's get out of here!" Kyle yelled above the beating wind, now mixed with droplets of rain and dead leaves.

Peter snapped out of his daze but not before spotting five additional shadows within the storm, trapped and barely held in place by some invisible barrier within the eye of it. He stepped back and pushed Argia behind him as orange eyes glowed brighter behind the mini-tornado that seemed to expand out of the cement sidewalk.

"Run!" He pushed Argia forward.

Argia's hand touched his briefly as she closed her eyes and

grasped his. They ran. And ran faster. Argia never let go of Peter's hand while keeping up with his rapid pace. Within minutes, the rain ceased, and the wind died behind them.

The runners slowed, and Peter tugged his hand from her tight grip. He placed his hands on his knees and caught his breath. "Scared I'd let you go?" Peter asked the girl.

"Hell yeah!" Gil released Peter's backpack.

Peter shrugged. "Scared ass. Why were you holding onto my bag?"

"Keep you with me, didn't want you to fall behind and get ate up by that freak storm that came out of nowhere." Gil stood and shuffled his feet while staring at Argia. "She was helping too."

"Look, uh, Argia...is there somewhere we can drop you? It's late and we have someplace to be." He adjusted his bag and started toward the city block. The entire street seemed to be littered with abandoned houses that were boarded up.

"I can't. It's hard out here for a girl alone." Argia searched behind them and visibly relaxed after a moment. "See what just happened? I could've been uh...recruited by one of those prostitutes. They've tried that before, but I ran." She yanked on Peter's jacket and whispered, "I keep running."

Peter jerked away, for her whispered plea made him feel uneasy. "From who?" he asked, then walking away.

She smiled in a dopey way, as if caught in a daze. "Bad people, like those prostitutes, and boys who run with gangs. Oh, and the ones who have guns or like to steal stuff...and mean men dressed in blue who drive cars with lights on them."

"The cops?" Kyle slowed his pace. "You run from the cops?"

Although Argia was petite for her age, she kept up with them and squeezed herself between Kyle and Peter. "Yep. They'll take me back. I'm never going back. Ever. Never. Ever. Never."

Gil moved his finger in a circle around his head and made a cross-eyed face. "Looney." He coughed.

Peter grinned. "Why do you need to hide from the cops?" He crossed the street and walked up the alleyway. He waited while Kyle kicked in a boarded window to the basement of an abandoned house on the corner.

Argia waited to answer him. Evidence of her inner debate was evident on her face. "Um. They aren't all nice. It is hard to know who is and who isn't." She grinned widely and hugged Peter. "But I know you are."

Peter untangled himself from her strong but thin arms. "No I'm not."

Gil laughed. "He's telling the truth. Nothing but trouble." He slid through the window, following Kyle.

"You can stay with us till we get to the next spot." Peter nodded toward the window. "Go ahead. You can trust me and those guys not to hurt you."

She smiled. "I know Peter. Safe with you," she sang in a similar singsong way Peter remembered Hanna doing. Then she slid through the window.

CHAPTER 11

Peter was tired. He needed to think. The crawlspace under the house they'd broken into was small, dusty, and dank, and they'd all tumbled down from a small drop from the window.

The others moved out a bit to get comfortable, but Argia stayed nearby and watched Peter closely. He tried to ignore her, because although Hanna had stringy blonde hair, a bad limp, and pale skin covered in dirt, there were undeniable similarities between them. Like Hanna, Argia had an airy disposition, the ability to hold on to some unforeseen river of happiness despite any bad situation. Like Hanna, Argia was homeless, roaming the streets, running from someone or somewhere. He regretted that he hadn't taken time to find out more about Hanna. He'd been selfish.

Peter pivoted from Argia's hopeful gaze. He didn't know what she was after, but he had a feeling she was trying to get closer to him, and that was the last thing he wanted. Peter tossed his bag down and slid his hand under the back of his head to get comfortable. He slid Angel's picture out of his pocket and smiled. Wanting to be with her was screwing with him. He felt starved and hungry, and the tingling anticipation of seeing her soon bounced off his skin. *Damn. Will she be mad it took me so long to get her?*

They were close to where the map showed Angel's location to be, but it wasn't exact. Pastor Finn had drawn a big picture of this place on the edge of the city, leading to Virginia, as if he'd know where to find her. But maybe Pastor Finn knew it. That's why he hinted to the sacred room. The hidden alcove Peter found had revealed so much more than Pastor Finn's map. Only problem was, the place where Rosa hid didn't appear. Maybe, she'd made a new Sanctuary. He'd have to take time to go through Pastor Finn's stuff again.

"Uh, Peter?" Argia whispered.

Peter jumped, shocked to find her lying right next to him, so close her warm breath tickled his ear. "Back off, would ya? Just because I'm helping you, doesn't mean you can take up residence in my personal space." He stared at her sternly, waiting for her to move away.

She grinned at him. "I need to ask you something, but I don't want the others to hear."

Peter sighed. "What?" He turned onto his side and slid a bit away from her.

"Do you hear them?" Her almond-shaped eyes skittered around the room, as if searching out multiple places on the cracked, dirt-packed walls. "They like you." Argia leaned in, almost touching his lips. "They're here to protect you."

Peter jerked back. "Get away from me!" The hairs on his neck stood up with awareness.

Argia touched his arm lightly, a tear falling from her eye. "Thank you. So much. I'm safe now." She stood and went to sit in the opposite corner, watching him with a broad smile while humming and rocking in place.

Peter jerked back. "What?! Get away from me," he stated harshly, the hairs on his neck standing up with awareness.

Peter turned away to spy Gil's comic expression as he twirled his finger at the side of his head and mouthed "crazy". Peter smiled. He couldn't help it, Gil was a fool.

Kyle laughed. "I second that!"

"Shut up and get some sleep, we got a lot of walking later today." Peter wanted them to be quiet, to leave him with his thoughts a while. He loosened his grip on Angel's picture and smiled at it again. "Soon babe, I'll be with you real soon. We'll fix this. We will." Peter dozed. Peaceful this time. The first time in a while. Every muscle within him relaxed, turned soft, and felt, safe. Just like Argia said, he felt safe.

"Peter!"

Startled, he jumped and scratched his curly black hair, then stared at Argia's worried expression. "What the hell? Really? I mean, can't you leave me alone even for a minute?" He shook his head at her. Peter was regretting bringing her, but something about her and her similarity to Hanna wouldn't let him leave her behind.

"I wanted to talk to you. The others are asleep." Her eyes darted from Gil to Kyle. "They are nice too. You picked your protection well."

Peter sat up, scratching his head more vigorously. "Look. I can't understand what you're saying. Why do you want to talk to me? Why did you even follow me? Girl, can't I just drop you at a hospital or something, you actin' like something is wrong in the head." He took his fist and knocked on the top of his head.

Argia sat back with a frown. "You think I'm crazy, don't you?" She crossed her thin arms in front of her small chest. Her torn, cropped jacket fell open to reveal a dingy blouse.

Peter smirked at her as his eyebrows rose. "Would you think you're crazy? They can help you at the hospital." He crossed his legs and got comfortable. It didn't appear that this girl would leave him alone.

"No they won't." Argia shook her head vigorously from side to side. "No hospitals. Never again! Not those places. I can't, just can't go back. I won't!" She stopped and leaned forward, till she was almost nose to nose with Peter. "They lock you up there," she whispered.

He scooted back. "Personal freakin' space. Stop moving up on me like that."

Argia gulped. "I'm sorry. I can't help it. You're just so...beautiful."

"Uh, look. I have a girlfriend. A serious one." Peter couldn't help feeling uncomfortable, so he slid back a bit further. "Besides you're too young for me." He glanced down at her tiny chest. "And not my type."

Argia looked down at her boobs. "Oh!" Her hand covered her mouth. "You like bigger? Well I'm still growing. But...it's not like that."

"Tell me about the hospital. What don't you like about them?" He tried to talk gentle, the way he felt he should've talked to Hanna.

"They put jackets on you. White ones." She tapped her chin with her dirty chipped fingernail. "Sometimes though, they have yellow ones. Well, not real yellow but dingy yellow. I don't like those. They smell. Horrible. They smell horrible. Stinky."

"Okay. Why did they put a jacket on you?" Peter asked, swallowing slowly. His skin started to tingle, and he watched Argia closely as she started to slowly rock back and forth, as if fighting a memory.

"I-I tried to run, but I learned...learn...learned to play nice, to behave. I stopped letting them know about...the voices." Argia's gaze jerked to a grumbling Kyle. As soon as she realized he was beginning to stir, she hurriedly crawled to the other side of the room.

Peter's jaw dropped. What the heck was the matter with him? Did he have a bat-shit crazy meter on his head? A beacon that got all the slightly touched girls on the street to want to follow him.

CHAPTER 12

Peter tried to ignore her. But Argia wouldn't be ignored. Although her petite legs placed her just up to his chest, she kept pace with him. Kyle and Gil followed as Peter weaved them in and out of the throng of people on the city street during the busy weekday. Here and there, an older person gave them a wary or concerned glance as if afraid they were a gang or something. Peter ignored them.

A few more blocks and they would be there. A place on the edge of the city that was supposedly in a bad part of town. It bordered on Maryland and had a reputation for being riddled with crime. The funny thing was, the more Peter roamed the streets, the more he realized that crime was everywhere. As rich and safe as Gavin Steele and his sidekicks seemed, those people in the Extraho of Obscurum were more evil and cruel than even the worst reprobates he'd come across.

"How much further?" Argia was slightly out of breath. The only indication that keeping up with Peter was a challenge.

"Not far. I don't know if we should, or can, take you in." Peter looked both ways before crossing the street, now void of people since they'd crossed into another part of town that consisted of mainly houses. No stores, businesses, or shops had been around them for a while. Only here and there, they'd passed a drunk or homeless person sleeping off their liquor.

"Hey." Kyle jumped between Argia and Peter. "Can you give us a minute?" Kyle pulled Peter aside.

Peter followed Kyle to the corner while Gil and Argia stood just staring at each other. Gil appeared uncomfortable with her.

"The girl. We need to ditch her." Kyle frowned at Peter. "Dude, she's out there."

"I know, but..." Peter dragged his brown fingers through is thick curling hair. "I can't."

Kyle nodded. "Yes you can. We can drop her at some shelter or something. Taking her with us..." He shook his head. "We just can't."

"I know you're not talking. You brought Gil with us. Because of you, his girlfriend, Chloe is having some wicked shit happen to her right this minute." He pointed at Kyle. "Your fault. Now you lookin' at me and telling me to ditch a girl who really needs our help. Unlike Gil, she's wasn't somewhere safe, somewhere she was being protected."

Kyle's blue eyes shimmered with guilt. "I get it. I'm real beat up about what happened. But that's not why I don't think we should take Argia with us. Haven't you noticed something strange about her?"

"Other than she seems batshit crazy? Naw." Peter crossed his arms in front of him as Argia inched closer to Gil and Gil stepped back.

"She makes us feel uncomfortable. The girl also talks to herself. But stares at you all—the—freakin' time."

"I know. Still. I'm not feelin' like she's a bad person. You get what I'm saying? I feel about her the same way I felt when I met you. I knew something bad was after you. I knew you weren't by most standards a good person—but I knew you were cool."

Kyle scratched his head, thinking. "I...uh."

"Think about what I'm saying. Put her strange behavior in the back of your mind. What do you feel when you're next to her? Danger? Or a feeling of heaviness, like the ugly feeling we got from those guys that we fought with? Tell me."

Kyle sighed. "You're right. I feel like something bad is around her, but when I'm next to her it feels like... Like, innocence." Kyle got this confused expression on his face. "But that doesn't sound logical."

"Logic left the room when we met up."

Kyle chuckled. "Yeah. It did."

Peter tapped Kyle with his fist. "C'mon. Let's get Angel."

◊

If Peter hadn't been around the block with strange and insanity, he'd've thought he was totally wrong about this place.

The Sanctuary he'd been expecting wasn't here. Couldn't be. In front of him was a city block. Every single house on it was abandoned. No one was on the street. And the block was in a weird place.

They'd crossed a large abandoned school's parking lot, then went through some type of city dump, which was completely void of anyone protecting it. No dog, no rodents, nothing. The dump had a fence around the back of it. They squeezed through a broken part of it, which opened up to this one complete city block with nothing but a portion of a park in the back of it.

"Now what?" Gil rubbed his arms against the fall wind blowing. "I'm cold, hungry and ready to go find Chloe."

Peter glanced back at Argia, who appeared uncomfortable. She was rocking a bit with a frown on her face. "What's wrong, Argia?"

Argia gulped. "Nothing. I. I'm tired. Tired." She sighed. "I'll wait here for you to come back." She sat on the bottom step of one of the houses. Humming some lilting tune, Argia dug in her satchel and pulled out a container of canned wieners. Daintily she chewed on one, then another. All of them stared at her.

Peter didn't realize she had food. The girl hadn't offered them any.

"You had food?" Gil asked.

"Yep." She kept humming.

"Got any more?" Gil stepped up next to her.

"Not for you. I'm only sharing with Peter. Meanie!" Argia stuffed the last miniature hotdog in her mouth and tossed the can aside.

"Cut it." Irritated, Peter tossed a power bar he'd taken from the last Sanctuary at Gil.

Gil grabbed it mid-air. "You've been hoarding food." He shook his head. "I thought we were friends."

Peter grinned. "Shut up. You're Kyle's friend, remember?"

Kyle laughed. "Peter, nobody really wants to be your friend. They just want to hang with me and know they have to deal with your attitude to do it."

"Again I repeat..." Peter nudged Kyle with his elbow. "Shut up."

"Let's go around the entire block. This street is deserted and I know there's a reason why." Peter noticed the stillness in the area. However, it didn't feel quite as serene as he usually felt when he was within a protected area like the other Sanctuaries. But he was close. Real close. Most all of them had this stillness and were void of people. Not only that, but this city street wasn't attached to any other street, they'd come through a junkyard that seemed to be some type of barrier or outer post.

Argia reached into her bag to pull out a book, "I'm staying here," she frowned.

Peter noticed a slight tremble in her hand, making him

wonder if the effects of the sacred grounds affected her. "You sure?"

Argia wouldn't look at him. "I'm s-sure."

"Why?" Peter wanted to know. Had to know if she was supposed to be with him or not. From his experience at Rosa's, one of the elder's Sanctuary, he knew that if anyone from the Extraho of Obscurum tried to walk on the sacred ground, they would feel sick or may even die. Which made him wonder what was up with Argia.

"I just don't want to go. I'll be waiting for you here. Uh, protecting you. I can do that. I'll protect you, Peter." She sniffled and wiped a hand on her now-sweaty brow. "They're looking for us."

Kyle crossed his eyes behind Argia's back and Gil nodded in agreement. Then Kyle mouthed, "Looney."

"Okay, well Gil, stay with her." Peter pointed and Gil stopped grinning at Kyle.

"Why me?" Gil snorted. "I think you play favorites. You leave me with," he caught himself from saying something mean around Argia, "this girl. But Kyle would be a better choice."

"No. If you plan on hanging with us, you'll stay here. We'll be back. If we aren't back before tomorrow...come get us," Peter pivoted away and started walking.

Kyle caught up. "You think that's a good idea? Strange girl with Gil the weak link?"

"Gil's stronger than you know. He has to be now. It's do or die. Right?" Peter shrugged. He wouldn't make excuses or pacify the kids who decided to follow him anymore. He'd warned Gill and Argia, hell, even Kyle. Even Chloe, Gil's girlfriend, wouldn't take the hint. Being with him, around him, near him, could cause death. So if he told them following him would put them in danger and they were stupid enough to keep on coming, then they'd better get some guts to survive. He was done dealing with the guilt of others' stupidity.

"No. He's not. Dude's been in that place most of his life. The only time he's gone out was with me and you that one time, then only with me. I think Chloe's been out more than he has."

"Since when do I care?" Peter turned towards Kyle, anger at being in this situation pounded through him. "I am barely able to stomach taking you with me. You know all I wanted to do was get Angel. And what pisses me off is you don't even realize what we're up against."

"What? You're kidding, right? I don't understand?" Kyle's fist pounded his chest. "I do! I was the one who watched you die at that place. I was the one who saved your ass twice from a bullet. But you still think I have to prove my freakin' judgment to you?" Kyle crossed his arms in front of him. "Get over it. You aren't the only one in this pound of shit. My parents died too. I survived years without their love and dealing with the demon spawn kids in my school who wanted to control me."

"But you don't know..." Peter couldn't say it. Not now. Not to Kyle. He was so screwed.

"Trust me, okay. I'm you friend. You're the best messed-up friend I'd ever had. We can fix this together." Kyle put out his hand.

Peter tapped it with his fist before shaking it. "You're right. I'm being an asswipe." He started walking again. He couldn't face Kyle with what he was about to tell him.

"Okay. Spill it." Kyle sighed as if he was getting ready to take a physical blow.

"I was set up. Gavin Steele, set me up. The demon he had inside him when we snuck into his house to save Angel wanted me to open that book we found in the Stronghold." Peter's palm started to burn just at the mention of Gavin.

"How could he set you up? They'd been stealing kids for decades. It's not possible he'd even known your name. I searched you on Google and it said you were considered dead. Your name wasn't even Peter Saints before, it was Peter Cone. Not as catchy as Peter Saints, but the Order apparently renamed you for some reason."

"None of that matters. He was searching me out, my family line. In the sacred books for both the Extraho of Obscurum and the Decretum Venia, it was clued in on an ancestor from each group touching an ancient relic that gave them a brief awareness of each other. The demon in Gavin knew the Angel whose DNA was purposely placed in my family line. That angel happened to be the scribe: a historical recorder who'd hidden knowledge about a thousand year war. I..." Peter gulped back the rise of bile in his throat. "I'm the last survivor of that genetic line. Only my blood could open the books in the Stronghold. And when I did it, I opened knowledge to both sides."

"Wait! What the f—" Kyle covered his mouth. "Are you saying that when we went to the Stronghold to open that book to find ways to save Angel and to fight the Order of the Dragon, we were actually helping the bastards?"

"Yeah. And do you remember begging me to leave it alone?" Peter's eyes watered at the sides. Stupid. He was so stupid.

"Vaguely. But it doesn't matter now. What does this mean for us? For the world—mankind."

"For us? We have to fix it. We need Angel to do it. Her ancestor was there. He was powerful. Besides, I love her, and I don't want anything to happen to her where they are holding her."

"How can we ensure her safety? We're barely staying alive ourselves."

"I don't know. The other books..." Peter sighed.

"The other books!" Kyle stopped Peter with his hand. "What the hell would we want to open them for?"

Peter shook his head. "Now we don't have a choice. The

demons, the ones working with the Order of the Dragon, they're getting free."

"Wait? They can't all get free!" Kyle rolled a string of curses.

"No, but the stronger ones can. Especially now that their demon is in Gavin and knows the secret of the first book."

"But how? How did he even know it was you?"

Peter dropped his eyelids down to stop, to push the words out to Kyle that needed to be said. "Hanna—the girl who gave me the brand—she had the ability to communicate with demons and angels. She was called a transcender. They were used to infiltrate the demon camps as humans to gather intelligence on the war plans of the demons. Those humans were given angelic powers specific to that ability. It took the Angels over half the time of the war to perfect it the DNA manipulations. But transcenders had crazy power. When they knew how to use it, they could entrap demons."

"Damn. So now we are royally smashed."

"Yeah. We are."

CHAPTER 13

This had to be the place. The way into the Sanctuary that held Angel. The structure in front of Peter resembled all the other brick houses that were connected in the completed replica of a city block. No alleyway in. No windows were left open; every window, doorway, or entrance was bricked over.

"What now?" Kyle asked, sitting on the cement bottom step of one of the row houses. "The place might look like a ton of houses stuck together, but it's really a fortress. There's no way in. It's like a bricked-up movie set...right off the freakin' *Twilight Zone*."

Peter eyed the place, keeping his hands on his hips as he looked up to the bright sun and caught a flash of light to his right. "There's always a way in. We've just gotta figure out what it is. Look around for symbols of the Decretum Venia. It won't be obvious, but if we take our time, we'll find it. All the sanctuaries have the symbol somewhere."

"Yeah, yeah, yeah," Kyle muttered as he got up and jumped off the steps. "I'm starting at the end of the block and will work my way back to you."

"Cool." Peter shook off the anxious tension in his neck and

started the tedious task of inspecting, touching, prodding, and pushing on every extended brick he could reach.

Hours later he and Kyle met up where they began.

A thin-lipped Kyle kicked the bottom step. "This sucks. We felt up every damn doorway, brick, and rock on this place and still got nothing."

"I know man. It does." Peter frowned as he tripped over a small pebble at the base of the step. He bent to pick it up to throw it, but the thing wouldn't budge. "Wait."

"For what? It's already night and we have to go tell the others to find somewhere to sleep in the junkyard. And that place smells worse than the mucked-up Sanctuary we were held in." Kyle pivoted away from Peter.

"Wait!" Peter squatted, adjusting his backpack while he tried to dislodge the rock. Then he heard the faint clicking sounds.

Click-click-click...

"What the f...?" Kyle muttered, hearing the faint sounds.

Peter stood and turned to see that several bricks were shifting at the base of one of the stairs. Within seconds, the design on the wall next to the lower set of stairs, on the replica of a brick house, was shaped in the rounded, intertwined three circles of the Decretum Venia. He stepped backward and glanced over to the nearby stoop, realizing that it, too, had bricks that shifted into the same design. "Check this out." Peter pointed.

Kyle's eyebrow rose, and he rubbed his hands together, as if a new spark of energy had flared up in him. "Whoa!"

Peter bent and pressed several of the bricks. "Nothin' not a thing. Damn!"

"Keep trying. I'll try the other one."

Standing up, Peter gave the top protruding brick a final kick. There was a grinding sound.

"Something's happening! Yeah dude!" Kyle exclaimed.

Peter looked over and realized that the bricked-up door a few steps up was cracking open. "'Bout time," he said as his heart began to beat in his chest at the thought that his Angel was on the other side of that door. The blood in his veins drummed, and a thick heaviness filled his chest with anticipation. *God, I miss her.* It felt like there was a hole in his chest, and the heaviness of anger, loneliness, and regret were constantly kicking him in the back of the head. It had literally felt like that every night since he'd allowed them to take her.

"Ready for this?" Kyle bounced on his toes.

Peter smirked and shook his head. "I knew you'd be trouble. Calm down and follow me." He glanced back, knowing that Kyle usually had a problem with adhering to orders. When it came to Angel, though, both he and Kyle had become protective.

Peter swallowed and squeezed through the thick door that had a brick front and a metal back, with no handles of any kind on either side. The hallway ahead was cement, illuminated with small lights encased in red bricks. He couldn't stop the hairs from raising on the back of his neck, nor could he stop thinking they were walking into a place just as screwed up as the sanctuary where'd he'd witnessed that murder.

"This place is freakin' cleaner than that hell-hole of a slum they put us in. Maybe she's better off here than with us." Kyle stated, his hand rubbing against one of the bricks. He stopped and poked at one of the encased bulbs within the center of the rock. "But who knows, I've been to places that rich people die to get into, but I couldn't wait to get out of them."

"Doesn't matter how good a cage looks, it's still a prison, and I know Angel wouldn't want to be here." Peter kept walking, listening for any sound that would indicate they'd been found out. "She'd want to be with me."

"I guess, but still, this place is first class." Kyle jumped up like he was trying to hit the ceiling. "No security cameras. Strange."

"Not strange. This place, like most of the Sanctuaries, was built a long time ago. They weren't afraid of thieves, they were afraid of other things. But that don't mean this place is safe. I thought at one time all Sanctuaries were safe, but people run them. And not everybody can be trusted." Peter focused ahead, making sure his steps were silent. The small lights within the bricks lit as he took each step, but as soon as he cleared the area, it darkened behind them.

"Why don't you just say it? The demons, or Order of the Dragon creeps, wanted in to places like this. But still, I'd rather they had some real security."

Peter shook his head. "Well fool, if they did get in, our asses would be toast. The only reason we made it this far is because of the blood in us. Because our parents were Decretum Venia recruits."

"Speak for yourself, I'm only half-blood. Remember my mom wasn't from the Order and my stuck-up—possibly dead mutilated father—never let me forget my blood was dirty with hers. Hell, if he cared so much, he shouldn't have knocked her up with me in the first place," Kyle snorted as he leaned in a bit to check behind them.

"Still, you wouldn't be able to get in here if you didn't have their blood in you," Peter stopped at the elevator door ahead of them.

"How do you know? I've been skipping into these places because you gave up blood—not I." Kyle's look of disgust turned into a grunt, as he straightened his shoulders then hunched a bit.

Peter smiled. "Rosa. I know because of what she taught me. She was the lady who ran one of the Sanctuaries where Angel and I hid out before we ran into you."

"Humph." Kyle tapped the elevator door with his finger. "No button?"

Peter frowned and searched around. "There's gotta be one

somewhere, but they're never obvious." He leaned against the elevator door and let his gaze travel the partially lit hallway floor, then to the bricks that held the small lights, and then his eyes circled back, surveying every square inch.

"This blows." Kyle kicked the wall, hitting one of the bricked lights near the floor.

Peter's eyebrow lifted. "Push the lights...any you can touch." He pivoted to the side and started pushing the small, flat, encased lights in the scattering of bricks within the cement wall.

"Ow! These things are hot!"

"No shit, Sherlock. Just keep trying."

Kyle touched another bulb and cursed under his breath. "What a dumb-ass idea," he said to himself. "I can't believe I'm following this genius." He pressed another light. "Dammit!" He blew his finger.

"Just keep trying." Peter pushed one more light. When he heard a whooshing sound, he turned and saw the elevator opening. Victoriously, he blew the tip of his finger like it was a smoking gun. "See? Told ya."

"About time." Kyle sauntered past Peter to step inside the lift.

Peter smirked at Kyle's cockiness. He couldn't help but hope there would be no more major issues getting to Angel. He hungered for her touch, and the ache was triple what he'd endured for all the months they'd been separated. Now that he was so close, the pain was almost unbearable. His love for her kept him sane and focused. In some small way, it even helped him love himself, something he'd never been able to do before.

"Well? Are you gonna push that or just stand there in a trance?" Peter nudged Kyle out of his spaced-out glare as he leaned over and pushed the blue button. It didn't have a number, a letter, or any kind of symbol on it, but it was the only button on the elevator, and he hoped it would take them to the level where the kids were kept.

Kyle frowned. "Just thinking."

"Oh. Well, I hope it didn't hurt too much," Peter chided.

The lights went out.

CHAPTER 14

G avin had to get the plan in motion. Jack had found another property that was potentially useful to gain the Order of the Dragon access to the precious blood of their enemy. It only angered him that Lucien hadn't been the one to find it. But Jack's ambitions would be dealt with - until he was no longer so useful.

The conference room on the main level of his mansion in Washington DC was the place where men of power had met over the decades, Presidents, actors, actresses, the multi-millionaires who could've been deemed the ones who actually ruled the world.

None of that power seemed to matter though. The minions of the Decretum Venia would find ingenious ways to block their most radical paths. Even though their numbers seemed to be dwindling, something gave them the power and the cohesiveness to subtly find the Dragon's weaknesses and derail them. But that was before Gavin acquired the power of the Dragon on his 18th birthday. His father's murder at his hand had been an honor to the old man. He'd died smiling, saying, "I knew it would be you, son."

Lucien though, would have to be dealt with. Unfortunately, it would have to wait till after his meeting—and after Lucien had healed from his last discipline.

Gavin felt Jack's entrance into the conference room. His senses seemed heightened ever since the master resided within him. Gavin knew who was coming, could hear them a great distance away—even smell them. Most especially the ones who'd given their souls to the Order of the Dragon, they held the scent of ash, as though part of them had already been to hell and back.

Jack watched him from the doorway.

"Jack, please enter and have a seat." Gavin waved his hand, then glanced up at Jack, slowly, allowing a smile to form on his face.

Jack cleared his throat, unfettered by Gavin's stance he sat down, appearing bored. "Your brother and the others are on the way. They had to finish with his cleansing. We're all sorry that Lucien displeased Master Balaal to such a degree."

Gavin slid into the chair at the head of the table. "And what of your master, Thanatos? Has he communicated with you?" Gavin studied Jack's face a moment. Thanatos was Balaal's greatest adversary, the one who wanted to take his position as one of the seven warriors named for the attack on the heavens and the Decretum Venia.

"I feel him. He is remorseful for the differences between your master and ours, but Thanatos has been tied to my family since the beginning. Even though Balaal and you don't believe it, we have been working toward the success of the Order of the Dragon." He cleared his throat. "As a whole, we are working toward the same goals." Jack raised a dark eyebrow. His thick mane of unruly black hair was trimmed just above his shoulders, where he bore a small tattoo of a demon, its body wrapped in a writhing serpent. "We set you both free with our peace offering of that child," Jack said assuredly. He nodded toward the map and continued, "And that property there... We believe someone you've been hunting resided there for a time."

"Is that so, and is it...attainable?" Gavin's skin warmed. Balaal was stirring, but Gavin was the stronger one, at least for the time being, so he pushed the demon back to its slumber. It would not take over, take the power from him just yet, not when he was so close to tracing Peter Saint's blood trail.

"Completely. The lawyers are working on it as we speak. It will be ours soon," Jack said, never pulling his smug stare from Gavin's.

"Within the month? We don't have much time, you know. The boy and the others they are holding there could escape anytime." Gavin certainly didn't want that to happen, for it would mean delaying his plan, thus giving the Decretum Venia time to come up with a way to stop the dragon. He didn't doubt that the boy, Peter, knew his plans, that the girl Balaal had planned to devour might have overheard his discussions with Lucien, who'd been tasked with keeping watch over her until the ceremony when her blood would be drained.

"We are watching the place. We've only spotted one man coming and going from the edge of the property. Unfortunately, there is an invisible barrier in place. Anyone from the Order who dares to step foot inside it is, uh..." Jack coughed. "They're incinerated, from the inside out."

The smell of fresh blood and tortured despair tickled Gavin's nose. His gaze awaited the appearance of his brother while he considered the information Jack had shared. The same incident had happened at the last property he'd purchased that was owned by the Decretum Venia. The only way they were able to get through was to give one of their guards a blood transfusion with the blood of one of the children they'd captured.

Lucien was accompanied by the witch, Mara, who was helping him walk. Gavin didn't miss how her blue eyes softened when Lucien wasn't watching. It came as no surprise, for women were always inexplicably captivated by his blond brother's good looks, until those same women were handed over to Gavin for his own purposes.

"Brother." Lucien struggled to bow his head. "I'm sorry I'm late. I had some, um...unfinished business."

Mara deposited a groaning Lucien in the chair next to Gavin and daintily sat down beside him with a wave of her midnight hair. Her sharp eyes danced over to him, and strength resided within them; in spite of her beauty, she held a hint of danger. Her wavy black tresses framed a gorgeous face. She was unafraid and felt equal to Balaal, since her demon mistress was Balaal's concubine. "Gavin," she said, but then her eyes narrowed into slits as she peered at him, as if she suddenly found something puzzling. "Balaal! Do awaken and join us, Master."

Then Gavin felt it: the piercing pain, the numbness, the fire, the ripping in his skin that seemed to come from nowhere. It was Balaal, returning to engulf Gavin's body, and he was pissed.

CHAPTER 15

Peter breathed slowly. The inky atmosphere seemed to press down on him. Kyle was grumbling. They'd been stuck for hours, blindly patting their hands around the cement enclosure trying to figure their way out.

"Well blood boy, any ideas?" Kyle smacked his teeth.

"Don't call me that. You really want to be punched in the face, don't ya?" Peter whipped a hand through his thick curls. "I didn't know what the button would do, but I'd think pushing it five, hell, a hundred times would make the damn door open." Peter kicked the wall. Wincing, he turned his anger inward, mad at himself again.

"Did it stick you? You know, like the other place did? Maybe it needs blood to open." Kyle ruffled around in the darkness again, and the sound of a bag dropping to the floor and a grunt echoed.

Peter tightened his backpack closer to him and brushed a bead of sweat from his brow. "No, nothing like that."

"I'm too tired for this crap. When was the last time we got some sleep?" Kyle snorted.

"Next to never. I haven't slept since I got the mark on my hand." With a huff, Peter gave up on finding their way out anytime soon and plopped down on the floor. He rested his back and bag against the wall. It was easier to talk to Kyle in complete darkness, because then he didn't have to see the looks of pity or disgust he knew would be staring back at him.

"The past sucks, but we've overcome that, right." Kyle started tapping on the wall. "How long you think we got in here before there's no air?"

Peter took a hesitant breath. "I dunno, but it's hot and getting harder to breathe. Of course, that could just be because we don't wanna be here."

"True, but..." Kyle's voice caught. "You hear that?"

"No. What is it? I don't—"

Tap-tap-thud...

A rhythmic pounding on the wall cut Peter short, followed by a creaking sound that echoed throughout the dark enclosure. A sliver of light broke through the back corner behind Kyle. The wall slid slightly open.

A mop of red hair, a riot of curls, framed the shocked girl's face. Her flashlight dropped, casting a glow on her surprised features. "H-how did you get in there?"

Peter jumped up. "Don't know."

"Yeah, but we're glad you found us." Kyle stood and walked over to the girl. He winked and slid past her to the other side.

Peter followed, ignoring her dropped mouth.

Suddenly, she reached out and grabbed his jacket. "I mean, how could you possibly have gotten in there?"

"I'm here to find my girlfriend." Peter brushed her hand away. "Can you help me? If you do, I'll tell you how I got in there."

The girl shook her head. "I just wanna know how to get out through there."

"Not tellin' until you help me find a girl named Angel." Peter's lips thinned as he stared down at the girl.

Her hand went up to her mouth. "You're...her boyfriend?" The girl mumbled something under her breath, then held her hand out to shake Peter's.

He stared down at it. "What?"

Diana shook her head from side to side. "Sorry, the girl mentioned she had a boyfriend who would find her," she cleared her throat, "when she first got here."

Peter narrowed his eyes at her.

"Never mind what I said." She waved a hand. "My name is Diana...and yours is?" She squinted at Kyle, who was rolling his eyes.

"Peter and," he elbowed Kyle, "Kyle."

"I know where she is, but you have to promise that if you leave here, I can go with you."

"Why do you want to? Isn't it safe here?" Kyle's eyebrow rose at her, as if on a dare.

"It was, but not anymore. Besides, I'm trying to find my parents. We got separated a few months ago and no one will tell me about them. They told me to meet them someplace if things started to get crazy."

"So what's crazy about being underground in the back of a junkyard?" Kyle snorted.

Peter couldn't help a grin at the girl's frown. "He's got a point."

"Look, do you want to find your uh, girlfriend, or not?" Diana crossed her arms.

"Yeah, I do. But I want to know what I'm walkin' into. What's this place like? How's she doing?"

The girl smirked. "This place is dull, and they keep re-teaching me everything there is to know about the Decretum Venia. My parents taught me that and more. So I'm bored sick. But a few weeks ago, they started taking blood samples from everyone. Then things got...creepy."

"What about Angel? How is she doing?" Peter's skin itched. He wanted to see her, but he didn't like what the girl was telling him.

The thought of someone knowing too much about the changes in her blood literally made him sick to his stomach. He knew something about him had changed when Kyle and he had left the stronghold, but he didn't know if the change had started earlier than that.

"Oh, yeah, they've been real interested in her. They held her... well, kept her for days while that Dr. somebody was here. If her friend Rob hadn't stepped in and pretty much sacrificed himself for her, I'm sure they woulda taken her with them."

Peter's jaw clenched. Angel had found someone else to take care of her. He swallowed. Peter didn't care. He held onto the love he knew they had. His old doubts and possessiveness had driven Angel away before. Not this time; he wouldn't lose her this time.

"We'll do it. You can go with us if you take Peter to her." Kyle placed a hand on Peter, trying to get him to back down.

"After I do, we can go the other way out. It'll be gross, but if we can't get out through the hidden elevator, we'll be toast." The girl rushed passed them in a whirl of red flamed hair.

Kyle smirked. "We always find the crazy ones, don't we?" He shrugged.

"You tellin' me?" Peter wiped a hand down his face. "You mean I do." He elbowed Kyle. "C'mon, before we lose her."

They followed closely behind Diana, barely able to absorb the dark, damp decor in the hallways they hurried through. Large pictures and statues of Angels dressed as warriors, and men wearing all forms of dress from different times in history, were scattered haphazardly throughout the place and Peter had to dodge a few here and there.

Finally, Diana came to an abrupt stop at a wooden door halfway down the hall. "We're going up to the floor, to the dorms. Lately, the place has been more like a prison. Anyway, it'll take us close to where your, uh..." She slanted her eyes toward Peter. "To where your girlfriend stays...with Rob."

Peter's heart shot up in his chest. He grabbed Diana's arm firmly, only releasing it when she flinched. "What do you mean, she's stayin' with this guy Rob?" Peter fought to control his breathing. Hell, even the dampness forming around the corners of his eyes. He would not lose it. It couldn't be what he suspected. Angel would never leave him—she promised she was different. That she loved him, despite everything he'd told her about his past.

Diana straightened up and backed away. "She sleeps in Rob's room. She usually sneaks in there after lights-out. I only know because...well, I had a thing for him a while back, and his room is next to mine."

Kyle placed a hand on Peter's chest as he tried to surge forward. "It can't be what you think." Peter flexed his fingers in and out of a fist. "Look...Angel, she's been through a lot. The nightmares she had might make it hard for her to sleep alone."

Diana raised an eyebrow. "You don't think the rest of us have nightmares? This place is a screamfest late at night. Besides, she's not in the room alone. She and her roommate get along well enough. But she just seems to feel," Diana shrugged, "safer with Rob. I guess. I don't blame her, he's pretty packed with muscle and he's just plain, Greek god looking. He could be like Thor's son or something."

Peter swallowed, and forced himself to make a calm reply. "Just take me to her."

Upon exiting the door on the above floor, Peter braced himself. The thought of Angel being with another guy made him sick. He wanted to hurt the kid, to kick a wall, to tear something up, but he knew he had to control himself. Most of all, he wanted to show her that he'd changed for the better, that he was worthy of her love this time, and throwing a temper tantrum or ripping the Greek god's head off wasn't going to accomplish that.

The hallway was more inviting than the one below. The walls were painted in a soft green hue and wooden doors with gold old-fashioned knobs made the place seem calming. Pictures and tapestry lined the walls with the three intertwined circles that represented the Decretum Venia's crest.

Peter held his head down as he and Kyle followed Diana. A few kids passed by and gave them strange looks, but after a frown from Diana, they hurried by.

"Don't mind them, the kids think you're new here. I have the esteemed task of orientating the latest indoctrinated kids to this 'safe house' so the people who saw us knew not to disturb me when I'm giving a 'tour' to a new tenant." She tilted her chin back at Peter with a grin. "Just around the corner there, and we'll be at Rob's room."

"Got it." That's all Peter could mutter. He was so furious inside it was barely containable. The name of the guy who stole an ounce of Angel's love from him made the storm of uncertainty and loneliness cave in on him. The burned symbol on his hand throbbed, not from impending danger this time, but because of the thrumming blood flow caused by his rapidly beating heart.

"Dude, don't worry about it. Angel wouldn't ditch you for some other guy. Trust her, she loved you from what I could tell when we were all together." Kyle bumped Peter with his shoulder.

"I do trust her. It's Rob I don't trust." The words were forced through Peter's clenched jaw.

Diana turned the corner. "Are you ready?" She stood in front of a door across from a bricked in window.

Peter could only nod.

When the door opened, he saw Angel—his Angel—sitting cross-legged on the floor, her elbows resting on one of the twin-sized beds. Peter stood there and studied her pale skin, framed by the long, wavy black hair that rested just above her slim hips. A guy with a riot of thick blond locks clipped to just above his ears was lying casually on a pillow, reading to her, but Angel wasn't looking at Rob; instead, her eyes were closed, and her eyebrows dipped as if she was absorbing his every word.

Peter swallowed back all the doubt and anger he had at knowing she had trusted another guy, and his chest filled with a burst of excited energy at seeing her face. He wanted her like nothing he'd ever wanted for himself in his life.

"Angel," the whisper slid out of his lips on an exhale. Peter stepped into the room.

CHAPTER 16

L ucien was sweating profusely, just as he had been ever since being brought back to life. He fell back onto the firm cushion of the leather couch that lined the wall of his spacious room in Gavin's mansion. Exhaustion and the taunting ache of bone-deep pain throbbed through him. The bastards had left absolutely no part of his body free of the whip and hooks they'd used to torture him. *Submission*, he thought with a grimace. It was all he'd known all his life, and all he ever gotten in return for it was pain. First, he was his father's abused puppet, and now he was his cruel brother's whipping boy. That wasn't what Lucien wanted, and it never had been. Before, though, he'd been too weak, too brainwashed to think it was worth it to fight the role he'd never asked to play.

Now, things had changed. That girl, Angel, had done that for him, and Lucien couldn't get her out of his mind: her pale skin, the scent of her hair, the calm way she spoke. Even the sick part of him felt at ease around her, the black, soulless part that would've made her a victim of his anger at his father, and the others in the Order of the Dragon, who had taken such pleasure in doing unimaginable things to his body for as long as he could remember. Angel was the first person he didn't secretly want to torture. He'd never been happy himself, so he usually wanted to destroy the happiness within others, but that was not the case with that girl.

Before Gavin's demon master commanded him to watch the girl, no one was safe from Lucien's homicidal rage. He'd killed so many in the name of the Extraho of Obscurum, for his family and for his own personal pleasure. Nevertheless, when Angel's green eyes fell on his, he was calmed. The effect was even more profound by the catch of her shallow breath and her words: "I promise not to hate you like he does, no matter what. I-I just want to help us both get away from him."

"We'll never get away," Lucien muttered, as if he was still standing in front of her. That was what he'd said to her, to the girl named Angel. "Humankind is doomed," he'd told her. "There are demons walking the Earth, on their way to the heavens because I helped my devil of a brother bring them here."

As he painfully reminisced about that confession, a knock sounded loudly at the door. "Lucien..." called an insistent male whisper.

Lucien's eye twitched slightly before he jerkily stood to open the door. He knew the voice; it was Jack's, the voice of the guy who hungered to take Gavin's place, but Lucien would never allow that. Using Jack to destroy his brother and the demon within him would be no easy feat, rather tricky, but Lucien had to grin at the thought. Trickiness was the one lesson his dear father and brother had taught him well.

Lucien purposefully hesitated a moment before opening the door, knowing that keeping Jack waiting would unsettle the man a bit. He finally flicked the lock and straightened his back to appear completely recovered. He even made sure to plaster a fake grin across his face.

"What took you so long?" Jack pushed past him.

Lucien flexed his hand into a fist before regaining his composure. "I was sleeping."

Jack's dark gaze studied him. "I got it." He pulled the dagger from the pocket of his suit vest and handed it to Lucien. "Only you can do it. It has to be wielded by someone of his bloodline."

Lucien looked at the silver, bejeweled knife that appeared almost translucent at the tip. "You're good." Lucien chuckled and walked over to the safe behind the picture of his mother. Her pale blonde hair matched his father's in color and texture. *That's to be expected, since they were distant cousins.* He slid the portrait to one side and placed the knife in the unlocked safe. With a few pushes to the keypad, the lock activated and secured the door, and he slid the concealing portrait back in place.

Jack stepped closer, his dark eyes filled with doubt. "I can trust you to go through with it, can't I?"

"Why should I?" Lucien smirked at him. "What reason do I have to kill my own brother and imprison his soul in the lower depths of Hell, when I'll likely end up there beside him?" Lucien leaned back on the wall, fighting a wince as he crossed his arms in front of him.

"I found the girl, Angelique Ramirez." Jack's cocky smile fit naturally on his darkly handsome face. "And my guys captured another of their blood from a subway station. She reeks of the Decretum Venia. We can use her for the final ceremony."

At that point, the cool, joking façade Lucien had worn for most of his life almost faded. "Really? Or are you lying to me in the hopes that I'll kill my brother and release your demon master before I have a chance to see if you are telling the truth?"

"No lying here. I have the blood of the innocent and the tool to eliminate the one who stands in our way. You, my friend, will kill him and his demon with the dagger. In exchange for that, I will tell you exactly where the Ramirez girl was seen just a few months ago. Not only that, but I will hand you the true deed to the property she was hidden in, so you and your team should have no trouble getting her," Jack said, unblinking. His hands rested comfortably on his hip, and a smug appearance of self-satisfaction curled his lips. "On the other hand, if you don't agree, the witch will tell your demon master, Balaal, that you plan to betray him."

Lucien swallowed, realizing there was really nothing to negotiate. "It will be done."

Jack sauntered to the door. "Good, but it must happen before the unveiling of the machine of light. My demon master's troops will be victorious in storming the gates of Heaven. You must complete your task just before the ceremony of the embodiment, just before the demons are released to take hold of the human host. You must comply, Lucien, for I swear to you that the hell my master has planned for you is much worse than your master Balaal's will be." With a curt nod, Jack slid out the door.

CHAPTER 17

Peter's fingers trembled. He wanted to reach out and touch Angel so bad it hurt. When her eyes finally opened and blazed right into his, his heart pounded in his chest.

Angel's jaw dropped, and the sound of the boy's reading faded into the background as she stood. "Peter?" A flash of longing, then remorse settled deeply into the recess of her green eyes.

"I've missed you." Peter's voice was hoarse with emotion. Moisture gathered in his eyes and he stepped forward.

Angel stumbled back, into Rob's arms, who stopped her fall. "I-I." Her head went side to side. "I thought I'd never see you again."

Rob cleared his throat. "So you're Peter? Peter Saints?" he asked, nodding at Peter.

Every muscle in Peter's body tensed when Rob's challenging blue eyes met his brown ones. "The one and only." Peter fought the urge to snatch the guy's hand off Angel's shoulder, but he didn't have to.

Angel's hungry gaze never left Peter's. "Rob, can you..."She shrugged off Rob's hand.

Rob sighed. "Sure, my room, is your room," he mumbled and brushed past Peter, bumping shoulders.

Kyle stepped up next to Peter. "Good to see you Angel." A lace of sarcasm littered his words. "C'mon Diana." He tugged the girl out with him and shut the door.

They stood there and soaked in each other's presence. Peter wondered at Angel's long sleeve shirt and jeans. He'd thought she would give up the clothes that hid her softly shaped figure.

Her hands trembled as she hugged herself. "I'm glad you came. So glad." Tears ran down her face.

"Are you?" Peter silently berated himself for being a prick. "I'm sorry Angel, can I hold you?"

She nodded, and Peter didn't wait a second before he gathered her closely to his chest. Angel felt so small, fragile in his arms. The top of her dark head barely rested below his heartbeat.

Peter couldn't help himself, his skin tingled; he just had to touch her. He gently kissed the top of her hair as his dark hand slid under her jaw to tilt her lips to his.

"Can I kiss you, please? God please don't tell me no." Peter hated himself for being this desperate for her love. Peter just hoped she could love him still, after what he had to tell her.

"Yes, but..." Angel sighed.

Peter didn't give her a chance to take it back; he kissed Angel's open mouth, forcing himself not to devour every single taste of her. Squeezing her firmly to his chest, he whispered, "I love you, always you."

Angel froze and pushed him away.

Peter released her. The last thing he wanted to do was to make her feel smothered. He remembered the bitter words she'd yelled at him just before she was taken, the night they'd had the fight that had caused her to throw out the cruel revelation that she wasn't in love with him anymore.

"Peter, I can't. We can't. So much...there's so much wrong with me."

He stepped closer to her retreating form, "I don't care. I never cared."

Angel put her hand up to stay him. "I was different then. Stupid, naive."

"No." Peter dropped his outreached hand; the round symbol on it throbbed. "I was stupid. I didn't mean to push you. To smother you. I just. Just loved you too much."

"You didn't smother me, I—"

A knock sounded at the door and Kyle peeked his head in. "Our golden opportunity to ditch this place is coming up. So make your reunion quick." His gaze skipped to Angel's. "Your friend *Rob* wants to come with." His eyebrow rose, then he shut the door.

"He can't." Peter crossed his arms, frowning. Just the thought of the guy made him want to hit someone—hit Rob.

"I won't go without him." She lifted her chin.

Peter swallowed down a roar that hung in the back of his throat. "You're in love with him?" His voice deepened.

"Not like you think. But I care about him. I owe him and I won't leave him here." Angel's fingers trembled as she reached out to touch his dark hand. "Don't be angry with me, it's not what you think."

Peter grasped her hand. "Make me understand."

Diana burst in. "We have to go. Now!"

"We'll talk on this later." Peter pulled her close and kissed her. Angel's slack lips hungrily responded before she pushed him away. "I love you, and I'm not losing you."

He tugged Angel behind him. Then followed Diana out and down the hall with the others. Within moments of them clearing the end of the hall, chaos broke out. Kids poured into the halls from all directions.

"What's the deal here?" Peter grabbed the shoulder of Diana's sweater.

Without turning around, she tilted her head and replied, "Lights out."

Rob slipped back to walk next to Angel. "We better get out now, before the room inspections."

Peter didn't miss the smug expression Rob tossed over Angel's head as if daring him. "Diana—which way?" He stepped up beside her, trying to calm the drumming of blood in his ears at Rob's challenge.

A small frown appeared on her face. "Sorry you had to see that, but that's been my reality since *she* got here." Diane grasped Peter's upper arm. "This way to the plumbing system, it'll lead us out."

Peter pushed his way through the crowd of rushing kids. Their chatter and irritated stares didn't stop him. The dark halls of cement walls and thick wood doors gave the place a medieval feel similar to another Sanctuary Peter hid in last summer with Angel and Kyle. The smell of kids, sweat, and some type of incense, permeated the air. The incense he remembered from the orphanage, it was blessed, some type of protection used to keep away pawns of the Extraho of Obscurum. After what he witnessed earlier in his escape – he wondered if it worked at all. But maybe it didn't control the twisted hearts of men, only the pure evil of the demons that tempted them. If that was the case, maybe human men were the owners of their own taste of evil. Blaming the demons was just their cop out.

Diana pointed to a short metal door at the end of the hall. Then she scrambled in front of Peter, bent and unlocked it.

"How'd you get that?" Angel asked.

"Ask your friend Rob. He gave it to me." Diana slipped through the door.

Peter pushed Angel after her and waited for Kyle.

"You go ahead, I'm following. I just want to make sure no one sees us." Rob used his wide form to distract Peter's entry into the door.

Peter didn't wait to hear Rob; he crawled quickly behind Kyle and watched Diana's pale hands grip a pole. She shimmied upwards into the darkness.

A door slammed in the distance, and a sinking feeling of disappointment sat in his stomach as Rob entered behind him.

CHAPTER 18

Peter crawled over Diana and pushed up on the round, seemingly cement door, opening it to the night. The moon cast a dull glow on the replica city street hidden behind the large landmine and junkyard they'd come through to get to the sanctuary. He climbed out and kneeled to help Diana and Angel out, then turned and stared up at the moon. A sliver of dark clouds floated under it, throwing them into darkness.

"Uh...a little help?" Kyle asked with a snort. "It's not just the damsels that are in distress here, ya know!"

Peter ignored him, all of them. *How'd it come to this?* Peter had a ton of baggage following him. Taking them to Rosa might be a good idea. She'd keep them safe, and he could ditch them, leave and face Lucien and the Extraho of Obscurum himself. But first, he had to get that information from her. The sanctuary that would tell him how to destroy them—all. Even though the brand could unlock doors hidden for centuries past, he still didn't know where or what all the sanctuaries held. But he did know, getting Angel to the one of the Strongholds would put an end to his recurring nightmare.

He would never forget what it felt like to inhabit the body of Luke 23, his angelic ancestor, the one who'd given his DNA to be merged into some synthetic weapon within Peter's ancestral line, his blood. Luke 23 was gigantic, over eight feet of pure muscle and equipped with weaponry. Peter couldn't even fathom belonging to his world, but even with Luke 23's strength, the demons who created the human Nephilim abominations from the Extraho of Obscurum were stronger. Not only that, but compared to the Decretum Venia, they seemed infinite in numbers.

A light touch on his shoulder jerked him out of his waking nightmare, but the fingers he'd know anywhere as Angel's fluttered away before he could capture her hand. "Where now?" she softly asked.

"This way." He didn't want to look at her and see that butt-wipe hovering over her like he owned her. One glance at Rob would have him acting like the needy fool he didn't want her to see. Peter made quick time down the deserted cement sidewalk that enclosed the sanctuary beneath them.

"How long before they'll realize you're gone?" Kyle's voice traveled as he caught up to Diana, who was now at Peter's side.

"Not till morning. They had some doctor guy visiting and the elders were in a meeting that was supposed to last all night. It's why I was trying to escape." Diana's hand accidentally brushed Peter's and she looped her arm around his.

Peter frowned, but didn't bother to pull away. He sensed the girl had something to prove, that she was using him to make the blond Adonis looking prick jealous. He glanced at Rob and noticed the dude's eyes were locked hungrily on Angel.

"It won't work." Peter jerked his arm out of Diana's.

"How do you know?" She smirked back at him.

"Rob's looking at her," Peter whispered then clenched his jaws shut as Diana's eyes left his to peer up at the sky.

"Oh, can you take her away or something? Make her leave with you?"

"I plan on it." Peter's palm throbbed. It seemed to be stronger if he was agitated, or when there was danger near. "Where were you escaping to?"

"My father sent me here to spy. Well sort of. He and the Decretum Venia had a difference of opinion."

"What kind?" Peter slowed a bit, wanting to get as much information out of her before the others listened in.

"He believed in the old ways, but this new doctor is leading up a study to unlock the secrets of the Order because he believes mankind should be punished for all they've done. He has many leaders following him and he and his team have been 'investigating' the holdings where we kids are supposed to be protected."

"What's he looking for?" The hairs on Peter's neck rose at the implication of what Diana was saying.

"Blood, DNA samples of us kids. For some reason our blood is different from average humans, or people—even from the elders. When we reach a certain age, the potency of the chemical dissipates. It's why they've hidden us kids for years. It's like we're some rare breed of super-human that can't be activated without some 'secret' turning of events that are the 'key' to the mystery. Only the elders knew this about us, and my father was one of them. After he found out that Elder Killian and his followers were gaining power, we fled Europe, moved to America, and he started to build forces that went into hiding."

"How many people are helping your father, and do you know how to find him? I may need their help." Peter hated to admit it, but the thought of going up against Lucien's group was daunting, and he needed a back-up plan. He didn't know if Gavin was still alive, but he was sure Lucien would happily take over.

"He has many people on his side. In fact, almost half the team sent to secure the future of the Order—to basically babysit us—

has sided with my father. The trouble is that they can't relocate all the kids at once. They have to do it slow and careful. I know most of the locations close to this sanctuary, the underground doomsday hiding places. They're totally off the grid of the Order. My father made sure of it."

"Why would he send you to this Sanctuary to possibly be found out?"

"I wouldn't have been found out. I'm that good. He knew it. I was well trained." She cast a saucy glance on him. "Looks like you were too."

"I wouldn't say I was trained, I didn't have a choice."

"We all have a choice, we could just end it all. Or fight to live, right?"

Peter grinned. He liked the way the girl thought. "I'd never give those bastards the satisfaction of ending my own life. Never."

"I hope not." Diana slowed as the came up to the stairs where Argia and Gil were huddled together asleep.

"They're with us."

Diana shook her head. "That girl over there, are you sure she's okay?"

Peter frowned. "Why wouldn't she be?"

"I don't know, she's got a glow about her, a heaviness around her."

"How would you know?"

"I know these things. It's my gift. Something I've worked all my life to strengthen. It allows me to know who's trouble, who I can trust, and who I shouldn't. That girl, I don't trust her. Something is around her that's not good."

"Don't worry about her. I can handle whatever it is."

Diana dragged her eyes off of Argia to gaze up at Peter. "I know you can." She tilted her chin in the direction of Angel. "But Angel...be careful of her. Your feelings about her may weaken you, like she has Rob."

Peter shoulders tensed. "You don't know Angel. You'll never know her, so keep your jacked-up opinions about my girl to yourself." Peter led Diana behind the others who'd gone to wake Gil and Argia.

"I don't think you know her as well as you think," Diana whispered before rushing ahead.

CHAPTER 19

Gavin felt the burning, the piercing, the cuts, the nails—all the tools Balaal had used to keep him in a perpetual state of pain and submission. But it wouldn't work this time. The boy, Peter, had done something to upset his connection with his demon master, but Gavin was thankful for that, for it gave him the power he needed to control the beast.

The witch thought she was smart, casting him back within this putrid darkness, but she didn't know this place gave him power. Energy—that fed his insatiable need to feel any type of torment. It seemed the time he'd spent in this lower level of hell gave him a greater tolerance for being tortured, almost to the point of addiction. Now that she'd left, he would cast Balaal back here.

With great effort, Gavin concentrated. Years of learning to channel his energy allowed him to easily push his mind, body, and soul forward while suppressing Balaal's strength.

"Ah!" Skin ripped from his torso, his face, and his legs. Gavin didn't care, though, for Balaal would be imprisoned within the darkness when Gavin's plan was finalized. All Gavin had to do to keep Balaal there was fight his own sickening need for punishment. That need, that longing for pain and torture, was the only reason he'd willingly allowed himself to remain trapped for so long.

Opening his eyes, he stared at the shocked expression of Lucien, who knelt at his feet in the dimly lit cellar. Cool blue irises, similar to his blinked up at him as Lucien struggled for composure.

"B-brother?" Lucien's hoarse question fluttered weakly through the dungeon.

The dark walls of the supplication dungeon surrounded them. "You've been begging Balaal, brother?"

"Y-yes, for forgiveness. For my weakness."

Gavin cracked his neck to the side and forced Balaal, who was now trapped in his conscience, to give some of his power to him, albeit just a bit. It seeped into his bloodstream like nectar, a drug so sweet he couldn't help but lick his lips. Gavin bent down and whispered, "Brother, I have a very important secret to tell you."

"You can tell me anything." Lucien kissed Gavin's feet and gazed humbly up at him.

"Good, because I am your only master now." The skin between Gavin's fingers ripped away, and the bloody, wrinkled excess dropped to the floor. Clawed talons grew out of his fingertips as his hand thickened into ropes of muscle, then spouted reptilian, scaly skin.

Lucien fell backwards and scrambled away on his heels. "What? What's happened to you?"

"The master? Pssh. I control Balaal now. He does my bidding, and I'm feeding off his power. The demons he controls are now mine to rule, as long as I keep him imprisoned in the depths of Hell where he tried to place me."

"Why would you want to do that? I don't un-understand."

"Oh, but you do. You, Lucien, understand me more than anyone. I've always wanted this power, but I never thought it possible to gain it. If we are going to see this all the way through, with you as my second-in-command, I must have more children to bleed out. I must kill Peter Saints and drain him dry."

Lucien pushed himself forward on his hands and knees. "I can find him. I have a lead."

"You will have more than a lead, brother. I will send demons to find him, and they will report back to me to tell me where he is, but there is one problem."

"I can help you," he muttered. "Just tell me what you want me to do." Lucien's head dipped to the floor, as though he was afraid to look at Gavin. "Anything."

"You must find me a psychic, someone with a second sight. We must channel Balaal's minions for information. I need one last answer to make the illuminae work, and I must kill someone to get it."

CHAPTER 20

Peter walked ahead of the group. After clearing the junkyard, they'd sauntered through what seemed like miles and miles of itchy, cumbersome cornfields. The dewy mist of approaching dawn tainted the air with the damp, sweet scent of corn.

While they trekked across the uneven terrain, Peter fought the urge to talk to Angel, Kyle, or any of the others. The edginess of a fight yet to come drummed through his blood. Something was wrong, and he didn't know what. Hanna's sickly face flashed through his mind, but in an instant, it morphed into Argia's. Both faces were sad and covered with blood. For so long, he'd forced people away, thinking he was saving them, but the truth was that Peter was trying to save himself from the pain, guilt, and regret of causing so much death. At the thought of Gil's girlfriend, Chloe, a sickness pounded the pit of his stomach. He'd fed Gil a lie; Chloe would never survive if they didn't get to her soon.

The symbol on his hand throbbed and burned. It trembled as he wiped it down his face. The transformations in his body never stopped. Ever since he'd been transported to that war, fought for a thousand years and hidden from man and demon-kind, he hadn't been the same. He knew, even Kyle knew, he died the day he opened that book. But what was reborn into something not human, not angelic, was only created to do something that could tip the balance of life as any being on earth knew it. To think that he, Peter, was at fault was stupid. Going up against the demon in Gavin was the stupidest thing he'd ever done for another person in his life—he'd risked the lives of others, to save her. Now he was being selfish again, something he hated about this situation. Using Angel to make it all right, to make him try to repair the damage he'd done. But who would pay for it this time? Fact was, he didn't know.

"Peter!" Kyle's voice sliced through the silence of Peter's angry thoughts. Peter stopped. "What?" he spat, a bit harshly, but Kyle was used to it.

"We're tired, dude. Everyone needs some sleep."

"Fine. Whatcha waitin' on me to find a spot for? I'm going over by that truck ahead." Peter searched around for another safe area to sleep, and pointed. "There, you take the others to the outhouse. See that storage shed?" The small building had seen better days, but it would do if it didn't rain. The holes in the wood were few and scattered, but the roof appeared stable.

"Dude, you seriously want us to sleep next to the poo? I thought we were friends." Kyle glanced back. "Oh, I get it, you want me to put Rob next to the shit."

Peter couldn't help a grin. "You could ask him to be lookout, first watch, and you and the others sleep in the shed."

Kyle smacked his lips. "I'll do you one better, I'll get all of them put away, and send Angel to you."

"If she comes," Peter muttered under his breath.

"She will. I've seen the way she stares at you when you aren't paying attention and that Rob freak isn't salivating over her." Kyle slapped Peter's back. "Besides, I want that red hot piece, Diana, to forever be in my debt. We will find a way to ditch the cretin. It'll be my sole mission as your best bro."

Peter shook his head. "We don't even look like bros."

"Says who? I'm your brother from another motha." Kyle winked a blue eye at him before jogging back to talk to the others.

Peter chuckled and walked to the rusted truck that would be his bedroom for a few hours.

He pulled the jagged door open and wiped the gray dirt and rust off on his jeans. It was getting cold, but Peter didn't feel it much. He tried to ignore the others, but every move they made seem to draw his attention. He could sense when they were hot, cold, shivering, or scared. Exhaling, he tried to forget his new hypersensitive abilities, but he was caught in a perpetual state of red alert, as if he was always awaiting a fight, a battle, or anything that might unleash the raging thing he struggled to keep at bay inside him.

~

Peter felt her presence before she uttered a word, and he closed his eyes briefly, taking several breaths to placate his need to grab Angel and pull her close to him.

"Hi," Angel offered a shy, whispered greeting.

Peter frowned. Angel was a lot of things, but he had never known her to be so timid. "Hey." He nodded. "Need a place to sleep?" he asked, desperately hoping she'd stay with him, that she would give some sign that he wasn't the only one who felt so strongly about them. He studied her beautiful face and caught the shame in it, and that made him want to punch something. His Angel had let that Rob guy in. She'd invited him into her heart— the place where Peter had been the first to reside. Peter felt like dying, but he wouldn't give up. He just couldn't, because he loved her too much.

"Yes, I'll stay." Angel granted him a hesitant smile.

Her small, denim-clad form climbed in and sat next to him.

Even in the long-sleeved shirt that was four sizes too big, she was the most beautiful girl he'd ever seen. "Thanks." He opened his arms, offering a silent plea for her to cuddle up next to him, to allow him to cover her with his warmth. When she nestled against him, he smiled.

"Peter I-I—"

"Shh." Peter gently touched his lips to Angel's, twirled his fingers through her hair. Peter nearly died ten times when she opened up to him and allowed him to deepen the kiss.

"Let me hold you." His eyes fluttered closed. "Just let me hold you...and rest."

CHAPTER 21

Peter pretended to be asleep. Angel's hand softly touched the side of his face before tentatively exploring the brand on his hand. He moved slightly. She stilled, then scooted away from the warmth of his chest to climb into the front seat.

"What's wrong?" Peter sat up and brushed a wisp of her dark hair from the side of her face.

"Everything." She wouldn't look at him.

"Angel, I don't care what went on between you and Rob." Peter swallowed down the lie. "I just want to be with you." A sliver of desperation weaved through his words. He'd tried to hold that back, but gave it up.

"I wish I could," a tear seeped from her eyes, and she sniffled, "but I can't, Peter." She twisted around, not fighting to hold back the pain and misery in her features. "I did this to you. Kyle told me what you did to save me." Her head moved side to side as if she was fighting her thoughts. "You don't know what you've done. When we were in the Sanctuary together, the one with the weapons where you, Kyle, and I stuck our hands on the symbol of the Decretum Venia, I read a warning in those books."

He frowned, wiping a tear from her upper lip, "I think I

remember you telling me about a warning, but I don't remember it."

Angel sighed. "You were deceived, Peter. Gavin—the demon in him named Balaal—has been deceiving you from the beginning." Her hands trembled as she used the back of her hand to wipe her damp face. "He used his slaves in the Order of the Dragon to kill your parents, and get the Decretum Venia to put you in hiding until he could lure you out at your prime—when your blood was most potent. Kids like Hanna are drawn to you because you held light, a specific light only for those who were given keys to the 'word.' The written historical word of angels. Only someone like Hanna would know you, because she is also a child of the Decretum Venia's elite. It's what she was created for, as someone who could control demons, but she never knew that. Outside of the Decretum Venia, she and others like her were considered insane or schizophrenic."

Peter's heart beat rapidly in his chest and he almost couldn't breathe. "You sayin' they played with her mind, drove her insane to the point where she would sacrifice herself to get to me?"

"Yes! They wanted her to die! Balaal wanted her to 'activate' the power in you so you could unlock the Strongholds," she sobbed, "and they used me too. Balaal knew you would want to save me, that it would push you to do something irrational."

"To save you." Peter felt a punch in his chest. He pushed back into the torn seat and rested his face in his hand. "It doesn't matter. I can fix it."

"You can't. You'll only make it worse." Angel's muttered words sounded broken.

Peter stared up at her. "I won't. It's as bad as it's going to get. I will destroy Balaal and Lucien. If they want to take a war to heaven, it won't be in my lifetime."

"You didn't see them. You only fought Balaal, but I was with him and Lucien for days!" The tormented shudder in her voice seemed to vibrate through her body. "You don't know the evil I've experienced, and they were just playing with me, like a toy."

"I sent Balaal back to hell."

"He won't stay. You aren't able to keep him there, and he knows it." Angel sniffed. "I'm sorry for leading you to that place. I should've just let them kill me, but they wouldn't."

Peter moved forward and kissed her, hungrily, as a tear slipped down the side of his face. "Don't you ever say that. Never. Give. Them the damned satisfaction. You will live." He pulled her to him in a tight hug. "You will fight, because you can. Promise me!"

Angel hugged him back. "I-I promise."

"We'll find a way out of this. I know a way, but we have to get Rosa's help."

Angel nodded. "Can you trust her? There are people in the Decretum Venia who've gone crazy."

Peter slowly released his hold on Angel, and nodded. "Yes, she can. I know where to find her."

A small smirk grew on Angel's face. "I think Diana knows too."

"You don't like Diana?"

"She didn't like me first," Angel muttered. "*Pero ella no sabe que no lo amo...*"

When Angel spoke in her native Spanish, something was bothering her. "Why, because you stole her man?" Peter spat, and regretted it the moment he saw the hurt on her face.

Angel shook her head. "I didn't steal him. He's not mine. She placed her hand on his, resting the other on the seat as she leaned over to kiss Peter's lips softly. "I was never his."

Peter leaned back, fighting against wanting to kiss her more and needing answers, "Then what is he to you? Why you lettin' him come between what we could have? Is it because of how I acted when we were together?"

She flopped back down on the front seat and sighed. "He...well, you and I. Oh *dios*, the reason I broke up with you had nothing to do with the way you treated me."

Peter frowned. "That so? Well when we argued you told me I was smothering you. That you just wanted to be left alone. Then you slept with me—only me, because we both had nightmares and you were used to being in the room with me." He reached out and touched his brown fingers to her pale cheek. "I remember that then...you only needed me."

"We were on the run, for a time, when you didn't trust me. And I was so scared of being by myself, I'd done it for a while, but I felt safe with you from the moment you bought me the milkshake at that dive in South Carolina."

"I still can't believe I didn't know you were a girl. But when we got to Rosa's Sanctuary and I found out you were uh, a girl, I wanted you so bad—like no one else."

"I knew how Shyan had hurt you, and I'm sorry it looks like I'm doing the same, but Peter, believe me, Rob and I don't have that kind of friendship."

Peter wiped his hand down his face and flexed his fingers into a fist. "It looks like you do. At least, it appears he didn't get the memo. And you're doing nothing to make him think different."

"I can't tell you his secrets. He has to, but he saved my life, and I owe him."

"What kind of friendship?" Peter sat back. "I'm sorry, I'm doing it again, starting an argument that's not solving this...this thing between us."

"I'm sorry, but we can't be together like we were. I want to, but I can't. If we do, I think I'll hurt you more than you know." Angel rushed forward and ran out of the truck.

CHAPTER 22

A piercing scream vibrated through the air, and Peter's palm burned like fire. He jumped out of the truck and darted his eyes around searching the chilly grounds in every direction. In spite of the sun being up, it was unnaturally cold. Peter shivered as he tried to figure out where the scream had come from.

Suddenly, Argia sprinted from the side of the outhouse, waving her hands. Above, dark clouds were rolling in, and the gunning of a truck engine sounded in the distance.

"Get back inside!" Peter raced to the hysterically jumping girl.

"They're coming!" Argia ran to Peter and twisted her dainty fingers in his shirt trembling uncontrollably.

"Calm down. It's just some truck driver cutting through here, taking a shortcut. C'mon. Let's get inside." Peter looked around for the others, confused as to why they hadn't followed her out.

As he dragged her back to the shed, she tried to wrestle out of his grip. "No! I c-can't go in there. The others! They'll find them. He's coming!!" Tears poured from her eyes, and she kept fighting, trying to wiggle out of Peter's arm that was firmly wrapped around her thin waist.

Thunder clapped. The ground shook as a stream of jagged light stabbed the dirt.

"Where are you going?" Peter wanted to laugh at the girl. She appeared almost frantic, but from what he could see, there was no one around but them. Except for the gunning truck in the distance that he figured was cutting through the path they'd crossed in the fields to find shelter.

"Away. Got to lure them away." Argia halted her steps. "Oh no, they smell us!" Then she crouched with both hands on her head, eyes squeezed shut, muttering, "No! No! I won't do it. Peter will get you." She mumbled, "Oh yes, we will get you..." Argia jumped up with narrowed eyes. "It's too late, they're here."

Two trucks were heading towards them. More clouds filled the sky. The others rushed out of the shed.

Peter grabbed Argia and ran towards the kids. "What did you say to her?" He pointedly stared at Kyle.

"Nothing, really." Kyle appeared irritated. "Dude, she was making weird noises and talking to things that weren't there. Even your nemesis over there, Rob, got spooked. We gave her an entire corner to herself, that's how bad her weirdness got."

"True that!" Gil spoke up.

Peter spied Angel and Rob heading into the field beyond the shed in the direction of the beating sounds of the speeding trucks.

Argia fought Peter harder and mumbled, "I should let them eat him. They would, would eat him."

Kyle drew a circle at his temple and pointed to Argia. Then spat at the ground, put off by the girl's rambling. "Yeah, definitely spooked us."

"You deal with her." Peter thrust the slender girl into Kyle's arms. "I'm gonna find out what those two are up to."

"Thanks a lot, bud!" Kyle called out. "Leavin' me here with Little Miss Psycho while you go play *Children of the Corn*! Real freakin' nice!"

Gil laughed in the background just as another clap of thunder assaulted Peter's eardrums. He broke through the tall stalks. In the dirt ahead was a small, broken sign that read "Corn Maze," written haphazardly in what looked like chalk.

"Angel, this way!" Rob's voice sounded through the corn.

Peter spotted them, climbing up a small lookout tower made of wood. The flat surface sat only four feet off the ground but would allow them to see over the tall stalks. He had to admit that it hurt to see Angel with Rob, but he wasn't leaving them alone for very long. He jogged in their direction, ready to warn them that something was off and they needed to get going.

Just as Peter turned the corner near the platform, Rob shot up. "Oh my God, man! Get down!" Rob dropped to his knees and pushed Angel off the platform.

She rolled to break her fall, and he ran to her. Rob jumped down. "What is it?" he asked. "What did you see?"

"They're on to us. There are guys in a truck, with guns hanging out the windows."

"Damn!" Peter searched for something to use as a weapon, since he'd left his gun and other gear back at the shed. His gaze landed on an axe and a large sledgehammer. He picked up the axe and tossed the sledgehammer at Rob's feet. "We have to try to fight them before they get to the others."

"What about me?" Angel demanded. "I can help. Give me something to fight with."

Assuming he and Rob were stronger and could more easily handle the heavier weapons, Peter tugged on the knife case at his side and handed the weapon to her. "I know it's not much, but it's all I've got."

"I'll make it work." She ran to the edge of the clearing and yelled at the guys in the truck.

"What's she...?" Peter swore and took off after her. He skidded to a stop behind her as she waved at the open bed truck in front of them.

The driver's face couldn't be seen, since a baseball cap sat low on his forehead, but the passenger was resting a large shotgun on the open window. The guy in the cab had a gun tossed over his shoulder.

"Hey!" Angel called. The truck came to a halt, barely missing her.

The driver only smiled sadistically, revealing white teeth in the semidarkness, beneath the brim of his hat.

Peter narrowed his gaze; something else peeked over the cab, and his hand burned. His eyes landed on the ash-covered demon with orange flames in its eyes, licking at the men. He clenched his jaw. He could tell by the look on the foul thing's face that it recognized him. Peter grasped Angel's hand with his heated palm. "Don't move." The searing tingle of power traced through the emblem on his hand, then surged through his blood. He felt as though he'd literally grown ten feet in size.

"Ow!" Angel tried to pull away. "Peter, let go! That hurts."

The guy jumped out of the back cab. With him came over a dozen ash demons, hungrily sizing Peter up. "Well, well, well. Looks like it's our lucky day, Earl," he spat. A long string of residual spit from his chewing tobacco dripped from his lips as he poised his gun up to take aim at Peter.

"Uh, we're just waiting for a ride," Angel explained, a frantic expression on her face. She grasped Peter's hand tighter, and he felt a small flinch.

"Oh, we'll give you a ride, darlin'. As for you, boy, your face is plastered on every wanted post I seen on the black internet. Mm-hmm. You got a high price tag on your head."

"Alive, Boone! They's gotta be alive." The passenger climbed out.

Peter's gaze never left the fire-eyed demons rustling around behind the guy named Earl. They were weak; they couldn't breach the barrier—they could only influence what was happening. He just hoped it would stay that way.

One of the demons, larger than the others, leaned over and patted Boone, and his head moved slightly, as if he enjoyed the caress as his demon master whispered on his head. Boone lifted his gun, and fired with a dazed look in his eyes, as if he was on drugs.

Peter pushed Angel to the ground. Then he jumped up and charged Boone before the assailant could fire again. The clouds played a menacing chorus of lightning and thunder. The demons behind Boone moved excitedly as Peter and Boone wrestled on the ground. He punched, jabbed, elbowed, and then threw a kick that sent Boone flying into one of his charging friends. Both men fell; the charging one was knocked unconscious in the collision.

Angel jumped on the back of the rifle-wielding passenger and held the knife against his sweaty neck. "Move, and I'll cut you," she said in a tone that gave him no reason to doubt her threat. Her small arm tightened around the man's neck like a vise, her legs locked just under his ribs. "Drop the gun."

Peter stood, but the muscles in his shoulders bunched when he heard a rip. That sound meant another demon, stronger than the others, was coming through.

Rob's expression proved Peter wasn't just imagining things. Shock melted into fear. Rob's face went pale, then as purple as Argia's hair. He froze, still holding the sledgehammer in his white-knuckled hand.

Power surged in waving throbs from the emblem on Peter's palm. As it pumped through his body, he couldn't help but smile. He pivoted and bent to pick up the discarded axe. The demon facing him was at least ten feet tall, but he would enjoy every minute of the battle. Its head surged out first. Its ashen, fiery body was covered with bronze-like armor that stretched from its chest and down its thick torso. Another rip in the invisible barrier revealed a bronze and green tail, similar to that of a scorpion.

"Whoa! Worst nightmare...?" Angel's shocked cry sounded through the thunder.

"Ah!" Peter's hand illuminated, and the light traveled down the axe and all over his body. He took aim at the beast's neck, said a silent prayer that his weapon would hit its target, then threw the axe with precision.

The demon barely released a roar, as the lit-up axe sliced through its neck, leaving its horned head hanging by only a small patch of torn flesh. Light exploded from the impact, knocking the truck driver's head into the side of the car. Peter charged the beast, pushing it backward, into the chasm between its hellish world and Earth. His burning palm lit with a red hue as he slid it down the jagged tear, hoping to seal it. In a flash, the shadowed demons disappeared, and rain began to pour from the clouds above, as if to wash the filth away.

Boone, furious, lifted a shaking gun at Rob, who snapped out of his daze just in time to throw the sledgehammer. The gun fired, knocking the guy down.

Breathing hard, Peter pulled the unconscious driver out of the seat and slid him onto the ground. "Go get everyone. We gotta ride...now!"

"You don't have to ask me twice." Rob looked around in stunned amazement and still trying to catch his breath.

CHAPTER 23

Peter's fingers were wrapped so tightly around the steering wheel that he thought it might crack under the pressure of his grip. He tried to loosen his hands but pressed the gas pedal harder, wanting to get as far from the macabre scene as he could.

"Peter, we need to talk about it," Angel's ragged whisper fought through the fog of Peter's thoughts. She placed her hand on his arm.

"I know. You saw one of them." He'd wished she hadn't. It seemed with more and more of the demons spewed by the Order of the Dragon piercing through this world from theirs, the fact that Peter had done something to strengthen them could no longer be denied.

Angel inhaled. "You mean there were others?"

"Yeah, lots of 'em." Peter blinked back the images of their charred skin, the one demon, the large one's one horn, mottled skin of red mixed with pale splotches littered with brown spots. Its teeth protruded on both sides, crowded and pointed. But the eyes, evil, cold, and so hungry the thought of it shot an involuntary shiver down Peter's back.

Kyle's head popped up between them. "Hey, what'd I miss?

Golden boy back here hasn't blinked or even swallowed since we got in the truck." Kyle's elbow hit Peter's as he tilted his head in Rob's direction. "You can tell me what happened since the others are in the cab. They won't hear."

Angel spoke up, "The guys in the truck, they weren't there by accident. I think someone sent them. They were yelling, 'come out, come out wherever you are.'"

"Either way, we all would've been in some deep crap if they got us." Kyle bounced slightly up and down anticipating the rest of the story. "But the gunshots? When did it come to that?"

Peter cleared his throat. "When they saw us."

Angel raked her fingers through her tangled hair. "I did something stupid, I ran out to them, thinking I could divert them and tell them we were just passing through."

"It didn't matter. They knew what they were looking for and they were looking for us," Peter spat.

"You didn't think the Order of the Dragon would stop hunting us, did you?" Kyle snorted. "The bastard kids I went to school with had this uncanny pit bull complex. Literally would have a victim and not let go till the kid or animal was a bloody mess." He shrugged. "Guess I know where the buggers got it from."

Angel folded her legs underneath her. "Still, I don't know how they could have found us – at least in a normal way." She laid her hand on Peter's arm. "We left no sign or clues."

"There's a hit out on us. But this is different. *Was* different," Peter uttered, so angry now he wanted to scream. Would it ever stop? Could he really end this? It seemed to him all the promises he made to Angel to protect her were now just empty.

"Was it like what happened to Chloe?"

"Chloe? Who's she?" Angel asked.

Peter sighed. "Gil's girlfriend. She hitched with us and ended up getting abducted when we cleared the subway station. It's like the scum had a scent on us or something."

Kyle bit his fingernail, then spit the remnants in Rob's direction. "Humph, Rob's still in shock." He shrugged. "You sure it ain't that girl Argia they want? Or who led them to us? I mean the chick did run out of the shed screaming, 'They're coming! They're coming!' You would've thought she knew about it in advance or something."

"I don't know, but when we met up with those guys who took Chloe, she wasn't with us," Peter considered. "But one thing happened when we went to save Angel that you don't know about."

Kyle cleared his throat.

Angel's face turned even more pale; her eyes grew wide with unshed tears.

"The demon, Balaal—he cut my face and licked my blood." Peter swallowed. "And said now that he tasted me, he'd have all my secrets." Peter didn't want to repeat the other taunting promises made by the demon he thought he'd sent back to hell. But either Balaal was pissed and sending his minions from hell to get him, or some other creature was doing it.

"Nah! You creamed him. It's got to be the weird girl you picked up from the insane hospital." Kyle leaned forward. "She mumbles all night and sleeps with her friggin' eyes open. Who the hell does that?" He shook his head. "Me and the others think we should ditch her."

Angel gave Kyle a doleful smile. "Peter used to say the same thing about you." She crossed her arms on her bended knees. "When we were all together."

Peter slid a finger down her cheek. "We're together now."

"Yes, but as bad as things were then, now seems even worse."

"Hey, so back to what happened then?" Kyle chopped at Peter's outstretched arms.

"There were other demons present that Angel and Rob couldn't see. They were hanging around those guys, even licking them and whispering to them. I wasn't too concerned since now I know they're bottom feeders. They can only influence the thoughts and actions of humans who are open to them. But then..." Peter swerved as a deer jumped into the deserted country road. He tapped its rear, skidding slightly before it scampered off through the woods. He slowed a bit to peer at the spotted rusty hood, to make sure there wasn't any damage before he hit the gas again.

"That scared the snot out of me." Kyle tapped his chest with his fist. "Anyway, like before, when we went to save Angel, you started having hallucinations about demon-folk?"

"Not freakin' hallucinations. The things were real. You saw them before we were fighting them at Gavin's," Peter stated, irritated.

"Affirmative, I was trying to forget that scene. I thought with everything going on, your hallucinations became mine, and well..."

"Oh shut up!" Peter couldn't help the smirk. He swore Kyle tried to get him ticked off as a weird way of calming him down and redirecting the anger. "They were just playin' with me until they called a larger, more powerful demon—one that had the ability to break the barrier and to show himself."

"Dayum! I missed that?"

Angel smooched the side of Kyle's head. "Peter's right, shut up Kyle."

"Not funny, man. You didn't wanna be there. I hadn't seen anything like that since the day...that day." Peter stared at the road, wanting to blot out the taunting memories.

"The day I saw you rise into the air, every bone in your body broke then you sprouted wings that were burned, then ripped from you." Kyle's voice went down an octave, almost to a whisper, "And you landed—dead. I tried for hours to revive you until you woke up like nothing had happened."

An audible breath escaped Angel's lips. "Peter, you never told me."

"I don't remember what Kyle saw, I only remember the hell I'd been transported to. I think when I opened that first book, the one that recorded the fall of angels, I freed something."

Rob let out a scream, the first sound he'd made since they got in the truck.

CHAPTER 24

L ucien was losing his patience with the man. The small office on the tenth floor, where he'd asked one of his guards to bring his prisoner overlooked the city skyline. The place was sleek, designed in grays and yellows, with cherry wood accents in the chairs, desk, and framed pictures. The staff had opened the windows slightly, and the cool breeze helped relieve some of the staleness, but even that didn't calm Lucien as it once had.

He stared down at the rugged-looking pastor, the one who'd had the audacity to shoot at his men on the border of the formerly protected woodlands Lucien had acquired. Unfortunately, Angel and all the other kids in hiding there were long gone before the Extraho of Obscurum arrived. Only two of the guards he'd sent to find the hidden kids or any relics from the Decretum Venia had survived. As soon as the rest stepped too close to the center of the decimated lands, they were burned alive—from the inside out. The others—those who'd been playing lookout in their cars— were promptly gunned down by the man who claimed to be called Pastor Finnegan.

"Again I ask, where are Peter Saints, and Angelica Ramirez? I know they were there!" Lucien slammed his fist on the desk, knowing the others would barge in any minute. "Their lives are in danger. I want to help, but first, you have to help me."

Pastor Finnegan's eyes narrowed. "Help you, a demon spawn? No way! Never! As long as I have anything to do with it, you won't find a single one of those children." He sneered at Lucien in disgust and shook his head. "Don't try to pretend you have good intentions, you beast. I was a police officer for many years before I changed professions. I know your type." He sniffed the air and wrinkled his nose. "The poison of your forefathers permeates from you."

"You are wrong about me, sir. You don't know me. I'm...different. But my brother has changed. Our demon lord has consumed him, and what he has planned for your kind—hell, for the whole world and the heavens beyond—is beyond your nightmares. None of us can contain it now. You must tell me where Peter Saints is. I need him and the Ramirez girl because only they know how to defeat him. If I kill my brother, the demon in him will still live. If he doesn't find a way back in this generation, he will destroy the next, and where will you be then? I need their blood to destroy not only my brother but also the foul one who inhabits him."

"Inhabits him? How is that possible? They can influence but never reside in human flesh again. That barrier was put in place centuries ago." The pastor stiffened. "You're lying, as your kind always do." Pastor Finnegan relaxed and waved his hand, then offered another shake of his head. "There'll always be one of us to stop your demon lords, whether in this generation or the next. The battle may rage on for centuries, but we will never give up the fight against your dark ilk."

Lucien grunted. "Your numbers have dwindled over the centuries. I know, because my brother, my father, and the other Extraho of Obscurum covens have been systematically finding your young and killing them." Lucien leaned forward on the cherry wood desk between them. "They die in the womb, aborted with poison, or else they succumb to what appears to be accidental death in school. Others are captured and tortured, and now that we know how valuable their blood is, we have no problems draining it."

Pastor Finnegan jumped up, fighting the handcuffs that kept his arms bound behind him. "Sick bastards! They're children!"

The door burst open.

Lucien shuddered but kept his eyes glued on Pastor Finnegan as his brother, or the thing Gavin had become, walked into the room.

"Brother, why is our guest not in the proper place for interrogation?" Gavin's calm voice thickened to an unnatural depth.

Swallowing hard, Lucien watched Pastor Finnegan's eyes land on Gavin. The man appeared visibly shaken. Lucien bought some time by smoothing down his suit jacket. "I was saving him for you to talk to alone, brother," he lied. "If he'd been kept in the dungeons, others in the Order would insist on being present." He cleared his throat, gulping down the bile that threatened to spill into his mouth. "Jack's lead secured the property for us and tipped us off to where they were hiding the Saints boy. They have a vested interest in this prisoner." Lucien's reasons for foregoing protocol was that he simply wanted to give the pastor a fighting chance. Although, facing Gavin wouldn't guarantee that, but the dungeons of the order were depths from which a man hardly ever survived.

Pastor Finnegan stepped back as Gavin came closer.

After taking one final breath, Lucien turned to his brother and stilled himself against Gavin's appearance. His brother's face was as pale as usual, his blond hair styled perfectly in a cropped, upward sweep, but his usually bluish-gray eyes were outlined in red.

"Shut up!" Gavin waved a hand at Lucien. A sickening grin appeared on his face as he grabbed Pastor Finnegan by the shirt. The tall, old man, dwarfed Gavin's six-four frame. "Peter Saints' blood lies in my belly." His face shifted, and his eyes slanted, doubled, then thickened. Gavin lifted an elongated finger, tipped with a horrifying curved claw, and slid it down the side of Pastor Finnegan's face, causing the man to tremble. "I will drag you to my master's hell myself if you refuse to tell me where he is."

Lucien wanted to close his eyes, to block out the grotesque transformation of his brother; he could hardly bear to look at the demon-thing Gavin had become. He knew, though, that if he showed any weakness, it would result in more punishment. Besides that, Lucien was determined to finish it. He could no longer allow Jack and Gavin to control him. If it was the last thing on Earth he did he had to turn the tables on them and their demon lords. It didn't have as much to do with Angel temporarily taking away his self-loathing as it did with the fact that, for once in his life, he had to know he'd fought back.

Pastor Finnegan's face was etched with true terror, and he cried out. Then, the pastor ripped from Gavin's hold and sprinted, toward the open window. The glass shattered, the curtains fell, and the pastor tumbled out of sight.

At least one of them got away, Lucien thought, careful not to smile, wary that his sinister brother was looking on.

CHAPTER 25

Peter and the others worked together to push the truck under the thick brush of bushes and leaves. The gas had run out about a mile back on the deserted dirt road that ran through the thickly wooded protected land. A sign indicated it was Indian reservation lands, which seemed odd considering where they were. But it didn't matter. This was where Pastor Finn directed him to find Rosa. Only thing was, the place was much larger than he anticipated.

"This should hide it good enough." Peter leaned against a nearby tree. The truck was now fully hidden.

Kyle turned his eyes to the side. "Glad the dude Rob finally shut up. Nothing like a good smack to bring a guy to his senses."

Angel was rubbing Rob's hands, attempting to unclench them. A shudder of jealousy rumbled in Peter's chest, but he fought it down. Or tried to.

"Yeah, thanks for lookin' out for us. You enjoyed slapping him just as much as I would've." Peter smirked.

Kyle laughed. "No way more than you would've. Your eyes have been killing the guy since you first met him."

"True. True. Well we better hurry and find this hideout. I

thought that Diana girl would know where we should go, but she's been no help. All she keeps doing is staring at Rob like a hungry fox."

"Well, it seems to me that demon scared the crap out of them. I think it would've sent that girl Argia way over the deep end." Kyle shook his head. "I'm still thinking she's got something to do with it. I mean, ever since we picked her up, it seems like we've had more episodes. I don't know, she just creeps me out."

"You? Bad man is all scared?" Peter taunted. "C'mon, let's find this place before nightfall. No way am I wanting to sleep outside again."

"Considering we haven't eaten all day, I'm right behind you." Kyle waved to the others and walked alongside Peter.

Peter stopped, went back, and grasped Angel's hand. "Diana, watch him." Then Peter gave Angel a slight tug, lacing his fingers through hers.

"Uh, hey, what are you..." Angel complained while she stumbled behind him, then reluctantly relaxed and held his hand.

"I couldn't take no more. Rob's got someone who wants to take care of him, let Diana have a chance."

"Really, Peter? Is that all you got? This is what bugs me with you. Can't you just know it's not like that between him and me?" She fell in step with Peter and braced her other hand against his firm arm.

"It's not about him and you," Peter lied—it was one of the things ticking him off, but it wasn't why he needed to touch her. "It's about when I touch you, I know, I really know, you're here and safe with me. You don't get how helpless I felt when they took you from me. We'd been together almost six months, sleeping with each other, keeping the nightmares away. Holding you at night was sometimes the only way I could sleep. I didn't care that it wasn't allowed. I didn't care about any of the stupid rules at that place, every night one of us found our way to each other's room to crash, and I lived for it."

"I did too." Angel bit her bottom lip. "I did too."

"I never pushed you, did I? I never made you feel like I wanted to do more than just sleep?"

Angel sighed. "No, you didn't."

"If I did, would you have wanted to be together that way? Were you ready?" Peter had never wanted to push her to be intimate, but he wanted Angel like that sometimes so bad it hurt. None of his past girlfriends had been as innocent, and years growing up in a mixed orphanage with girls made it easy for him to pursue them. But Angel wasn't like those girls. He thought she'd been close to taking things further, but after her capture by Gavin, it seemed that if he'd tried to touch her in some places she froze, and pushed him away.

"My heart was ready but," she blinked away a small tear, "my mind wasn't."

A twinge in his gut gave off a feeling she was holding something back, and it wasn't about the intimacy of their relationship —but he wouldn't push her now. "Okay." He stopped.

The expanse of the woods thickened in a few spots. Several paths crisscrossed throughout. Peter had only taken a few steps when Gil yelled. Around them, the trees and bushes rustled. Several men and boys emerged and surrounded them with guns drawn.

"What the fu—" Kyle's curse was cut short when the guy behind him hit him with the butt of his gun. Kyle dropped, out cold.

Peter stepped forward. "We're here to meet someone! Rosa! Pastor Finnegan sent us." Peter rushed out the words.

The thick guy ahead of him stood almost nose-to-nose with Peter. Only a gun was sandwiched between them.

The guy put up a hand. "Your name?"

"Peter...Peter Saints."

The man grinned. "You're him? Damn you're a big kid. Whatcha been eatin', boy?" He slapped Peter on the arm. "I'm Sam. This here's my place," he nodded around, "and my boys—some of them by birth, some adopted. You're welcome here. This place has been locked down by Ms. Rosa. If you weren't a good guy," he winked, "you'd be burning up from the inside out. That lady really knows how to bring down the enemy."

Peter eyed Sam. The guy's demeanor had totally transformed from a hard-assed, killer, to someone almost jolly. "Yeah, she does."

Angel stepped up. "She blew up a barn the last time we met her." Angel smiled. "I thought she was crazy. She'd made me dig holes to plant bombs."

Sam nodded. "Oh, you missed the show, huh? We had video feeds set up on the sanctuary she protected. The bastards fried that day, they did. And ones who didn't fry got blown up. I enjoyed every damn minute of it. That day there was a great loss." Sam started under the brush.

Peter grasped Angel by the hand and followed. "What happened?"

"The slime-heads got something. The Extraho of Obscurum's been sniffing around our kind since the beginning of time, I guess. They're figuring out our secret weapons," he glanced back at Peter, "...our kids."

CHAPTER 26

Peter followed Sam through a small tunnel on the side of the meadow and moss-covered hill surrounded by trees and squishy wet foliage. The tunnel was packed tightly with clay and branches and smelled like fresh dirt mixed with various plants, as well as some unknown herb he couldn't place. The scent was similar to something at the rundown farm where he first met Rosa. She used oils and herbs to create some type of barrier to keep out evil things. Now, walking through this packed tunnel, he was finally able to relax. Nothing could hurt them here; at least for now.

"How much farther?" Peter asked, his fingers still interlocked with Angel's as he tugged her up beside him.

"Not far, folks," Sam's voice echoed in front of them.

Peter nodded at an anxious-looking Angel.

"Thank you," she said. "Thanks for bringing us, Rob and me, to this safe place. He really needs this." She smiled.

"Ya know I can't say no to you, Angel. You've got my heart." It probably wasn't wise to keep reminding her how he felt, but Peter couldn't help it.

"And you have mine, Peter," Angel replied. She then shyly

turned her eyes forward and focused on Sam and his men, who were leading them down some dirt steps.

"Stay close, kids...and watch yer step!" Sam called over his shoulder, pointing his flashlight beam ahead, their only illumination in the dark, cramped space. "There are some nasty drop-offs and booby traps around."

"Why? I mean, isn't this place safe? Rosa kept the Order of the Dragon out at the barn. Why do they need traps here?" Peter asked.

"That only works 90 percent of the time. Lately, they've been able to breach a place or two, and we haven't figured out why. We think they're somehow using the kids they kidnapped."

"They are," Angel uttered.

"Well, that's why we gotta keep the traps set. They ain't just for those goons from the Order of the Dragon. We also have to look out for traitors to the purpose of the Decretum Venia. There's some poison in the Decretum Venia that could be the death of us all." Sam flickered his flashlight down a steep set of steps, shining it on some disturbed dirt on the floor. "Jump to the left of the dirt. If ya miss, we'll be digging you outta one of the traps, and you don't wanna hang out down there with all the deadly spiders."

Peter felt a tremor in Angel's hand. "Wicked." He couldn't help the grin, because he'd made a hobby of catching eight-legged creatures at the orphanage where he grew up.

"Yeah, I had fun designing this place." Sam chuckled, then fumbled around on the dirt wall, flashed his light on his hand, then pushed a hidden button. Instantly, the place flooded with light from the ceiling. "This'll help you out."

Impressed, Peter whistled. "Damn...er, wow. That's just—"

Sam laughed again. "Look, kid, I know Pastor Finnegan's a bit of a tight-ass, but I sure as hell ain't. There ain't a four-letter word I haven't heard or said. You can always speak yer mind with me, son." Sam jumped to the side off the step.

The mud walls and cylinder shape of the room made Peter feel a bit claustrophobic. Sam wiped dirt from a section of the wall to reveal a wooden door.

"Don't worry about it bein' exposed," Sam said. "For some reason, the dirt here rises, and it'll dust the door over again in a day or two."

Sam opened the door; Peter's jaw dropped as he gazed into a hallway encased in metal with doors on each side. "And this is...?"

"The basement. The place goes up about three levels. Down here, we store all our supplies, food...anything we need. We've got enough to survive for up to a year."

"Doomsday preppers? Great!" Argia called from behind. "It's our doom!"

Angel sighed beside Peter. "I hate to agree with Kyle, but she's pretty...out there."

"Ya got that right, sister!" Kyle poked his head between them.

Peter mashed Kyle in the face and pushed him back. "Too close, man. Way too close!" He didn't let go of Angel's hand as they walked through the door and down the hall behind Sam and his guys.

Sam pointed ahead. "The elevator's slow, but it works. Go up to the first floor. There are two rooms y'all can bunk up in for a bit. I'll bring Rosa to you." He waved goodbye before he and his crew went in another direction, leaving Peter and his companions there. Peter released Angel's hand, pressed the elevator button, and waited. "Kyle, when we get upstairs, put the others in their room, then come with us."

Kyle nodded and turned to talk to the others.

The elevator opened, and Peter walked out into another corridor that was the same metallic color. All of them were quiet, scared to actually anticipate that true safety and comfort could be just on the other side of the door. They spotted the doors a short distance from the elevator, in an alcove.

Peter looked around and scrunched up his nose, a bit disappointed that there was nothing else on the floor but those two rooms. "C'mon." He placed a hand on Angel's back and nodded at Kyle.

"Hey!" Argia complained as Kyle pushed her into the room across from Peter's.

"Yeah, stop it," Gil whined. "You don't have to be such a freakin' bully. You're not herding cattle here."

"Just get a mooooove-on, would ya?" Kyle said, wearing his characteristic smirk. As soon as the others were situated in their room, he turned and followed Peter and Angel.

"That was...udderly stupid," Angel shook her head at him.

"Oh yeah? Then why are you still milking it?" Kyle punned back at her as they followed Peter into the room.

CHAPTER 27

S ilence hung in the large domed room. As with the hallways, it had metal walls, no pictures, and pull-down bunk beds covering every free space. Three levels of bunks lined the walls with thin mattresses, thin sheets, and no pillows. The only comfort in the room was the large wooly yellow carpet that lined the floor.

"We have to talk." Peter leaned against the door, pushing it closed with his backside. He crossed his arms to stop himself from pulling Angel into them. It was killing him to give her this space.

Angel waited a moment before pivoting to face him. "I know." Her voice was quiet, almost regretful. "I owe you that much. It's j-just been hard to get up the courage to tell you everything." She rubbed her hands on her worn jeans and tugged at the sleeves on her baggy shirt.

He pressed his lips closed, hoping it would stop him from talking too soon. He knew she'd been worth the risk he took in going to the Stronghold; he just hoped she was still worth it. If she threw away what they had, he'd never be able to go up against the Extraho of Obscurum, not with everything he valued on earth ripped from him. Not without Angel.

155

"I love you," she sniffed, "but I can't be the girlfriend you deserve. Not with all that's happened." Her hands covered her face.

Peter stepped forward and grasped them. Kissing them gently while he interlaced his fingers with hers, he slid his hands around her waist. "There's nothing that would stop me from forgiving you —from loving you," his voice deepened, "Tell me Angel, don't you know by now there's nothing I won't forgive of you? No one I've ever loved like you?"

Tears fell unchecked from her eyes. "Yes." Strength seemed to blossom on her features as she inhaled audibly before baring it all. "The things Gavin and his brother did to me while I was there...horrible things, made me wish I would die. But I fought them with everything I had, because I didn't want them to find you."

Peter couldn't control the tremor of anger that coursed through him. The brand on his hand instantly heated to the point he had to shift it off Angel's hip so as not to burn her.

"Go on," Peter encouraged.

"They nearly raped me, but before then, they cut me—everywhere." She started to sob. "That demon thing that was Gavin licked it like it was some drug. He told me my blood gave him my secrets, and he would find you and do to you all the things they'd planned to do to me."

"Shhh. It's okay." He kissed her. "Let it all out, I can take it. Let me take it off you."

Her hands hesitantly slid around his waist and she rested her forehead on his chest. "The worst thing was, when Gavin or whatever he was, scratched me with is finger. It—God, Peter," she shivered, "Gavin's human hand turned into a claw or something. When he slid it down my face, I felt it to my soul."

"I know what he was. I killed him. I killed it." Peter held onto her shaking form.

"But the worst was what I did to get away from Gavin, I-I told his sick brother Lucien I'd be his, I'd do anything, as long as he got me out of there." Angel exhaled a stilted breath. "I didn't mean it. Peter I didn't mean to lie, but it just hurt so bad. The beatings, the cuts, the nightmares...and Lucien's touching..."

Peter felt ill. His eyes watered and he fought against the tears to stay strong for Angel. "But you're here now with me. You are safe with me. I promise we'll bring them down, but I need you. I need you to help me do it."

Angel shook her head. "I don't know, I don't want to go back."

"You can do this. You're stronger than them. I know it doesn't feel like it, but I know who you really are, Angel. I know the Angelic DNA bloodline that runs in your body. I've seen it, experienced it. But mostly, I know the Angel I first met. The girl I thought was a tough boy who wouldn't let me leave him behind. Then I knew you as my friend. A real friend. And I need you." Peter leaned down and kissed her, relief flooding through him as she opened her lips to deepen their kiss. Reluctantly, he pulled away, "And Rob?"

Angel frowned. "He and I share a similar story. It's his story, so I won't tell you everything—I can't do that to him. He was captured by the Extraho of Obscurum. He and some of the kids got away, but not before they experienced all types of abuse by the men, women, and even the children."

Peter ran a hand through his thick curly hair. "Damn. I'm an ass."

"No, just protective...and slightly possessive. "She smiled. "That's okay because I was about to punch Argia if she mentioned how much she had to protect you and how she loved you."

"What?" Peter raised an eyebrow. "I hope not. I didn't do anything to make her feel that way."

"You don't have to. When you're around, people just feel safe. I mean gosh, you've changed so much since we last saw each other.

Your height, the muscles...the anger. What are you, like 6 foot 4 now?"

Peter held her close, bent to land another quick kiss. "So, you're not a midget. Well, maybe a little." He patted the top her head, which came up just beneath his heart.

She laughed. "Well, it seems I missed out on the giant gene." Her Hispanic accent wove into her words.

Peter released her waist and lay on the carpet, the only place in the room that really seemed comfortable. He held out a hand and was warmed by the need shining in her eyes when she took it and proceeded to lie with her head resting on his chest.

They stayed like that for a moment, then he had to ask, "Can I see them?"

She froze. "The marks?"

"Yeah, I don't want that to be something between us. You don't have to show me all of them, just what you're comfortable with."

Angel's hand fisted at his shirt; slowly she relaxed. "Alright." She sat up, then stood slowly, her eyes not meeting his.

"Look at me, Angel, just me, okay?" Peter rested his hand on her worn tennis shoe.

With a nod, her gaze met his, then her hands tugged the bottom of her shirt before her eyes closed and slowly pulled it up.

Peter's breath caught in his chest at the sight of her skin, puckered with scars from, not just cuts but burns, on her once-smooth pale skin. They dotted closely together, more on her lower belly, and scattered up her chest to just under her sports bra. Where her full breasts met, there were more red welts from cuts and burns.

"I'll kill them," Peter spat, low and deep.

Angel's eyes watered as she slid the shirt over her thick, black hair. "There's more on my legs, my feet, and...behind." She glanced away. "They teased me, getting closer to my...uh, sensitive parts when I wouldn't give them information about the Decretum Venia, or you."

"Who did this?" he asked quietly, not wanting to upset her further.

"Gavin, but at times, he made Lucien do it while the others watched." She swallowed. "The day you came to get me, they were going to start draining my blood for some ceremony."

"I'm sorry, babe." Peter stood, leaned down and kissed her, then trailed his finger over a scar on her shoulder. "That's why during the few weeks we were at the holding sanctuary, you stayed covered up?"

Angel nodded. "I didn't want you to know."

"Beautiful." He touched his lips to hers again. "Everything about you is. The scars remind me of what we went through to be here together."

She lifted his hand; turning it, she traced her finger to the brand. Her pale hand against his dark one appeared small. "It's still there? The girl, Hanna, who gave it to you must have been special."

"Hanna was...like Argia. Off the rock crazy as bat-shit." He smiled. "And she obsessed over me too. Followed me every time I snuck out of the orphanage. It's like the girl had a radar."

Angel caressed the side of his face. "You do. I saw it. Weird, but I felt comfortable around you. I can't explain it. That's why I followed you that day at the diner. I hid in the bushes till you left. I wanted to be where you were because something inside me just *knew* you."

Peter felt uncomfortable with her revelation. All the kids who seemed to seek him out and tag along, had said that, except one person. "Kyle didn't feel that way." He grinned at her.

Picking her shirt off the floor, Angel pulled it over her head with a muffled laugh. "I don't know, there must have been a good reason he was around when that Carnie guy tried to kill us."

Peter snorted. "Yeah, right. More than likely to try and rob us."

"No. If he wanted to do that he could've let the guy shoot you."

"Kyle doesn't care what he has to do to survive." Peter crossed his arms and watched as Angel tucked part of her shirt in her pants.

Kyle pushed the door open. "Talking about me behind my back again, bro?"

"Always." Peter pivoted towards Kyle.

Slamming the door, Kyle rested against it. "Don't make me stay with those guys over there. Argia, she's making them feel on edge and that Rob guy"—he slid a glance at Angel—"is still quiet after the big scream episode."

"Is he okay other than that?" Angel stepped towards Kyle.

"Fine, if you consider not blinking, slight rocking and pale-faced stares okay." Kyle chuckled. "I actually like him a lot better this way."

"Shut up." Peter slapped Kyle's arm.

"I won't keep taking your bullying, sir." Kyle used the nasal joking tone to goad Peter on.

"You know I hate when you sound like that," Peter spat.

"Yep, that's why I do it."

Angel wrapped her arm around Peter's waist. "Did you find out what's taking Rosa so long?"

Kyle nodded. "One of the men watching this place stepped off the elevator before I came in here." He rubbed the top of his buzz-cut. "He said she'll come in the morning and that they would leave food for us outside our doors. Then he left."

Peter's shoulders relaxed. "I can't say I'm mad. I'm so tired I could fall asleep standing up."

"Me too? So uh, can I crash?" Kyle asked, hopefully.

Peter kissed the top of Angel's head. "What do you think, Angel, should we let him? Or do you want him to go keep an eye on Rob for you?"

"Low, real low, dude." Kyle narrowed his eyes.

Angel laughed. "Stop Peter! Yeah, Kyle can stay."

Peter couldn't help it; he smiled, and for the first time in so long he had a feeling everything was all right.

CHAPTER 28

Some time later, Peter woke—or at least he thought he did. He was there again, staring at the angels from the brutal battles he'd witnessed every night in his dreams since he opened the book of shadows. The smell of sulfur and burning flesh and the sounds of screams pummeled him. Peter staggered, his breath caught in his throat as the pressure on his chest deepened. The grass beneath his feet was drenched in blood, and he noticed a disturbing sight: a small hand, from a broken doll being tossed about by the deafening wind and the black, cloud-like tornado in front of him.

"Peter!" Angel yelled. "Peter? Peter!" she chanted his name over and over again.

"No, no..." His voice cracked, his voice dry, though he felt as if he was drowning in the putrid air around him. *No! Not Angel. I won't let them take her again.*

"Wake up! Please wake up!" Angel cried.

Kyle's deep voice penetrated Peter's foggy mind. "Get up, dude! You'll hurt her!"

As if he'd been smacked in the face with freezing water, Peter's body began to shake while he was ripped from the depths of his nightmare. "Angel! Oh God! I'm so, so sorry."

Angel dislodged herself from the crook of Peter's arm. "It's okay. You just scared me. You're burning up, hot and sweating."

"And crying, dude. You were freaking crying." Kyle's wide eyes taunted him.

"Shut up!" Peter wiped the back of his hand across his face to clear away the dampness left from his tears. He stood and whipped a shaky hand through his unruly curls.

"Peter, what's wrong?" Angel's concerned eyes searched his face as she placed a hesitant hand on him.

He wanted to relax under her touch, but he couldn't. Every part of him burned. It was if he was on fire inside and out, and he was terrified. The lifelike dream was worse than any of the taunting warnings his mother's presence had given him before he'd done the unthinkable. He felt like he had cotton in his mouth. Releasing a cough, he slid away from Angel, unable to face her. "I only made things worse."

"I don't understand." Angel's voice skipped, as if she was afraid of what he might say next.

Kyle spoke up. "Pete, you don't have to do this. Stop tearing yourself up over this, man. I was there too! I'm just as guilty as you are, dude."

Peter shook his head. "No, you tried to stop me, like any friend would. You fought to get me to stay away from that book, but I nearly killed you to get to it. I was so desperate, so needy to feel connected to anyone, to anything that would fill the painful emptiness inside me." Peter covered his eyes with his hands. "I can't lie to you anymore, to anybody. I have to stop lying to myself about the real reason I touched that book and opened the stronghold."

"You did it to save Angel. We had no choice," Kyle tried to reassure him.

Angel's breath caught. "Peter, no!"

"Kyle, you're wrong. At first I thought I had to open the book to save Angel, but with each step I took toward it, the energy from it revealed my true intentions. I only used Angel as an excuse for opening it. There was far more to it than that."

"Then why? Why'd you do it, if you knew from the books we'd read in the buried sanctuary that it was dangerous to uncover it?" Angel's voice grew stronger, tinged with a hint of anger.

"Revenge."

Kyle cursed.

Angel dropped to the floor.

"You don't understand. The Order of the Dragon, Gavin... He represented everything that took my parents from me. I'll never forget seeing my father drown, that car sinking into the water, or my mother's body jerking around from the gunshots that killed her while she screamed at me to run. Then..." He gulped in some air, and every breath was still a struggle. "I was weak. I couldn't save them, couldn't save anyone, but I wanted to save you." Peter turned to Angel and lifted her with his shaking hands. "I wanted to kill them, all of them who'd been hurting me and the people I loved for so long."

Angel moved her hand up to caress him. "It didn't work, Peter. It never will. There will always be something evil here. This is where it rules. From the beginning of time, this has been the source of the Dragon's power. We're only to be here for a short time. Even if we stop them temporarily, they'll keep coming back."

Kyle moved closer and rested an arm around them both. "Then so will we. The Decretum Venia will always work to protect everyone. It's what we were created to do. Even though I'm not full-blooded like you and Peter, I know what those Dragon bastards are made of, and there's no way I'll give in to them, at least not without a good fight."

Peter couldn't stop the grin from sliding across his face, and some of the pressure seemed to leave his chest. "I know. That's why I keep you around."

"Nope. You keep me around because no one else likes your angry ass."

There was a brief knock on the door. It swung open before anyone had a chance to answer it.

Peter stood and smiled at the sight of the small, plump woman who entered and closed the door.

Rosa spread her arms wide. "Peter! Oh, Peter, come here and let me hug you."

Mixed feelings flooded Peter's chest. He wanted to run into her arms, but part of him was ashamed to. Sooner or later, he would have to tell her the truth. To make things right, he had to tell Rosa everything, and he only hoped that wouldn't break her heart, or make her hate him.

CHAPTER 29

Peter went to her, bending for a long hug. He didn't want to let her go, but the need to make sure she was real overrode his guilt. Rosa's softness and the smell of lavender comforted him. Not since his mother's death had he felt so comforted.

"Rosa, I ruined everything."

She pushed him back to study his eyes. Her sanguine smile and forgiving features hardened. "The past can't be undone, but this we can fix, my son." Rosa nodded absently as her thumb tapped his chin. "We will."

"How?" Peter stepped back out of her arms. "You don't know what I've done." Peter shook his head. "I don't even want to repeat it again, it just cuts me how stupid I was."

"I know what transpired because I'm a seer. I've been trained to protect you—your family line—for as long as I can remember. Only a few of the elite elders in the order even understand why you were given the code-name Saints. Even your name carried with it the depth of your importance to the order. Peter Saints... you were born to be a leader." Rosa reached for his hand and turned it to inspect the red puckered brand that grew and throbbed under her inspection.

Peter pulled back his hand. "It goes away—sometimes. When I'm not agitated, ticked off or...uh seeing things." He swallowed.

"Demons. You see the demons. That's unusual for those like you. Only seers, like me—like that girl Argia you brought with you —can see and hear the Angels and the Demons."

Kyle snorted. "Argia is crazy and sees dead people, things, and probably her own shadow. Not to mention, she may be a little on the schitzo side."

Rosa shook her head. "That's how it seems to people who don't know her true power. Unlike Peter, her strength is ever-present. Unfortunately, her handler died and she got lost like so many others in the system the Order of The Dragons built to capture and control children like her." Rosa twisted around and pointed at them. "All of you."

"I don't know why, but I keep picking up special people like her," Peter cut a glance at Kyle, "and him."

Rosa smiled. "Oh, he's useful."

"Most times." Angel stepped up next to Peter.

Peter placed an arm around her. "The problem is, I'm not the only one seeing the demons now. And it's because I opened something that was meant to stay hidden."

Rosa shook her head. "Do you believe that you—a child— would know any better? The Extraho of Obscurums have been controlled by their demon masters from the moment they raped human women to breed slaves to do their will."

"It was an abomination that should've been destroyed." Kyle crossed his arms. "I went to school with those kids and they're evil. My father's journals had been passed down from generation to generation. He never thought I was worthy enough to touch them, but when I did, I thirsted at every word. He was a scientist. His family worked with herbs and medicines that miraculously healed people."

Peter cocked an eyebrow. "I keep finding out more and more

about you every day. From school drug dealer, rich kid, to son of a chemist. Man..." He shook his head. "Kyle, do you make this stuff up?"

Angel frowned. "No Peter, Kyle's been truthful...for the most part. But Ms. Rosa, if the Decretum Venia knew about us kids, why'd they let so many go unprotected?"

Rosa snorted, and placed her hands on her rounded hips. "Disorganization and egos. These past few years, the craving for power within the Order has made me sick and scared. I'm scared because it's the kind of animosity that grows deceit. I'm sad to say, the Order who once protected you kids is falling apart, from the inside out. We have some poison in our midst, several traitors against mankind, who feel punishing humans by unleashing evil will set things right. It has never been the way things were meant to be done."

"Is that why no one came to help my father when he asked for it? Before he made my mother drag me out of bed to hit the road?" Peter spat. "He was complaining about no one coming to help us. He thought he'd been betrayed. I never knew what that meant, but now I'm getting ticked off just thinking about it."

Rosa patted his shoulder. "What happened was on purpose. One of the groups within the Decretum Venia, seeking to pervert our purpose, took that call. He didn't tell anyone you were in trouble. Your father knew your importance. His father, and grandfather revealed your legacy to him. You and only your bloodline held the key to a secret. One of which was never to be revealed. With each generation, that secret was held in the blood of the son. And on your 18th birthday, if the blood wasn't 'activated' or taken, it would go dormant until you had a child."

Peter felt ill. "You're sayin' the Extraho of Obscurum basically hunted my family for centuries? Until they had one shot to make one of the kids mess up? And the dumbass who did it—walked into their trap—was me?" He stumbled back.

Rosa's hand shot out to grab him. "No, it wasn't that easy. They used a seer to find you, to sniff you out. Her name was Hanna and she was institutionalized as a young girl. She was extremely gifted as a seer, but her mother died and the authorities got to her before our people did. While she was in the hospital, one of them learned what she was, and the demons started communicating to her, mixing the signals of the Angels that were to guide her. Then..."

"What? Then what?" Peter's voice broke. The accident, Hanna's blood from the injuries of the hit and run driver, and her dying in his arms, came back in a guilt-ridden flash.

"She found you before we were able to reach her. The guy who was with her was one of the Dragon's men. We killed him, but she ran from us."

Peter sighed. "Yeah, she ran to me. That night, she followed me and I couldn't shake her. That was the night she died and gave me this," Peter lifted his palm; it glowed illuminated and unnatural, "with her blood."

"Yes." Rosa smiled. "She heard them, the Angels."

"But why would the Angels want her to activate me? It meant the Order of the Dragon was closer to their goal?"

"They knew you were ready to end this." Rosa grasped his hand. "I know you are. We can put this to rest for the next thousand years and stop both of the Orders from destruction and save everyone."

Kyle snorted. "Aren't we a bit late for that? Everyone is seeing demons. Gavin is building some machine to take over heaven, and none of us are ready to fight them. Unless you've got some weapons, we're toast."

Rosa smiled. "You kids are the weapons. Peter, you must finish what you started. Open all the books and they will reveal how to set things right."

"How?" Angel said. "We have to fight Steele Industries, the

Order of the Dragon and demons strong enough to hurt us. That seems impossible. I know," she shivered, "I've seen them—felt what they do to us." Rubbing her arms, tears started to fall.

"Your pain can become your strength if you see this through." Rosa pulled Angel into a hug. "I know this and I trust that you kids are stronger than you think."

Peter wiped his hand down his face. "Pastor Finn said the other kids were in trouble. The ones at the orphanage."

A flash of pain fluttered over Rosa's face. "The kids are safe, he got them out just in time." She swallowed. "But Pastor Finn," her eyes watered at the edges, "he was taken."

A flash of fury as hot as molten lava pushed through Peter. He grabbed Rosa by the arms, a strangled cry forced from his lips. "No! No! God no..."

"He's alive, but just barely."

Peter released her, fell to his knees, and grabbed her around her calves. Sobs wracked his body.

He had no words.

The pain in his chest for the closest he'd had, as a father, kept him frozen in a constant wave of pain too heavy to take.

He blacked out.

CHAPTER 30

"I'm sorry I teased you about crying earlier. That was a gank move, dude. I admit it." Kyle's gruff voice chanted, "Wake up. Wake up, dude. I promise to give you all the street cred you deserve, but you have to wake up."

Peter's mouth was dry, he slit his eyes open to see Kyle pacing next to the bed. "Can you just shut up?" He vaulted up with a scream. "My head hurts and I'm pissed."

"Yeah, I got that emotion. You're not the only one those bastards stuck it to, you know." Kyle's voice dipped, a slight quiver to it. "I may have had bad parents, but they were mine—all I had."

Peter nodded. "I know. Mine were good to me. They loved each other and I—never saw this life, I've been dumped into, comin'. I was stupid," he spat, "dumb to think I'd ever have that again."

Kyle smirked. "Yep, that's a stupid dream. But you, me, and Angel can have our own peace. We could do those bastards in and just—disappear."

"Disappear?" Peter jumped up, stretched his arms over his head, and scratched at the brand on his hand. "Impossible. Too many people want us dead or would torture our bodies any way they could."

With a chuckle, Kyle gave a punch to Peter's arm. "I've got more skills than you give me cred for, bro."

Peter rolled his eyes. "Stop trying to talk gansta to me, you're white and it sounds just—wrong."

"Says who? The girls at that last place liked it well enough. They ate it up." He leaned on a white metal dresser.

"That's because they didn't know any better." Peter went to his bag and grabbed a clean black t-shirt. "So, how you thinkin' we got a shot at going ghost after we do this to the Extraho of Obscurum?"

Kyle smiled. "One word. Stronghold."

Peter stilled, then tugged the t-shirt over his hips. He couldn't help the smile on his face. "You're right."

"When we were at the only Stronghold I've walked into in life, I had some time, while you were knocked out, to search the place. It's totally livable. Food was even there, the dried kind like have on spaceships. It didn't taste too good but it was edible. We could stay in a place like that for months before we'd have to go out and get supplies."

"There's not many Strongholds. Only a few scattered in unknown places. I believe you only find them if they need to be found. The Sanctuaries are known to the Elders, but some of them thought the Strongholds were only legend."

"Well, we'll make it work wherever we land right?" Kyle's eyebrow lifted.

"We will." Peter went to Kyle and slapped hands with him. "Thanks, bro."

Kyle's eyes widened, he hit his hand on his chest. "Dude, you're gonna make me cry." Then a smirk blossomed on his face.

"Low, real low." Peter pulled on his worn tennis shoes.

"It's cool. I bawled too when I found my parents' blood in the house. Their bodies weren't there, but it was obvious what happened. I cried like a baby and rolled myself into a ball until this voice in my head said, 'Dumbass, you better run before they come back for you.' It was loud," he tapped the top of his head, "in here."

"I'm not likin' this sensitive side of you." Peter shrugged, hoping to shake off the sinking feeling in his stomach, bringing back the loss he felt at Pastor Finn's slipping from life.

"Well, I still cry, I just don't do it when anyone's around. It sucks, but I hate my life. At least I did until I found you and Angel. The only thing that would make it right was finding my own girlfriend."

"You'll find her. Argia seemed interested." Peter snickered and tossed a pillow from the nearby bed at Kyle.

"That girl scares me. Makes my man-parts shrivel up." Kyle faked a shiver. "She's pretty, in a weird, goth sort of way. But that's it. Not even on the coldest night would my lips seek hers out."

"Damn, that's mean." Peter ruffled the top of his curly dark hair." She's harmless."

"Enough about my sorry love life." Kyle waved. "I came in here to see if you were awake because the pretty boy wanted to talk to you."

Peter's eyebrow lifted. "Rob?"

"The one and only. What I can't understand is what parent would name their kid Rob? Sounds old."

"Why? I thought he wanted me out of the way so he could have Angel to himself."

Kyle whistled and started to tap his foot. "Well, uh, someone," cough, "like me... may have yelled at him when they were stressed that their best friend or ah brotha from another motha was having a nervous breakdown."

Peter snorted at Kyle's ploy to deflect from the fact that he'd approached Rob about him and Angel. "It's not your business, man. Why'd you say something to him? Angel—I don't want to hurt her, or make her think I'm a possessive freak who won't even let her have guy friends."

"Why fake it? No guy wants a blond, muscle-head, pretty boy sniffing around his girlfriend. I did you a favor, okay?" Kyle went to the door. "Angel will just blame me."

"No she won't."

"Okay, then you can beat me up after you talk to him." Kyle turned the knob. "And about that other thing, we'll talk more after we leave here," he tilted his head toward the door, "without them."

Peter rubbed his chin with his thumb. "Right." Part of him wanted to laugh and the other wanted to throw something. Kyle could mess up the fragile relationship he was rebuilding with Angel because of this.

A tentative knock sounded at the door. It opened a moment after. Rob did a quick peek out before closing it. He swallowed. "Hey."

Peter returned a grunt. He didn't hate the guy, but seeing the boy in front of him, who'd held even a fraction of Angel's attention, made him want to attack.

Rob appeared to force himself to relax. "Look, I need to tell you one thing before we go into the 'Angel' situation." He cleared his throat. "I appreciate this." He waved his hand, "Thanks for bringing me here. And for saving my life by introducing Rosa to me, I'll never be able to repay you for letting me have Angel to help me through a rough time. Without her there to talk to, I would've gone insane." A nervous laugh escaped his lips. "Who am I kidding? I will always be insane," he muttered.

Peter smirked at him, taking some pity on the guy. "It's awright. I woulda done it for anyone."

A tentative smile bloomed on Rob's face. "Angel. She and I showed up at that last place at the same time. We were processed together. See, I'd been captured by the Order of the Dragon after they killed my parents and my brothers to get me."

Peter sat, preparing to hear a similar story to all the kids he'd met throughout the years after his parent's murder. "I know them. Sick freaks. All of them."

"You were captured?" Rob asked while nervously tracing his finger on the wall and biting his lower lip.

Peter shook his head. "No, I only dealt with them when I went to get Angel, but the things I saw hanging on the people there would make your hairs stand."

"I don't think I'll ever witness anything as bad as that monster we saw in the cornfields. I thought I'd imagined it, but the smell..." His eyes studied Peter's. "And you—you fought it."

Peter crossed his arms in front of him. "Yeah, I did."

Rob plopped on the lower bunk next to him. "The things the Order of the Dragon did to me, Angel tried to help me hide. She was the only person besides myself who I knew got away. What they did to me made me want to die, the pain bit at me so deep, consistently. When Angel started convulsing from the drugs they were giving her to sleep, it sparked something in me. I fought them. I woke her. After that, they left us alone. The head elder figured he'd just watch us and see how we'd recover so he could use that information to help other kids."

Peter walked over to Rob. "All I care about is, are you in love with her?"

Rob looked away. "In my own way, I am. But I'm not strong enough to love her the way she needs it. I can't protect her. When we saw that demon, and its eyes ate her up with a hunger I'd never perceived before. I froze. I was weak. But you killed it. The power you have can save her. And I love her enough to know she's worth saving."

The pain in Peter's chest at knowing someone loved Angel as much as he did left him conflicted. He felt bad for the guy, but also he felt victorious. "Did you..."

"I never approached her in that way. I took whatever she gave and begged her to sleep in my room because of the nightmares. The things I did to myself in my sleep scared me more. She tied my hands for me so I wouldn't rip the skin off my chest and back. Angel removed anything I might use to stab myself with, and she'd watch me sleep, chanted over me like Rosa taught her."

Peter sighed, guilt eating at him. "I'm sorry."

"It's not your fault—it's theirs. The Order of the Dragon and the things, unimaginable acts the women and men did while torturing me." Rob patted Peter on the back. "But thanks to you, and to Rosa, I'm willing to die to stop them. Rosa has healed me of the dreams and the pain. Her herbal medicines and her chants, her power, cover me. I see everything more clearly now."

"Yeah, Rosa's special."

"And so is Angel. I want you to know that she never returned my feelings. She always dreamed of you during her nightmares when I watched her sleep in the early mornings. You were her anchor. She'd be fitful in her sleep, but then she'd call your name and calm down."

"Thanks." Peter smiled at him.

"Well, I was also supposed to let you know that everyone is learning some fighting techniques from Big Daddy and Wonder Woman." Rob rolled his eyes.

"You're kiddin', right?" Peter laughed.

Rob shook his head. "Nope, these people have code names for themselves. Especially the adults. I don't think they want the rest of us to be able to speak their real names if anything ever happens."

"Where are we meeting?"

"Up a level. There's stairs at the end of the hall."

Peter stood. "I'll be there. I just need to get my head straight first."

Rob nodded and headed to the door. "I'll let the others know."

When the door closed, Peter's fist hit the wall. The decision made, he'd have to leave this place soon. Take Angel and Kyle to the one place that would give them the advantage. The only thing that ate at him was that when he opened the next sacred book, his enemy would also have more knowledge.

A prickle of apprehension tickled his neck. A warning. One, yet again, he'd ignore.

CHAPTER 31

Gavin saw the world around him from a new perspective, and it pleased him. Nevertheless, he couldn't smile, for his insipid brother stood in front of him, struggling to hide his discomfort while caught in Gavin's hard stare. "We can't keep meeting like this, brother." Gavin tapped his chin while he scanned the wooded area that led to their newly acquired property. It was once a protected area of historical woodlands and a hideout for his earthly enemies, the Decretum Venia.

Lucien released a sigh and snaked a hand around the petite dark-haired girl hanging on to his arm. "Gavin, they can't get in. It's like the last place, the barn we own. The protection they've placed around it is deadly to all of us. I hope the men won't blow up this time."

Gavin grinned, knowing he no longer had to stand by and helplessly watch. He nodded at the girl. "Send her forth. Maybe it only works on men."

Lucien held the shivering girl steady. "You don't want to risk her do you brother? Her talents will aid us in other ways. She's in training as a psychic. Perhaps she's too valuable to—"

Gavin waved his finger at Lucien. "We've plenty of young ones in training. You know they're all expendable, yet you've grown piti-fully attached to this pathetic creature. You've always liked them young, haven't you? Barely on the verge of the ripe old age of eigh-teen, you lascivious soul."

Lucien gulped. "It's not that kind of relationship. I've gotten over my affliction, my, uh...need to relive the pain I endured as a child by passing it on to others." He lifted his chin in defiance.

"You'll get no congratulations from me on that. It was one thing we had in common, Lucien, our need to make others suffer." He wrapped his hand around the girl's neck, tugged her close and gazed into her eyes in a hypnotic manner. "Walk, girl! Keep walking until you find the entrance they are hiding." He leaned forwarded until his lips touched hers, and she lifted, as though in a drugged daze. "Go!"

The girl staggered back several steps. "Yes, Master," she uttered before twisting around and running toward the woods.

"No!" Lucien yelled just as the tips of the girl's dark hair turned orange.

The veins in her hands seemed to catch fire from within, and she screamed. The high-pitched song of her pain seemed to go on forever, until her petrified, oddly twisted form turned to ash.

Gavin sniffed the air. "Lovely."

The other men gathered around, awaiting Gavin's instructions, but Gavin's eyes fell on Lucien.

"But that was J-Jack's daughter!" he said, hardly able to stop his trembling as his hand went to his chest. "This will mean war to him and his master."

Gavin laughed, full and deep. "I know, and he'll learn not to deal with a weak human but to deal with me instead!" He stepped forward, and the group of men parted for him. "Now, I will get us in. It's doubtful they've erected power enough to stop me."

The ground gave easily under Gavin's feet as he followed the path taken by his sacrifice. It was the first ingredient needed to weaken the defenses, the blood of a youthful virgin. Now it would be easy for him, in his new form, to completely breach the hiding place. The barrier was invisible to the naked eye, but it glimmered in front of him. Gavin couldn't contain his addiction to the strength that holding his demon master captive gave him.

He lifted his hand, only easing out a bit of Balaal's power through the tenuous prison he'd worked so hard to suppress his demon master tightly within. Gavin only had to concentrate steadily to extract the charge he needed to rip though the protection ahead. Absently, he wiped his bleeding nose, a minor side-effect of his exertion. The pleasure and pain of tearing skin made him lick his lips; he yearned for pain and salivated at the taste of blood, even his own, but there was no time to enjoy the bliss of the torture he craved. The demon-clawed bones tore through the fingers of his hand; he let out a slow breath of concentrated air, and easily ripped down the barrier.

The others couldn't see what he saw, but it made Gavin smile. "It is time!" he declared in a guttural command, then called forth the master's demon minions, those just strong enough to cross over. They seemed to materialize out of thin air and began walking about on the so-called protected land.

One battle won.

A dozen or so of Balaal's servants surrounded Gavin. The ashen, glowing, demons with flaming eyes and huge, muscled forms seemed anxious. Their mouths were slack, dripping fire, and their grins showed their hunger for flesh.

With a sharp demand as he passed through the barrier, Gavin uttered, "Peter Saints! Find him! Find him now!"

CHAPTER 32

Peter stood just inside the door to the training room. He'd seen nothing like it before. Rows upon rows of shooting ranges for various types of weapons—with kids lined up taking turns for instruction. His eyes never left Angel's steady form as she shot arrow after arrow with a precision and calm that reminded him of the first confrontation they'd had with a gang shortly after they met.

Stepping forward, his path was blocked by a redheaded kid that came just under his nose.

"Well, well, if it ain't Peter Saints, crashing my new digs." The boy spat on the ground. "Remember me? Ren Thomas? The guy who used to kick your sorry ass at Pastor Finnegan's dump?"

Peter lifted an eyebrow. "I think you've got the story confused. Must've been when I knocked your big head up against that wall before I left. Rattled your brain."

Ren tapped his chin. "Don't remember that. But after you split, I became the king dog. Had kids giving me all their money, and the girls giving me all the goods." He winked, "You know what I mean?"

"Why do I care?" Peter shoved Ren back. "How did you get here anyway?"

"The old guy started smuggling us out shortly after you split. He told us we were going to safe houses that would increase our training and teach us to protect ourselves in case we found trouble." Ren shrugged. "How have you been?"

That's when Peter noticed it. Fear, deep within Ren's eyes. "Surviving? You?"

Ren sighed. "It was hard getting out alive. I was one of the last ones to leave. He got the younger ones out first." Ren stepped closer. "My group ran into some trouble and our 'handler' told us to run, but not before I saw one of the guys chasing us grab him and ask..." Ren's voice got lower, "for you."

Peter frowned. "Me? Just me?"

"I don't know. I didn't stick around to find out." Ren gulped. "I just...wanted to tell you. I thought you should know."

Peter grinned. "Thanks." He moved past Ren and headed towards Angel. He never would've thought he and Ren could come to a truce. But life and death changed things. Changed people and made the differences he'd had with other kids in the past seem petty.

Angel didn't notice as he slid into line behind her. She'd moved on to the gun range and was running her fingers over the weapon before lifting it.

"How'd you get so good at shooting things?" Peter asked.

She didn't jump, but her eyes blinked in surprise. "I didn't hear you come up behind me. Isn't that dangerous?"

"Yeah, I read the sign on the pole, but I didn't care."

A small dimple appeared on her cheek. "I knew you wouldn't."

"Did they teach you to do this at the last Sanctuary?" Peter reached over and flicked the switch to pull the target closer for inspection.

"No, they were too busy trying to get information out of me

about my parents, Gavin, and you." Angel grabbed the target to inspect it. "I learned this from my father. After he realized we were being followed, he'd started to get more serious about my lessons. He wanted me to learn more than martial arts."

"Sick of everyone wanting to know where I'm at," Peter spat. The frustration of always being on the run hanging on him like armor. "It just gets real tired."

Angel giggled softly. "You always talk slang when you get angry."

Peter followed her to the next station where handguns and knives were neatly laid out. Each had a picture and directions on how to use it with accuracy. Without glancing at them, Angel picked up a jeweled handgun.

"I guess. Kyle does it so much I'm starting to think he grew up poor and in the city, even though he claims to have had rich parents and went to private schools all his life."

Peter stepped close behind Angel as she fired off a round of shots. All of them hit the middle and center of the bull's-eye.

"He just wants to find a level to bond on with you." Angel reloaded the gun, flicked the lever, and sent out a new target.

Peter stood steady behind her as she shot. This time he studied her stance, and her shoulders, smiling to himself that the old Angel was back. Her fear and brokenness seemed to fuel her anger. A new strength he hoped he'd given her.

She dropped the handgun on the table and didn't bother to pull in the target. "I'm done. You want to go to the hand combat area?"

"Yeah, you ready to fight me?" He grinned and rested his arm around her shoulders. Waiting for the small wince that used to come, his hand flexed, only to relax when he noticed she was supple under his touch.

"If you want me to teach you a thing or two." Angel leaned into his arms. "I'd like that."

They walked through the small clusters of kids along the narrow passageway in the back of the shooting and weapons area. The rounded lights on the wall cast a dull glow on the jagged rock surface. The kids excitedly bragged about their progress, but Peter didn't miss some of their questioning and accusing eyes following them.

"So I see you kept busy while I was blacked out, huh?"

"Yes, I wanted to stay with you, but Kyle told me you'd be ashamed to de-man yourself further in my presence, and if I cared one ounce for your dignity and manhood, I'd leave him to take care of you."

Peter chuckled. "You kidding, right?"

Angel shook her head. "No. And he was serious. He wouldn't even let Rosa or Wonder Woman in to see you."

"Wonder Woman?" Peter placed a hand in his pocket. "Oh yeah, I remember Rob telling me the adults here had code names."

Angel stiffened. "You talked to Rob?"

"Is that a problem?" Peter tightened his arm around her and pushed her slightly forward.

She recovered and pulled away then walked more briskly down a small corridor to the right of them.

"Talk to me." Peter pulled her arm and pushed her against the wall as a few kids barreled behind him. "Don't hold anything back from me. I thought we were more than that. More than secrets, more than friends. Something deeper that makes it easy to expose faults, mistakes to each other." Peter leaned in and kissed her. He couldn't help himself, his need of her was palatable. "I will forgive you anything. I love you so much, Angel."

Her eyes watered. "I love you to Peter, but I..."

"Shhh, not now 'kay?" He touched her lips briefly with his. "I'll let you kick my ass, then we can talk alone later."

Angel sniffed and nodded. "Okay, but don't go easy on me." She pushed at his chest, "Because I won't on you."

She marched forward, her back straight, her long dark braid slapping her curved hips, and he was proud. This was the Angel he'd fallen in love with from the first. The only hitch was in his chest: a fear he would snatch that away from her when he revealed the darkness they were up against. The evil he'd unleashed thinking he was doing something good. Resigned to deal with those thoughts later, Peter followed.

Angel's stance was deceiving. Casually, she bit at a fingernail. A habit Peter hadn't noticed when they were together. Her eyes followed his movements subtly, from under thick lashes.

Peter wasn't fooled, but he was cautious. Other kids gathered in a circle, eager to see a new fight and already throwing bets that the girl would lose. Kyle was there, grinning like a fool as he was taking bets that Peter would lose. The bastard.

Before Peter's eyes left Kyle's spectacle, a firm hit of Angel's swinging foot tripped him.

"C'mon!" Angel yelled. A small smirk lifted her full lips. With a flip and a slide she landed a punch to his chest.

Peter wouldn't hit her, but he'd show her he was the stronger competitor. He ducked and blocked her rapid punches. Then, Peter grabbed her fist in the palm of his hand. Angel's leg formed a perfect split upward and landed a kick to his jaw.

"That's all you got?" Her usually soft voice was harsh. Aggressive.

And Peter loved it. She was coming back to him. His Angel of fire. For a moment he was dazed as he caught a second of longing in her eyes. Followed by her punch, he dropped down just in time.

"Fight me back!" Angel taunted.

Peter slapped her punches out of aim, smiling at her, toying with her. Angel kneed him in the stomach. He jerked forward, smacked at her face and pulled her hair. Then jerked her head back, making a slicing motion at her neck. "The base of the neck, right there, is how to kill the demons," he hissed.

Twisting out of his grasp, the flat of Angel's palm hit Peter's chin, loosening his grip. Stomping on his foot, she jabbed two fingers at Peter's eyes.

Peter stepped back. "That's a good place too, but if you've got knives..."

Angel growled, jumped up, snaked her arm around Peter's neck, and flipped over, using her weight to force him backwards.

They landed on the ground. Angel's leg firmly around Peter's neck. "Could I break their necks like this?" Her back bowed, in position to snap his neck.

Coughing, Peter nodded. "Yep."

Angel tightened her leg. "You give up?"

Peter suppressed a smile. "Yeah. This is all you," he coughed, hitting his hand on the ground to signal defeat.

Kyle stepped into the middle of the circle. "The winner is... Angel!!! Peter Saints again, beaten by...a girl." Kyle belted out a whistle.

CHAPTER 33

Peter opened the door to their room. Relieved Kyle didn't follow them. He needed this time with Angel alone. Time to set things right, if he could.

Angel tossed a small leather satchel on the lower bunk. Then she rested her knee on the chair with her hand on the back of the chair, her head down.

Peter watched her for a moment, absently scratching his palm, before clearing his throat. "Rob told me how you helped him. But he also admitted he was in love with you." Peter knew he should've confirmed Rob's admission that Angel hadn't loved him back, but Peter selfishly wanted Angel to re-confirm the fact.

"I kissed him. I slept next to him and I started to care about him because we had that terrible place in common."

"But were you in love with him like he was with you?" Peter's heart clenched; he wanted to let it go, but he couldn't. And this brought them to one of their major issues from before, his fear of losing her to someone else.

Angel turned around, her eyes red from her tears. "They told me I'd never see you again. That it was for the best. Part of me fell in love with Rob, but he wasn't what I needed. Everything in me—

in my dreams—wanted you. Not just because you were my first love, but because I knew that you and only you knew me."

"I think Rob knew you." It killed Peter to say it, to give Rob a heads-up on him. "He was there for you too. And it's okay."

Angel's eyes narrowed. "Be honest with me. Tell me what you really feel."

Peter let it go. "I hate it. The truth?" He let out a broken chuckle. "My heart feels like it's bleeding in my freakin' chest. I hurt so bad from wanting to push you away to needing to pull you close, it's driving me crazy. But I'm tryin' here. I'm trying to be the guy you need me to be, because your life right now is muffed up because of my mistakes."

Angel shook her head. "No! I was born to this life. My parents warned me. It was even more dangerous for me because my father was groomed to be a plant, a spy. He reported information about Steele Industries and Gavin to the Decretum Venia. It wasn't until I had lots of time to think about it that I realized why we moved so much and why he constantly drove his career with the focus to work every department at that company."

"You were too young to know your father's motivations." Peter shrugged.

"It doesn't matter, Rosa confirmed it for me." She stepped to him, placed her pale hand on his dark cheek. "Stop blaming yourself. I want to put everything behind us and just love you like when we first met. Unfortunately, there are nightmares in between. I feel so guilty for easily falling into a relationship with Rob where I had to pull strength from him."

Peter kissed the inside of her hand. "So where does that put us, Angel? You now know I've been faking my patience to an extent. I'm dying here. I can't see my life without you."

"I can't either. I've told you everything. I did tell Rob that I love you. However, if he needs me still, as his friend, I would ask you if it was okay. If you didn't want us to stay friends, I'd let it go."

Peter bit his bottom lip. "I don't want you to do that. If you love me, you have to just live through this part of it—the painful slices. Pushing away somebody to make me feel more secure isn't fair to you. It's phony, because it's not something you're ready to do yourself."

"Okay, I stay friends with Rob, and Argia stays friends with you." Angel laughed.

Peter rolled his eyes. "I don't know if she's a friend. She just reminds me of Hanna, and I want to make things right by protecting her." Telling Angel the entire truth had to be done for them to fix their barely-there relationship. "There's one more thing I gotta tell you."

"When you speak in slang, it scares me. You only do that when you don't feel comfortable about something."

"Yeah, right. See, when I opened the book in the Stronghold, I found it was me who set things in motion. And I have no choice but to finish it."

Angel slowly nodded.

"See, I need your help to reveal the next part of the puzzle. I can open the next sacred book, but I need you to find out some information for me." Peter rubbed the back of his neck. "I only find out information revealed by what my DNA reveals, but if I had more...someone else's DNA who was one of the major players in the war that started this, I may be able to figure out how to stop the demons from crossing over."

Confusion marred her face. "I don't understand."

"When I opened the Stronghold, I unleashed knowledge—awareness of this thousand year war. But the war was won, the secrets of both sides were hidden away, never to be found. My blood opened the first book. I think someone was there with whom you might have a connection. I'm not positive, but something besides my love for you is haunting my dreams to take you with me."

Nervously, Angel rubbed her arms. "I don't know, Peter. Is that wise? If you take me with you to do this, won't you be playing further into The Extraho of Obscurum's plan? Why can't we just get all the information we need about Gavin's company and work with the people here to fight against it?"

Peter grasped Angel by the arms. "You don't get it. We will lose. They aren't just fighting with people. You saw it! The demons are visible to any human they want to be. If we don't stop them, more and more will cross over. They have the power to do it because of what I did."

"What's to stop them from doing it anyway? If they do, they don't have any real power. It will cause the Decretum Venia to come out of hiding and start a war. I thought you said only a few of their demons, the strongest, can cross over."

He released Angel and pivoted around. "They want to use humans – like us. Kids of the Decretum Venia, to possess, to hide within so they can cross over. Our connections to our Angelic host conceals them. If they can't get their hands on us, they can use someone with psychic ability to mask the evil contained. Remember, that's what you told me Gavin revealed when you were captured. They couldn't do it before I went to the stronghold. Many of them weren't strong enough to cross over. If we open the next book, it reveals how the weapons were made—were used. We can use those weapons to return the stronger demons that broke through. If we cut off the demons' way of communicating with the Extraho of Obscurum human pawns, we can stop them. That way the Order of Dragon puppets would only be able to do evil here on earth, where the Decretum Venia can control it."

"Alright. I'll do it." She stood on tiptoe and kissed him.

Peter kissed her back, lifting her in his arms. He stepped ahead and sat her on the ledge of the window, devouring her mouth as though he was starving. A knock came at the door. He reluctantly pulled away. "I love you."

"I know." She smirked.

Kyle's whistle broke through their moment, and Peter turned as Angel jumped off the ledge behind him.

"Timing. I've got perfect timing." Kyle held open the door. "I've got some bad news."

CHAPTER 34

L ucien was ill, and throwing up in the private bathroom in his office didn't make the pain go away. Gavin was no longer his brother; hell, he wasn't even human.

Only his dreams, visions of times spent with Angel, gave him peace. It afforded him any hope that even his twisted soul might find rest. Lucien didn't understand why he felt that way about her, as he'd never felt it for any other captives. The only thing he could recall was a strange kinship with her, but finding her and ensuring her safety was an obsession. Even the demonic uttering of Gavin's dark master demon didn't consume his thoughts quite the way Angel's voice did.

He stumbled out of the bathroom, trekking through the dark wooden door that perfectly matched the paneling in his office. His workspace was smaller than Gavin's, though he refused to decorate his walls with garish paintings of his parents or former Order of the Dragon members. He, instead, demanded pictures of the sea, fish, birds—anything to take his mind off the madness that had been his life for as long as he could remember.

Lucien fell back into his chair and willed his false appearance of calm to surge through his body. His attempt at de-stressing was quickly destroyed when someone barged into his office.

"I should strangle you!" Jack cried. "How could you let your brother kill her?" He charged at Lucien, grabbed his shirt, and practically pulled him across the desk.

Lucien slapped his forearm over the man's wrist, breaking the hold. He shrugged his shoulders calmly and stepped back. "I couldn't stop him!" Lucien spat. "Gavin hypnotized her or something."

"What are you talking about?" Jack's fist hit the desk, and his perfectly styled dark hair fell forward.

"I'm telling you, my brother has changed. Balaal isn't running the show anymore. Your d-daughter did exactly what he told her to do, as if she thirsted for every word. It was...unnatural." Lucien straightened his tie. Observing the tortured wrinkle in Jack's forehead, he felt a moment of regret for the man. The pity quickly passed when Lucien recalled that Jack was just like Gavin: greedy for power and rarely given to emotional attachments.

"She was my favorite daughter out of the five. She had the strongest psychic ability and I was grooming her to be a witch." As if defeated, Jack plopped down in the thick leather chair across from Lucien.

"I'm sorry. He used her to break into the property. When we walked a little farther, we discovered the place was destroyed beneath the surface. I don't know what they used, but it was some type of acid-filled bomb. Thinking they were walking on solid ground, several of my men fell hundreds of feet to their deaths. To answer your next question, no kids were there. My men found a small group traveling, and although they got away, we were able to capture their handler."

Jack grinned. "Yes, and I heard he's been...handled."

"You didn't hear what Gavin did to drive the man to jump." Lucien shuddered inside just thinking about it.

"I had no idea your brother was involved."

"He won't rest until the Transfero of Lux Lucis is built. We need the children, but even more importantly, I must find the one I'm looking for. Remember your promise not to let the others know of her whereabouts." Lucien sighed, trying to think of a way around the disaster.

"And how do you intend to keep this morsel of flesh, this Angel Ramirez, to yourself, before the other leeches find out? Your brother's master will force you to sacrifice her, just as he so willingly sacrificed my daughter." Jack waved his hand. "We can still kill him, you know." Jack leaned in and rested his hand on the desk. "He and his demon master are...unstable. That may work in our favor."

"I have the dagger. Are you sure that's all I'll need? There may be more we have to consider."

Jack's eyebrow rose. "What else could there possibly be?"

Lucien swallowed. "He controls Balaal's demon warriors. I didn't see them, but I swear he was summoning them after he broke through the Decretum Venia barrier."

"Mara." Jack's eyes shuttered closed.

"We can't let her know our plan. I doubt even she can handle Gavin. He'll kill her, and we need Mara for the ceremony that will weaken him before I stab him."

"Fine. Gavin's your problem, but if you want to know where this Angel is heading, you'd better figure it out quickly. The Transfero of Lux Lucis is only weeks from completion. Thanks to the intel from my contact, I'll be delivering a group of kids with Decretum Venia blood." Jack jabbed his finger down on the desk, as if to emphasize each word. "Whether or not your toy will be delivered alive is ultimately up to you."

Lucien's steady gaze met Jack's. "I'll do my part. Just do your job and tell me where she is. Don't bring her in with the others."

Jack grinned. "I never said she'd be with the others. I'll give you her location. Just be prepared."

"I am."

"For Peter Saints?" Jack chuckled and spun around, then sauntered out the door.

Lucien's jaw clenched. His memory of the boy, the one of Gavin's obsession, was brutal. Even so, Peter Saints was only a kid. *What harm could he possibly do?* The one thing he did know for sure was that killing the boy before Gavin would bring him the greatest pleasure, and that was something he longed for.

CHAPTER 35

Peter used every muscle in his body to keep from pounding the wall. His fist balled, his breathing labored. He kept it together.

"He's dying," Kyle repeated.

Angel placed a hand on Peter's upper arm to soothe him. "Are you sure? What are the details?"

"When Rosa was speaking to the man running this place, she said your guy, Pastor Finn, jumped out a window from several stories high. It was a miracle he survived long enough to drag himself to a hiding place. The Decretum Venia had a man following him and other spies inside the Extraho of Obscurum. They saved him before he was found."

"Did you overhear who did this?" Angel asked hesitantly.

Kyle folded his arm and a ripple of fear passed over his features. "Gavin Steele."

Peter shook his head. "He's alive?"

"More than. Rosa suspects he's back to his old self. That the demons that control the Extraho of Obscurum are stronger and so is he. She mentioned they'd found out he'd been in a coma since we vacated the premises where we saved Angel."

"Coma?" Peter couldn't believe it. "How'd he wake up?" Pacing, Peter suppressed the fear that threatened him; twisting it around in his head he turned it to anger. "Does this mean the demon I ripped from him isn't gone?"

Kyle sighed. "I don't know. I didn't hear anything else. I uh, had to get out of the room before they knew I was eavesdropping."

"We've got to go. I will kill it. If Gavin Steele is like I left him the last time, he's more than dangerous. He's now pissed and angry."

"And smarter," Angel whispered, sitting in a chair against the wall. "The Decretum Venia should know how to handle this."

"They don't. If they did, it would've been handled." Peter snorted. "It's me he wants. But if I'm going to take the next step in this set-up Gavin's manipulating me into, it'll be on my terms."

Kyle nodded. "That's what I'm talking about."

"We leave, in the morning," Peter said.

The door opened. Argia stepped inside. "Hi."

Kyle muffled a curse. "Really? Stop sneaking up on people like that. Why aren't you downstairs practicing fight skills with the others?"

"I don't like them." Her eyes bounced from Angel to Peter. "Can I talk to you? It's important."

Angel picked up her bag. "It's okay. Kyle and I need to find Rob and the others."

Peter waited for the others to leave. Forcing himself to appear relaxed, he waved at the seat Angel vacated. "Wanna sit down?"

She eyed him. "How long has she been your girlfriend?" Argia twisted purple and black strands around her finger.

"A while. Why?" Peter shrugged. "I told you I'm not interested in you that way, remember?"

Argia shrugged. "I know. I'm not interested in you the way you think either. That kind of relationship wouldn't be good for me."

Peter frowned. "Why? Because you creep out most of the guys around you?"

"No I don't. Kyle likes me. He's just afraid to admit it."

Peter studied her a moment. He chuckled. This Argia seemed different than before. More focused with clarity, and less mentally unstable. "You...ah, seem calmer."

The largest smile blossomed on Argia's face. "I am. Rosa did it for me." Tears gathered in her eyes. "I know how to shut out the voices now. I slept, really slept, for the first time since I can remember."

"I'm glad. Yeah, Rosa is something."

"So are you, Peter." Her almond-shaped eyes widened. "Do you know why I followed you?"

"You mentioned it. Something about a glow, a light—hell I thought maybe you needed food." Peter crossed his arms and leaned on the wall. "Or to steal money."

"Some of those things drew me to you, but around you, the bad voices were quiet." Argia bit on her chipped polished nail. "Here, in this place, I feel safe. Part of me wants to stay here and never leave. I don't think I can though. Walls make me physically sick, nauseous really. The time I spent in and out of psych hospitals makes me feel like walls are closing in on me."

Peter stepped closer and placed a hand on Argia's shoulder. "I brought you here because I want you to remain safe. Stay as long as you can. It's not a good world out there for us—kids like you and me. Ya know?"

Eyes narrowed, Argia jabbed a tiny forefinger into Peter's chest. "You will not leave without me."

"I didn't say nothin' about leaving." Peter forced his features to remain placid.

A nervous laugh escaped Argia's lips. "You think I'm stupid? Crazy like they say. I can look at the energy surrounding you and tell when you're lying, hiding something, angry...in love."

He shook his head. "No one can do that."

Argia nodded. "I can. For you to be so strong, and so different than the rest of us, you are stupid. There's people like me and Rosa, but there are others much worse who work for the evil one. Not just people with innate gifts, but wicked people who are twisted. I know them. I saw them. I ran, and found a way to hide from them."

"I'm sorry about what happened to you, Argia, really I am, but it's not my issue. Not my problem. I've got my own. I'm not someone you want to follow. The road I'm walkin' is dark, and you need to stay out of the darkness. It can kill you like it did a friend of mine."

"So you're leaving?" Argia blinked as if holding in tears. "I don't know these people. You—I don't feel safe when you're not there. Your strength keeps them at bay." She grasped his shirt tightly, her nose almost touching his. "I will never let you leave me. Never!"

Angel walked in the room. Her stunned expression rendered Peter temporarily speechless. In that muted second, Argia ran out the door, pushing past Angel with a sob.

"What did you say to her?" Angel whispered as the door clicked closed.

"Nothing. Just...just tell Kyle, we leave tonight."

CHAPTER 36

Peter left a goodbye note for Rosa with instructions. They'd 'borrowed' one of the cars in the hidden garage. It was a bit old and rusted. The vehicle had a trunk full of supplies, thanks to Kyle's planning.

"You sleep?" Peter asked Angel, who sat up front with him, her head resting on the window. The snoring in the backseat said Kyle was out cold.

"Not really. I'm trying though, but I give up. Stupid nightmares," she grumbled.

Peter couldn't stop his need to touch her. It was hard to believe she was sitting there with him.

"What did your note to Rosa say?"

Tightening his hands on the wheel, Peter sighed. "I told her to meet me at Gavin's. And I told her I made Gil a promise to save Chloe. I asked if the rogue Decretum Venia guys could make good on my promise I'd be grateful. They have the equipment and, according to Kyle, they know the locations of the Extraho of Obscurum properties and holdings."

"Hmm, they'll find them. But how will we know where Gavin is?"

"He'll be where his stupid machine is. Kyle found out the location, and it's just a day's ride from where we're going." Peter threaded his fingers through hers.

"Are you sure about this? I just have this feeling I'm about to open up Pandora's Box or something. After we do this, there'll be chaos."

Peter shook his head. "We are already in chaos. Doing this will give us the upper hand. I know it."

"I hope so." Angel blew her breath on the window and traced a heart in it.

"Do you trust me?"

A dimple appeared in her cheek as she smiled at him. "Yes."

Peter lifted an eyebrow, pushing his luck a little, he asked, "Do you love me? Is that heart you hide—mine?"

"Only if you fight for it." Saucily, she pouted.

"Always." Warmth filled Peter's chest. Seeing Angel's old self made him feel like maybe they did have a chance. Maybe, just maybe they would heal after this.

For a moment, a somber expression passed over Angel's face. "Do you think he'll make it—your Pastor Finn?"

Peter swallowed. "I hope so. If Rosa knows where he is, then the Decretum Venia must have him somewhere safe at least."

"Tell me about a dream you have. Something happy." Angel forced a sanguine smile on her face.

Peter knew she was trying to get his mind off of his pain. "I dream of you. Me," he tilted his head in Kyle's direction, "and knuckle-head back there—of us living somewhere far from here. Some island where it's just us. But Kyle's got a girlfriend. I don't dig him getting touchy-feely with you."

Angel laughed. "No way would Kyle have a chance to steal me from you. He's way too needy."

"Yeah, well, I don't want him gettin' any ideas. He's a hound. At the last place we were holed up, he flirted with anything female—

anything. Some butt-ugly girls went around thinking he wanted them."

"Ha! I see that in him. I think he just flirts with them because he's a softy who wants everyone to feel wanted."

"I bet. Kyle told me, 'I keep my options opened for dry spells'." Peter rolled his eyes.

"I bet it's just a front. He's as scared as we are."

Peter shrugged. "I don't know. Some nights I stay up and can't sleep, that bastard sleeps like he didn't experience the hell we've been living for the last year. Peaceful as a baby."

"Oh." A pensive frown appeared on Angel's face. "What happened with Argia? She seemed really upset."

"She figured out I leaving and she was afraid to stay there alone."

"Hmph, come to think of it, no one's seen her since she left your room. It's been hours."

"The girl's got some uncanny hiding places. She is sort of off about some things, but Rosa's been working with her."

"Yeah, Argia hasn't been spooking out the others as much. Rob is actually starting to like her. And he said she can sing too."

Peter kissed her hand and squeezed her palm as he cleared his throat. "So what's up with you two?"

"Nothing really. Rob admitted he didn't want to pressure me to be anything more than friends."

"Why do I get a feeling, the bast—the guy said more?" Peter forced calm to flow through is tightened muscles. He knew Rob would try one last time to see if there was something between him and Angel.

Angel giggled. "You don't have to play stoic with me. I wanted to scratch out Argia's eyes when I walked in and it looked like she was about to kiss you." She brushed a wayward curl out of her eyes. "He also told me to be careful with you. That Argia told him something evil is trailing you, and now her, since it knows you and she are together."

"She never told me. You sure he's not lying on the crazy girl?"

"He wouldn't do that. He appeared really concerned and a little spooked by it. Rob said Gil told him some of the things Argia does in her sleep, screams and whispers. She unsettles them so much they basically give her a corner by herself."

"Well, if she made it through the herbal barriers at the last camp, she's safe. Rosa would've told me if she thought Argia was a threat, or being used as a pawn."

"I thought you said Rosa did mention she and Argia have some ability to be used by both dark and light forces."

Peter tapped the brakes and started to turn off the main highway leading to an abandoned house Kyle found using a cell-phone he'd taken from the camp. "Yeah, I said that, but Rosa made it a point to say that Argia's been doing a good job at keeping the darkness away. We've had it bad, but that chick—she's had it worse. She's been living and hiding on the street for years after she escaped a psych hospital."

"Isn't it funny how that works out. Someone's always got a worse story."

"True." Peter warmed at Angel's kiss on his cheek. He gunned the engine and drove on the bumpy paved road that led into a densely wooded area. Thick trees lined the one car rock road. Tiny Chinese-style multi-colored lanterns hung low, lighting the way.

"Is this it?" Angel asked.

"I think." The hairs rose on his neck. Why'd Kyle always find the worst places?

Kyle's groggy form slumped over the car seat. "Looks like the picture on the rental website."

Peter frowned. "Did you pay for us to stay here? How?" As far as Peter knew, Kyle didn't have any money or credit cards.

"Yep, can we say PayPal?" Kyle grinned.

"How did you do it? I don't want us traced," Peter ground out. Kyle really knew how to tick him off sometimes.

"One of my dad's old accounts. Did I mention he came from money? I only planned on using them in case of emergency. The electronic payment account I opened is linked to one of the smaller banks."

"I don't know, Kyle. Pastor Finn made it clear we should only pay for stuff in cash. No traceability." Peter frowned as he pulled up in front of the house. The light wasn't on. Its yellowed exterior had seen better days and there were a few broken windows at the front. A small porch, just big enough for two people to stand on at a time, had some broken wood planks.

"No worries, dude. I checked out this place. It's owned by some woman who's hardly here. This is one of many properties she owns. The key is in the mailbox on the side of the house. There's a main house about a quarter mile through the woods that's wide open. This used to be a servant's quarters."

"It looks okay," Angel muttered groggily. "I'm just tired."

"I'm hungry. I'll get our stuff out of the trunk while Peter here does the honor of opening the crash pad. I paid for two nights so we don't have to hurry off if we don't want to."

Still doubtful, Peter wiped his hand down his face. "Who comes to check on the place to make sure people vacate? Who cleans it?"

"They stated in the contract that the renter has to clean the place. So that's what we're doing. Now, if your inquisition is over, I'm getting our bags and the chips I have in the trunk waiting for me." Kyle slid over and opened the door.

Angel followed. "C'mon Peter, it looks fine."

Peter grudgingly opened his door.

Kyle cursed. "What the hell? How'd you get in there? And you ate my damn food!" Kyle kicked the bumper.

Peter and Angel went to the back of the car.

Argia's hand waved hesitantly. "I couldn't let you go unprotected."

Kyle hit the open trunk with his fist. "There you go! The slightly mentally unstable Jane Doe is protecting us?"

Peter held out a hand to help Argia to the ground. "You shouldn't have come."

"Nonsense. You need me. I even brought some herbs to protect us. This place isn't safe. We're wide open. They can smell us."

Kyle leaned almost nose-to-nose with the girl. "Who, Argia? Who can smell us? I wish you'd just stayed back there." He snatched the backpack of food from the trunk with a small laptop he had tucked under it. "We'd be safer with you gone."

Argia appeared unfazed by Kyle's outburst. She grinned. "Your light is brighter now. So much power." She sniffed the air. "We'll show them."

Peter frowned. "Yeah. Right."

Angel stepped up. "Hello. Do you want to help me grab the rest of the stuff?"

Argia held the small satchel hanging from her shoulder close for a moment before dropping it and landing a glowing smile at Angel. "Yes. I'd like that."

Peter pivoted away and jogged to Kyle who was just opening the door.

With a glance back at Argia, he cursed.

CHAPTER 37

He felt Argia staring at him. Peter couldn't shake the girl. He'd left Kyle and Angel in the kitchen of the over-furnished home that smelled of dust and mildew. Spotty water damage, from years of neglect, stained the walls that were decorated with a massive amount of artwork the owner appeared to use to cover up the imperfections.

Peter flinched when he felt the girl's timid tap to his shoulder. "Are you mad at me? You can tell me."

Letting out a pent-up sigh, Peter pivoted around. "No. I just wanted you to stay there. Dammit, you can't go with us."

"You keep saying that, but I'm still here. I'm good at keeping up with people who don't want me around." Argia worried her full bottom lip with dainty white teeth.

Peter considered her pretty, with the exception of her youngish appearance. "I don't care. Look, you don't know me or what I'm capable of, but before I'll take you where I'm going, I'll stuff you in one of these closets, tie your hands behind you, and leave a note for Rosa and the others to find you. You shouldn't have followed me. Another one like you did it, and she didn't live to tell about it."

Frowning, Argia stepped closer, her slightly rounded chest nearly touching Peter's shirt. "You killed someone?"

Peter pushed the girl back. "When are you going to get it through your head?"

"Never. So give it up." She grasped his hand tighter than Peter would've expected from someone so slight.

"What are you..." Peter tugged his hand from hers.

"I've seen it. The symbol. You do know it's an ancient language, right?" She eyed him but didn't make a move toward him again.

"How would you know?" He folded his arms and frowned at her.

"What I wasn't taught by listening to my captors, I learned from the voices around me. The angelic ones constantly fed me countermeasures, strength, and peace, while the demonic ones tormented me, taunted me, and caused me confusion."

He raised an eyebrow. "You? Confused? Naw," he snorted.

"You don't think I have feelings?" Argia jabbed her tiny finger into his chest. "It makes me want to cry every time Kyle calls me names. I've felt like dirt every time I went around other kids and they ran from me or called me names. But I'm strong. I shake it off because the angels tell me I have a purpose. So...I fought to find someone like you." Tears welled in her eyes. "Someone like me."

Peter felt like scum. He dropped his hands to his sides then rested them on her shoulders. "I'm sorry. I don't think you being here will help us. As far as I know, you're letting our enemy know where we are."

Argia shook her head. "No. They're hunting you." She leaned close, whispering, "He knows the taste of your blood."

Peter pulled back from her. "They also know you." He narrowed his eyes.

"Not really. They try through me, but I'm good at keeping my essence out of their reach. However, being around you is a bit dangerous."

Peter snorted again. "I bet." He placed his hands on his jeaned hips. "So where does this put us? You won't go, I want you gone, and even I don't want to hurt you like I threatened."

"Just take me with you. At least as far as you can."

"Kyle made it clear he doesn't feel comfortable with you around." Peter searched behind him to make sure the others were still upstairs. "And you're making things with me and Angel uncomfortable."

"I see." Argia tapped her lip with her finger. "She's jealous and thinks I'm in love with you?"

Peter smirked. "You think?"

With a shrug, Argia smiled. "I got it! I'll start acting like I'm in love with Kyle."

"Uh, no. That wouldn't be a safe bet for you. For some reason, you make Kyle angry."

"Only because deep down, he's drawn to me." She slanted her eyes at him and winked. "I think he's got a curiosity about Asian girls."

"What?" Peter waved his hands and stepped back, trying not to laugh in her face. "Kyle specifically thinks you're wacko. It's got nothin' to do with you being Asian."

"That settles it then. I will do whatever it takes to make your girlfriend feel comfortable." Argia jumped up and clapped. "And I'll make Kyle like me too."

Peter gave up. There was no way he'd get through to her, and he was tired of trying. If she survived the trip to the Stronghold, he just might take her all the way. "Fine."

Argia hopped past him and through the doorway just as Angel entered.

"Hi." Angel's smile appeared pensive as she sidestepped Argia. "We can't sleep in the bedrooms."

"Why?" Peter's hand ached to hold her, but he held back, sensing an unease in her.

"They're packed from floors to ceilings with boxes."

"Let me guess, Kyle's going through some of them?"

"You guessed right. There're some expensive items in them. Mostly art." Angel gazed around and let out a small giggle. "You could easily guess that."

"Yeah." An argument issuing from the other room made Peter step forward. Then, he shrugged it off, figuring he'd let Kyle deal with Argia.

"So ah, she appeared happy."

Peter slid his hand down his face. "Yeah, she's determined to stick with us. I even threatened to tie her up and stuff her in the closet to keep her from following."

"You didn't!" Angel pursed her lips. "That's wrong. You know the girl has some problems."

"No, she *is* the problem. But it doesn't matter now. We're stuck with her."

Kyle barged in the room. "You!" He pointed at Peter. "Owe me big time." Then he pivoted around and stomped out.

Angel laughed. "Oh, my gosh, is he mad."

"Serves him right. He's always picking up strays for me to deal with." Peter plopped on one of the many couches in the room. It was soft, with crazy patterns that clashed with the art on the walls. He was just glad it didn't smell.

Angel joined him on the couch and slid her arm behind him. "You mean Gil?"

"Yeah, and his girlfriend Chloe." Peter flexed his hand, his palm heating as a constant reminder that his life was no longer his own. "She was abducted by those bastards. I don't even want to think about what they're doing to her. It makes me too damn angry at them...at myself, for letting Kyle talk me into bringing Gil into this screwed-up situation."

"I'm sorry." Her eyes filled with sadness and she leaned in to kiss his cheek.

Peter turned and captured her lips, kissing her with all the hurt, anger, and desperation he felt. "God, I love you." He kissed her again.

"Get a room." Kyle snorted with Argia behind him.

"I got one. You both take one of the others," Peter mumbled between quick kisses with Angel.

"Not happening, dude. Both those rooms are packed. We're crashing in here, because there is no freakin' way I'm sleeping alone with this one." His head tilted towards Argia. "She scares me."

Argia wrapped her arms around Kyle's waist. "I won't hurt you."

Kyle mouthed. *Help me.*

Argia landed a kiss to his lower jaw. "He'll come around." She winked at Peter. "But he's right. We can't sleep in either of the rooms. Besides, I forgot to protect the outside perimeter of the house."

Angel snuggled closer to Peter. "What does that mean?"

"From the enemy." Argia blinked. "I was supposed to lay the herbs around outside, but it's too dark now, so I've started inside. I've covered the other few rooms I just have this one left, and we should be able to sleep like babies."

Peter raised an eyebrow. "Unlikely."

"I don't think that shit works anyway." Kyle removed Argia's arms from around him. "I'm tired and that other couch is calling my name."

Peter lay down fully on his couch and Angel intertwined her legs with his. "We call this one." Smiling at Kyle, Peter chided, "You and Argia should fit well on the other one."

"Hell if," Kyle spat and grabbed a quilt off the arm of the clashing plaid couch then laid on the floor.

Argia looked at him, almost as if she was hurt by his response.

"I'll sleep on the floor." She sighed. "I prefer it since I move a lot when I sleep."

Peter watched their interchange and noticed the guilt-ridden expression on Kyle's face before he quickly recovered. Peter couldn't help but smile.

Kyle climbed on the couch, but threw down the back cushions for a makeshift bed. "Suit yourself. You can have the covers."

Peter cleared his throat. "Kyle you suck." He threw a pillow that collided with the back of Kyle's head.

CHAPTER 38

"K nocking? Someone's knocking," Peter mumbled as he twisted his body at an angle that kept him on the couch, close to Angel's warmth.

"I'll get it," came a groggy response from Argia from across the room.

"Don't," Peter uttered, but it was too late. By the time he got the words out, Argia was at the door. His eyes shot open as he ran up behind her.

"I..." Argia stuttered, clearly at a loss of words.

Peter studied the woman at the door. Her eyes were red and bloodshot, as if she hadn't slept in days, and her face was a pale, sickly color, framed by wild, greasy strands of hair that looked as if it hadn't been washed in months.

"So sorry to bother you," the stranger said, "but I manage this property. I wasn't aware anyone was renting it." The woman rubbed her hands on her thin arms.

"We paid for two nights." Peter stepped up behind Argia.

Argia placed a hand on Peter's wrist. "She's not alone."

The woman grabbed Argia with both hands and with a growl,

dragged her out of the house. Argia wrestled with the woman as she was dragged down the steps.

Peter charged after them, but the moment he stepped over the threshold, his chest began to pound fiercely, and his hand burned. He cursed as he realized the alleged landlady was being puppeted by a demon, its sooty black form barely noticeable in the depths of the night.

Peter ran after them, into the woods. He knew it was a trap, but he refused to think about that. Peter's arms pumped faster as the woman turned, dragging a struggling Argia by the purple and black hair.

His palm itched, heating up more and more. A light would soon burst out, and he willed it to calm itself. Pushing the weaker demon to fight wasn't what he wanted. It was too weak to hurt the woman anyway, and on some level, the lady wanted to do its will. If she wasn't compliant, it wouldn't have been able to so easily control her. However, if he wanted to get Argia away without hurting the seemingly innocent woman, Peter had to figure out why she'd been taken. "Hey, lady!" he called.

Her only response was a growl, and she threw a dazed glance his way. He could have sworn the soot-bodied demon blinked its fire-orange eyes at him before a slip of a smile cut through the darkness of its face.

Then it happened: a ripping sound echoed in front of him. Just like that, the woman came to a halt.

Argia screamed, "It's coming out!"

Behind her, it was as if someone tore a seam of fire within the fabric of the woods. From somewhere, about twelve feet up, a frightening roar emitted, and the ground shook as a large, trans-parent-skinned demon burst through the line of fire, its body a swirl of red, orange and black, like flowing, molten lava. Its black, bottomless eyes seemed to pierce through Peter.

Standing his ground, Peter growled and let the heat of power burn. From his palm, up his arm, around his neck, and completely through him, light pulsed. He narrowed his eyes, flexed his hands, and demanded, "Let her go!"

The vile thing laughed, then grabbed the woman by the neck and lifted her several feet into the air before opening its mouth several sizes beyond what would have been considered natural. Its horned, crowned, misshapen head tilted back, and saliva dripped from its gaping mouth as it stuffed the woman's head between its jagged teeth.

Crunch!

The grotesque sound echoed in the air as it bit her head clean off her neck, searing the flesh closed. Her twitching body fell to the ground, and Argia's hysterical screams grew louder.

Peter charged at him. Growing stronger with each step, he willed the multiple ropes of lighted power to push out of the symbol on his hand. They twisted and pushed forward, thick beams with sharp, hooked tips. Like whips, they wound around the beast's head before piercing its thick neck.

It roared.

"Die!" Peter spat. He wrapped his fingers around the lit ropes expelled from his hand, tightened his grip, and yanked.

The demon fell to its knees and let out a whimpering growl.

Ignoring Argia's frantic warnings Peter jumped on the thing's shoulders. His heart beat rapidly in his chest as both his hands tugged hard on the lit ropes while the suffocating beast bucked wildly. Gurgles of liquid grew louder through its growling and jerking. It tried to free itself from the illuminated ropes, but its hands only burned and melted away with each attempted touch.

"Go back to Hell!" Peter commanded with a smile on his face. With all the growing strength within him, he twisted the lit ropes around the demon's head. Harder and tighter he pulled, until he ripped the beast's head off.

"Throw it through the fire!" Argia yelled, her voice more steady and sure.

"Done!" Peter twirled the ugly, separated head above him and tossed it behind him and through the fire-licked hole, to the dark abyss, all the while willing the ropes back within his body.

"I got this!" Argia pushed the body backward as Peter jumped forward.

The sooty demon disappeared as Peter landed in its direction. Twisting around, Peter frowned at the open hole, seemingly a portal from his world to another. "How do we close it?"

Argia smiled. "Like this." She placed her hand on the bottom of the line of fire, closed her eyes, and chanted.

"What the...?" Peter took a step back, realizing Argia was just the kind of ally he needed. For the first time, he was glad she was there.

CHAPTER 39

G avin stared across the room at the woman he was destined to marry, and he wanted to kill her. The witch, Mara, understood him too well, knew his demon master in ways he couldn't fathom. For that reason, she was a threat, a danger to his newfound power.

"You've changed." Her lilting, deceptively innocent tone seemed to taunt him.

"Not changed, my dear. Improved. I'm just...smarter." He grinned at her. "Our time of pursuing our own interests will soon come to an end, and we must finish this thing between us."

She raised an eyebrow. "You mean marry? What about your brother?"

"What about him? You can't have him, at least not as your husband. I know you want him to hold my position, but we both know he's far too weak to sustain Balaal – or *you*." Gavin didn't know why he was wasting his time with her or Lucien. If things went the way he'd planned, he wouldn't have to marry her anyway, for he'd already accomplished what he was born to do.

"I sense your mind is elsewhere, Gavin." Coyly, she dropped her gaze while absently playing with the tassels on the sleeve of her gown. Mara always kept her legs beneath elaborate layers of fabric in ornate prints and patterns. Her pale skin, black hair, and strange blue eyes seemed to hide the multitude of scars left by her punishments and witch training for the Extraho of Obscurum.

"Only on your beauty, Mara." Gavin watched her and pushed his attraction away. He didn't have time to want Mara, but the feeling seemed to carry the same ferocity with which he longed to kill her. It didn't help that whenever the witch walked into the room, his control of Balaal slipped.

"My demon mistress wants him but can't connect to Balaal." Mara stood and sashayed over to Gavin. She sat on his lap as a lover would and leaned in close enough to kiss him. "Are you hiding something from me, my love?"

The door burst open, and Lucien and Jack rushed in.

Lucien frowned at them before placing a staying hand on Jack's chest. "He wants to talk to you about some information he got from one of his contacts. It's about that Peter Saints."

Mara smirked and whispered, "You're secret is safe for now, Gavin, but I will find out what you're trying to hide from me." She kissed him passionately, as though they'd been lovers all their lives. When she pulled back, her eyes narrowed. "Balaal will be free." With those last uttered words, she slid off his lap and walked out the door, closing it behind her.

Lucien swallowed. "Is everything all right, brother?"

"Yes." Gavin bit his lip. The demon Balaal's burning essence pushed at every orifice of his body, causing him intense pain. He tightened his hands on the arm of the couch as beads of sweat littered his brow.

"Are you okay?" Jack studied him with a hawkeyed gaze.

Stop, you bastard! Gavin pushed the mental blocks up again, securing Balaal deep within the hell they shared. He released a sigh. "I'm fine. Now, what is it you need to talk to me about?"

"Start by telling me why you killed my daughter!" Jack charged Lucien, who stood between them.

Gavin stood, completely composed and back in control, just the way he liked. He smiled and sauntered over to stand in front of Jack. "You two will serve whatever purpose I deem necessary for us to power the Transfero of Lux Lucis. Her sacrifice has carried us one step closer to finding the blood sacrifices we need to power it."

"I could've done that without you killing my child!" Jack's hands shot out and grabbed Gavin by the shirt.

Gavin glanced down at Jack's fist. He leaned in, staring deeply into Jack's stormy eyes. The smile never left his face as he rested a finger over Jack's, and almost swooned from the intense, painful pleasure of the transformation of his finger into a demon-fashioned talon. "You have forgotten your place." Gavin ripped through Jack's hand, slicing through to the bone. He didn't flinch as Jack's knees buckled and a finger dropped to the floor.

"Wh-what are you...?" Jack's trembling plea fell from his lips, between streams of tears.

"Balaal and I are one." Gavin stepped around Jack's fallen body. "Lucien, clean that up, and I will tell you where you can find the children we need to feed the Transfero of Lux Lucis."

CHAPTER 40

Peter ran with Argia close behind him, in spite of her smaller stature and much shorter legs. He climbed the steps and barely made it to the top before his fist hit the door. Thankful for the sliver of daylight hitting the tree-covered sky, he was ready to go.

The door opened slowly, and a groggy Angel stared back at him.

"We're leaving now!" Peter rushed past her to grab his bag. His heart thudded almost audibly in his chest, and dread hung on his shoulders like a metal cape. "It's getting worse."

Angel stood in front of him and laid her hand on his. "You're burning up. What happened?" She placed her other hand on the back of her head. "I didn't even hear you leave."

"Kyle, wake up!" Argia's insistent voice broke the stunned silence of the room.

Shaking off Angel's firm hand, Peter stood and slid on his backpack. "Help her with him. I'm starting the car. We'll talk on the road."

Peter was grateful for Argia's help, but the demons were growing bolder. For the time being, something held them back.

Peter didn't know what or who it was, but he was sure they'd eventually catch up if they stayed in one place for too long.

He rushed out the door, nearly tripping down the steps. He yanked open the trunk, tossed in his bag, then thought better of it and closed the trunk. He plopped in the driver seat and threw his bag on the passenger side floor just before Angel slid into the car with a cursing Kyle and silent Argia. He gunned the engine and fishtailed around to speed down the lit pathway, running over several of the colored lights that bordered the dirt driveway.

"So? Do you mind telling the rest of us what the hell's goin' on?" Kyle tapped Peter's shoulder. "And why was Little Miss Cray-Cray alone with you in the woods? Tell me she didn't start spitting pea soup with her head spinning around, dude."

"Stop that! Argia saved us." Peter glanced at her through the rearview mirror, not missing the tear she brushed away from Kyle's hurtful comment. He also noticed the longing in her eyes. "Leave her alone. I'm what they're after."

"What happened?" Angel's soft hand touched his arm.

Peter moved his hand, his palm still throbbing, to grab hers. "Feel that—the heat?"

"Yeah. Your palm is burning up." She lightly kissed the back of his hand, "Something was after you?"

"No. Something *found* us. The landlady knocked on the door at some godforsaken hour, and Argia got up to answer it."

"She wanted us to come outside," Argia's raspy voice joined in. She cleared her throat, and continued, "The barrier I placed wasn't far enough out around the perimeter."

"So they can sniff us out, like bloodhounds? I thought Rosa taught you some sacred chants and herbs to protect the sanctuaries," Kyle asked in disbelief.

"Yes, but I already knew them. The angels that whisper to me told me what to do when the demons were close. It's how I stayed alive long enough to find Peter. I think this was about a year ago when his name came to me. Then, when I saw you two that day, I can't describe how relieved I felt. To not be alone. I've been alone a long time."

Kyle grunted in agreement. "I'm sorry for being an ass. Peter treats me like crap and I think I like to take it out on others."

"Bullshit, Kyle. Don't put your stupidity on me," Peter spat.

"Stop it, Kyle." Angel's firm command followed Peter. "You treat Argia horribly and she tolerates it because she doesn't want to get left behind. Play nice."

Kyle grinned. "Sure, I can do that—for a while." He patted Argia on the shoulder. "If she does."

"What happened to the landlady?" Angel asked.

"She was eaten." Peter tightened his fingers around hers.

"Her soul was theirs," Argia added sadly. "I saw it as soon as I opened the door. I was trying to close it, but was too late."

Peter wrapped an arm around Angel's shivering shoulders.

Angel sighed. "I can't believe this. It's like every nightmare I've had since I left home is coming true."

"Home was my nightmare, but this is much worse," Kyle stated.

"How can we fight this?" Angel wanted to know.

Peter gripped the wheel harder. "There's a way. I just don't want to spill yet."

Kyle leaned up between them. "Why not? You don't want our visitor, who may be playing for both teams, to know?"

"Shut up." Peter rolled his eyes. "Anyway, we've got a problem. It's not Argia those things are sniffing out. They use people to get closer to us, because they can hide within them. The weaker demons that can influence people, but don't take a full physical form, are tracking us. The best we can do is stay away from people until we get to where we're going."

Angel pointed at the dashboard. "How are we going to take care of the gas problem?"

Peter groaned. "Can things get any worse?"

"Always." Kyle smacked his teeth and leaned back, balancing his feet on the edge of Angel's seat. He pushed one of his dirty shoes hard against the window.

"Do you mind?" Angel snapped.

"So that's it? I'm the bad guy now, just because she's here?" Kyle shifted away from Argia.

Peter glanced back at him. "Do you ever stop whining, man? You got any brilliant ideas about getting gas? We've got another eight or so hours of driving ahead of us."

"Cash rules, and I've got some left over from our previous travels. You?" Kyle whistled low.

"Yeah, I have some in my bag. Pastor Finn's first gift of money and protection is getting us further than I would've thought. We should be all right in daylight. Even if we go somewhere there might be people. Can you check the route to keep us in the middle of traffic for a while?"

Angel reached into her bag and pulled out a candy bar, stuffing some in her mouth while she talked. "I don't think that's a good idea. Especially if you said the demons are using people. It's hard to figure out who they would use and who they wouldn't."

Argia sat up. "Not for me. I'd know. I sort of feel it or see it. Then the voices warn me. Sometimes though, like last night, I listen too late."

Peter smiled at that. He'd made the same mistake, but not anymore. "That's because you doubt yourself—your strength. We need to stop doing that. We've won this war. Remember that."

"How do you know?" Kyle asked.

Peter laughed. "I saw it, just not clearly. I felt it, the day I went there—to a time in the past that was supposed to remain dead. The memories I woke. They haunt me every night. But someone once told me, I've won the war only if I'm willing to fight it."

"Who said that?" Angel asked.

"Someone named Luke. Luke 23, and he was—indescribable." Peter felt comforted when he allowed himself to dwell on the peace he'd felt when Luke 23 confronted him in his angelic form. All he'd seen in Luke's eyes was comfort and a bit of disappointment at Peter allowing himself to be manipulated.

"That's a weird name," Angel replied.

"It's an angel's name," Peter responded. "We are genetic enhancements they engineered to protect their secrets. Secrets of the war they fought here, and the shame they had for over a thousand years from losing the war against the demons. Those demons raped women whose kids became the leaders of the Order of the Dragon. While our makers used the advancement of science beyond anything we've ever seen. They took the best part of themselves and the best parts of what humans had to offer, and changed our DNA without violating the bodies of the humans they felt they served."

Angel's fingers absently traced his. "That sounds amazing."

"It was. They were warriors. Fighters you only hear about in movies. Huge—they stood about 9 feet tall or more, muscles everywhere, and power they seemed to pull from inside themselves to take down masses of demons."

"Did they kill them all?" Angel asked.

"No. There were just too many. And they had poisons that would kill the angels. But the worst was the Wall of Ash that ate up any angel, human—anything that tried to pass to the demonic plane to save humans."

"Who'd they need to save?" Kyle leaned closer to hear the details.

"Their humans and one guy who'd started the fight. Jakaan. He built the machine that transported him to the heavens. He was the cause of many of their falls from grace—jealousy."

"Figures, everyone falls for that emotion," Kyle spat.

"When they went to try to save him, nothing worked. Then

Micheal 2 created weapons that would kill huge numbers of demons, but no one knew how to penetrate the Wall of Ash. That's what we have to find out. The end of the story: how they penetrated the wall and how they forced the demons back to their own dimension."

Dread bubbled up in his throat, but he forced it down. In order to get those answers, he'd have to force the one he loved to give her life for that secret. Peter wasn't willing to share that bit yet.

The car jerked. "We need gas, or we won't make it," Angel pointed out.

"I got it covered, but I'm not feeling good about stopping, not after what happened in the woods. Don't blame me if things get sticky." Kyle directed Peter to the nearest gas station and rest stop.

CHAPTER 41

Lucien stood in the back of the huge warehouse, near the door. His brother, or whatever foul thing he had become, was in the front, standing on the platform to the side of the Transfero of Lux Lucis. The mechanical evil creation that had been his family's obsession for as long as he could remember. The only thing they fixated over more was pain: giving it, receiving it, and using it. He hated them, but he also feared them, and despite all his fighting, he'd become like them, only weaker. Lucien was never disgusted at the small part of him that cared, even though his father and brother were. They saw it in him and detested it, like a beacon of light they were determined to extinguish.

"Your brother is more dangerous than I suspected," came Jack's urgent whisper from behind him.

Lucien fought the urge to move away from the man. Jack disgusted him even more than his brother, and when he killed Gavin, stabbing Jack to make sure his demon would never rule their kind, would be his next mission.

"Do you hear me? Can you handle him?" Jack demanded.

With a sigh, Lucien answered, "He's my brother. If anyone

knows how to bring him down, I do, but timing is everything. Now leave me, before he eyes us together."

The air shifted behind him as Jack moved on.

Lucien perked up at Gavin's deep, cold voice. Gavin pointed to the map—the location where he was sure the kids would be, the children with the blood that could be transfused into sons and daughters of the Extraho of Obscurum for carrying their demon masters to the gates of the heavens for war.

Gavin's voice grew insistent, and his blue gaze pinned Lucien to where he stood. "The boy, Peter Saints, is traveling with others. I've sent my brother's team to retrieve them. They will not dare return without him. The boy's blood is more than enough to cover thousands of us, but the others with him are likely just as strong."

Feeling unhinged, Lucien asked, "How'd you find them?"

Gavin's blue eyes flickered with a golden glow, almost reptilian, which passed as fast as it came. He smiled. "I have my methods. I'll show you later, brother." His hand went to his chest, and he bowed slightly. "You have my word."

Lucien couldn't control the apprehensive shiver that slid over him. Lucien waited him out, knowing Gavin would eventually bore playing mind games with him. It didn't take long. When someone else asked a question regarding the finishing touches on the Transfero of Lux Lucis, Lucien took the opportunity to sneak out.

He had to move quickly. Gavin knew where a cluster of kids from the Decretum Venia were holed up, and he also was privy to Peter Saints' location. Better yet, Lucien knew that wherever Saints was, Angelina Ramirez would be with him.

He rushed to his office, thankful it was in the far end of the facility, away from prying eyes. There, his assistant and her contact were waiting for Lucien to go over the genetic information he'd asked them to research on Angelina and himself. The connection he felt to the girl wasn't typical. Not only that, but he'd read something in the historical document archives that seemed to be strange and a bit disturbing. He smiled, proud of the forethought he'd had fresh out of college, to ask one of his staff members to transpose the documents into his own personal database. Lucien had learned long ago that his father and brother were hated as much as they were feared, and that gained him many adversaries within the wretched, damned family. Tied to demons, weakened by their human flesh, it was a losing battle. He didn't understand why the others didn't realize the demons didn't want humans and refused to take care of them. They were fools to fall for all the riches that had been promised, wealth beyond imagination. Everyone had a vice, and the Order of the Dragon had no trouble unearthing it and using it to their advantage.

After crossing the threshold to his office that resembled a small apartment, he walked through the front room, filled with couches and books, to a room off to the left. He made his way around the large desk, to the lab behind it, to where his assistant was waiting. Tiffany and he shared a strange friendship, one built on being the siblings of sadistic older brothers. As children, they were tortured together in the dark dungeons, and Lucien had comforted her. He could even admit that she was the only woman he'd ever considered falling in love with, if that was even possible, but Lucien knew he was too twisted to ever really love someone. He did care for Tiffany deeply, though, and he smiled at her chestnut hair as she tied it into a bun at her nape, a habit she'd developed to keep her cruel brother from yanking on it when he beat her. Lucien then spared a glance just past Tiffany, at the scientist anxiously waiting behind her.

"Glad you made it back, sir. We've got some interesting news about the subject you gave us," Tiffany said.

The scientist behind her cleared his throat. "I had to steal the equipment from the company and the historical data regarding your family DNA." The scientist's eyes hungrily scurried to

Tiffany, barely hiding his adoration of her, but Lucien didn't mind; in fact, he'd used that weakness to seduce the man into working for him.

Lucien clicked on his computer and sifted through the database of sacred documents from the Order of the Dragon and his family history. His eyes narrowed as he typed in several words. The sentence that had sent him on the chase stopped him cold every time he read it: "And the angel of light that was trusted with the most precious of gifts left his brother behind, stabbing him through to go into the darkness..."

"Tell me," Lucien said, flexing his fingers. "Tell me this so-called interesting news you found."

"You and the girl...are related." The scientist took an audible breath. "That means there could be a connection between your people and the children you seek from the Decretum Venia."

Lucien put up a hand. He didn't want to hear the words; a sickness settled deep in his chest. He wondered why Gavin didn't feel the connection he felt to the girl. *What does it mean?* For all those years, Gavin had thought the children they'd captured were killed by Lucien to fulfill the sick, twisted needs inflicted on him as a child in the Order of the Dragon, but that was never the case. Lucien had killed them to save them from the fate he knew awaited them if he allowed them to live. By killing them, he rescued them from being tortured by his peers in the Extraho of Obscurum or by his brother. Also, he denied the evil bastards use of the children's blood to carry out their insane desire to conquer the Heavens. Lucien had let them think he couldn't help himself from torturing and killing the young ones, but he really, truly regretted taking their lives, so much so that he drugged them to put them peacefully to sleep. What he didn't regret was saving them from being taken to the hell he'd lived in all his life.

The girl, Angel, was different. She was stronger, and she had the power to fight them, even though Lucien had never figured out why. He'd sent one of the spies to help her after he'd let Peter Saints believe he was near dead. The spy was a guard, sent to them from the Decretum Venia, though he had no idea that Lucien was aware of who he really worked for, why he was there, and the subject of his true agenda. It served Lucien best that way.

"And my brother? Is he related to her?" Lucien forced out.

His father had many concubines, but only his father's wife had produced Gavin. Lucien was his bastard, the spawn of a donated female who was sacrificed to Balaal upon Lucien's birth. Lucien was handed to his father as a servant to his legitimate son, Gavin.

"No relation," the scientist stated.

Relief filled Lucien. He couldn't believe the girl was any part of the evil that was his brother. "Tiffany, what did you find out about the children Gavin's security team was tracking? How did he find them?"

"I-I don't know, sir, but I do know there are enough of them to power his machine. The only problem will be getting them out of the church in the middle of the city without them being burned alive in the fire your brother ordered the Extraho of Obscurum plants in the Fire Department to start."

"And the girl and boy?"

"Peter Saints and Angelina Ramirez are not thought to be there. Your brother sent a separate team to seek them out, but nothing in the system reveals who those orders were given to."

Lucien ran his hand down his face. His brother was unnatural, and God help him, he'd kill him before he took them all to Hell. "So he didn't give orders to humans? What the...?"

CHAPTER 42

P eter gunned the engine in the car as long as he could. The gas tank was past empty and the rest stop ahead was the only place they could get gas. He dreaded it, but they didn't have a choice.

"I'm driving the next round, dude. You look wound up." Kyle dug in his bag to inspect one of the guns they'd collected.

"I don't care, the girls need some rest anyway. They've never seen what I'm about to show them."

"True that, my brother." Kyle hmphed.

"Really? Why you always tryin' to act black?" Peter laughed and reached behind him to mooch Kyle in the head.

"'Cause when I'm with you, I am. You're influencing me." Kyle slapped Peter's hand away from his face, "Turn there, we should be good. There's a cop car there."

Argia spoke up, "So. They're not always nice."

"Well, we've had some luck with them in the past. I like to think most of them are okay—or at least have a small conscience." Peter drove into the relatively empty rest stop. He stilled himself saying a silent prayer that none of *them* followed him there. "Argia, do feel anything?"

Peter watched her in the rearview mirror as he slowed next to the pump. The place was well lit, and a few cars were scattered with people in them appearing normal.

She frowned. "I feel something icky, but I'm pushing them away—the voices, the good ones are telling me to be cautious."

Peter nodded, his eyes meeting hers in the mirror. "Right, I'll go give the attendant the cash. Kyle, have the pump ready to go, then get us out of here."

"You know I've got you." Kyle stuffed a gun down the side of his pants. "We'll make it there if my life depends on it."

"Or mine." Peter got out the car. He leaned his head to the side as if he was stretching but he was studying the people around him. The cop was checking them out, but was playing it off. There was a woman putting bags in her car. Two guys drove in just ahead of their car, pulled out a credit card to pay, but seemed to be working real hard at not checking them out.

Angel climbed out of the car. "I'm going to get some water and snacks. Can I come with you?"

Peter couldn't help the smile that formed on his face. Just being with her made him have hope. Hope that she was his future, that the connection he'd sought all his life would be with her, and only her. Then she returned his smile, and he felt like he could do anything. Peter walked to her, slipped his arm around her shoulders and leaned down to kiss her cheek just under her ear.

"Stop that! Stay focused," Kyle warned with a pointed finger.

Peter nodded, casting a glance at the two men up ahead. He had a feeling about them—and it wasn't good. Leading Angel into the Dash-in, she went to the drinks and grabbed stuff in a hurry. He went to the counter and bought a lighter, gum, and some candy.

The lady behind the counter popped her gum and rang him up. "You want cigarettes with that? I won't card ya." The girl looked about eighteen years old and was a little plump. She smiled and winked.

"Nah, I'll pass, but do you have any tools? I got to fix some things on my car."

Angel came up beside him and pushed her items forward before whispering that she was heading back to the car.

Peter nodded, barely catching what the girl behind the counter said.

"Here's some extra stuff the mechanics keep around here. You can take it, I was going to throw it out anyway." The girl handed him a black trash bag of stuff that was obviously metal since it clanked together.

"Appreciated." Peter smiled at her, flattered she was being so nice.

"Well, it's not often I see people my age around here. This is near a retirement community. People come here for the warm weather and cheap prices, but I'm stuck here on punishment till next year to take care of my grandma."

"Sorry 'bout that." Peter handed her some money, and on second thought dug deeper in his pocket for a hundred dollar bill. "Here's money for the stuff." Balling the bill in his hand he laid it on her other palm. "This is for you, but don't look at it till I leave. Consider it a getaway present."

Her face beamed. "Thank you! Now git. That cop is near your car."

Peter rushed out. Once his foot hit the curb, mayhem broke out. The cop was arguing with Kyle. Argia's mouth hung open as the guys in the car across from them snatched out a gun. Two additional black cars screeched into the station. Angel tugged Argia into the backseat.

Running, Peter frantically dug into the bag the girl had given him, dropped it on the ground and grabbed several of the tools. He slid to a stop, threw the hacksaw and hammer at one of the men holding a gun. One of the tools hit its target, jarring the man's wrist and setting off a series of gunshots. The smell of leaking gas filled the air.

Pop!

Sparks flew at the ricochet of a bullet, then flames snaked around the pumps. Peter ran for the car as Kyle turned from the cop to get in the driver's side.

"Go!" Peter slid over the hood and hopped into the passenger seat. The car stalled. A lump formed in Peter's chest. His eyes froze as the dark, inky forms rose from the ground near the gunmen who kept firing. Slivers of orange fire-licked veins ran in paths around their ash-colored, humanoid replicated bodies.

The brand heated. He flexed his hands ready to do whatever needed to be done to get them out of there.

"Freakin' car! C'mon!" Kyle cursed.

"Oh my God! They'll kill him." Angel gestured at the police officer who attempted to charge the men running towards them.

"Do you see those! The demons?" Peter leaned his head out of the car.

"No? Just the men! More are here." Angel slapped Peter's shoulder, pushing his head in the direction of the speeding cars at the other end of the station beyond the blazing fire.

"Thank you, thank you!" Kyle hit the gas and fishtailed past the guys running at them. The thud of shots pounded the metal around them.

"Keep going! They're not stopping," Peter ground out as demons poured from the ground and jumped on the cars pursing them.

"The policeman, he's following us," Argia called. She'd turned around to face the rear. "There's about six cars behind him. It's like he's barricading them by swerving side to side."

"He's on our side," Kyle said. "He warned me to get out of there. We're apparently famous. The cops have my name, Angel's name, and a picture of you. He told me that underground, they're paying over 5 million for each of us—alive only."

"Why's he on our side?" Peter twisted his body slightly out the window, watching the demons jump off the pursuer's car to land on the cop's hood. Several pounded on the hood, then one reached in. All Peter saw was the beast's elongated fired-tipped talons as it sliced open the cop's neck. The car careened into a ditch.

"He's with the Decretum Venia, undercover. Some of them are still looking out for us and not trying to sell us out for Armageddon."

"Gun! Give me a weapon, Kyle!" Angel demanded. "Spontaneous fire chasing us is a clue those guys work for the Dragon."

"Bag. Under the seat. Don't hurt yourself, or shoot near me," Kyle laughed.

"I know how to shoot." Angel tossed a gun to Argia. "Can you help?"

"I guess." Argia leaned out her window and shot at one of the pursuing cars.

"We don't just have them to worry about." Peter braced himself between the door and the window as two of the larger demons sped up, with a blaze of fire behind them. The car rattled as one, then the other landed on the roof. "Demons!"

One clawed its way up the back hood, fire-tipped claws pierced through smoke. A loud roar vibrated in the air as it revealed itself. Flames danced in its eyes, sunken within the depths of black gray ash. Its yellow-tipped horns jutted out as it licked the window.

"Uh!" Argia's back hit the seat. Her gun dropped to the floor.

"Fight them like before!" Peter demanded of her and he released the power within him.

"Shit!" Kyle jumped.

Peter didn't bother responding as his veins filled with the power he'd held back since the day Hanna branded his hand. A white surge of electricity zigzagged through his body, revealing itself through his skin. He slapped his hand on the dashboard. A pulsating electric flood of light and power engulfed the demons who'd been tearing at the hood. Another shied back, slipping a bit off the rear of the car. But a larger, stronger one seemed to cut through an invisible barrier to jump over the weaker one.

"Me! Come with me, little Peter!" it growled.

Peter tuned out the screams from Angel and the others, realizing this demon was strong enough to cross completely over.

"Hold the car steady, Kyle!" Peter slid out the window and onto the hood. Stomping down, he forced the power to his feet and willed it to stick, giving him balance just before the red-skinned demon's clawed feet and armored body cut through the trunk to charge him.

Peter smiled, couldn't help it, because now, he didn't have to hold back. "Die!" Power surged through him. Forcing out a light beamed whip from his hand, he ducked away from the beast's slashing, clawed fingers. The whip sprang piercing pins as Peter swung it around the neck of the demon.

"Not good enough." It laughed and sliced down the side of Peter's face.

The burn, the pain, seeped into Peter's soul. Frowning, he envisioned his fingers growing into sharp claws. He sliced across the neck of the beast. The whip wrapped around the demon's thick torso. Peter twisted his hand and the whip extended sharp pins that sank deep within the beast.

It roared.

Peter grinned, feeding off the flow of power shooting out of him. "Now, this... This is good enough!" Twisting the whip, Peter yanked.

The flame within the demons eyes ebbed. Its mouth hung open in surprise, in pain. With a hiss, it disappeared. Peter fell back against the hood of the car.

Kyle jerked the vehicle to the right. Peter scrambled to hold on as they slid to a stop. Flying over the hood onto the grass, the heat from his palm retracted against the cool ground. He rolled to the side and slid his hand down the side of his face. A thin line of burnt flesh throbbed back at him.

All he wanted to do was sleep.

The darkness claimed him.

CHAPTER 43

"**G**et up!" Someone slapped his face.

Peter groaned. Everything hurt: his face, his chest—every last inch of him. Worst of all was the throbbing burn on his face; waves of pain that seemed to sink deep within him like poison. It weakened him, but he fought, clawing against it, struggling to get closer to the soft lilt of Angel's voice. A kiss touched his cheek, soft and insistent, followed by a bite.

"Wake up!" Angel yelled in his ear.

Peter jumped, but still the fog in his mind pulled at him.

"Those things... They did something to him. I shoulda closed the door they came through. I just..." Argia's mumbled ramblings filtered into Peter's other ear as the car jolted to the side.

"He's strong. He'll fight back. I know," Kyle confirmed.

Another kiss, then dampness, like tears, dripped on his cheek.

Peter pushed himself, willed and fought harder to wake up. "Angel? Baby, I'm sorry I blacked out." His voice was gruff, his throat sore. But he reached for her as his eyeballs jumped behind lids that felt glued shut.

"I'm here. Open your eyes, sleepyhead." Angel kissed his cheek and slid an arm around his waist. Her fingers pried his lids apart.

Peter put his hand to his head, blinked to focus and realized he'd slept all day. "Tell me what you saw." He had to know; sometimes he thought he was going insane. His entire body felt like it was dancing with electricity. It had to be in his mind because it didn't stop Angel from holding him.

"I saw smoke, fire...then a red demon. I thought I was having a nightmare with my eyes wide open." Angel's voice quivered. "What about you?"

Argia spoke up. "The weak ones. I saw them, they tease people, get them to do bad things. Try to get me to do bad things. Around Peter, they get scared and mad. The voices warn me about them."

"I bet they do." Kyle snickered.

Peter kicked the seat. "Shut up! She's telling the truth. I see them too. I've seen them a lot...ever since we went to the stronghold together."

"Speaking of that, we're almost to the destination. It's just a few miles up this dirt road, through the woods, and... Wait. Is this starting to sound like a bad plan to anyone else? Doesn't it sound just like the plot of one of those dumb slasher films?" Kyle said.

"No. There aren't a lot of places for us to hide, but this place will be safe, at least from them. It won't be easy to get into though. They never are." Peter thought briefly about the last stronghold he'd breached. It was dangerous, even though his ancestor had created it in a way that he would have access. It was obvious Luke 23 never wanted him to go there, for both he and Kyle had nearly died getting in.

Kyle weaved off the road and drove down a sandy path speckled with wood and debris. It led through thick brush and shrubbery, and the car slid as the tires spun in the uneven dirt and grass that comprised the dark road. "What the...?" Kyle slammed on the brakes when a wrought-iron fence seemed to come out of nowhere.

"We're here." Peter sat up straighter and just stared. *This is it.*

Now his deception would be revealed to Angel. He only hoped she could be as forgiving of him as he would always be of her.

Angel leaned closer. "This is a sanctuary? Like the one we found inside that grave?"

Peter shook his head. "No, not exactly. It's a...stronghold, a place most in the Decretum Venia aren't even aware of. It's where the strongest angelic ancestors of the Decretum Venia met and collaborated about how to send the demonic monsters back to Hell where they belong. The only problem is that the bastards are determined to take every living soul with them, but here is where it will end."

Angel placed her hand in his. "Then I'm in. I'm tired of running. Lead the way, and let's put an end to all this."

Peter smiled at her, then kissed her hungrily. "Trust me on this, okay? We'll make it through...together."

"God, could you two cut it out? Some of us don't have anyone to kiss to relieve our tension, man." Kyle slid a glance to Argia, who turned away. "Stop flaunting it and just let us in this place."

"Hater," Peter joked and climbed out of the car behind Angel. He quickly moved up ahead of the others, pushing tree limbs out of the way. The dull ache from his battle with the monster seemed to ebb away the closer he got to the fence.

The fence seemed to stretch for miles, separating them from the crashing sea. Twisted, pointed, sharp shards of glass riddled every inch of the fence; if sunlight had been able to touch it, it would have looked as if it was covered in sparkling diamonds. Besides the sand, the surf, and the thickening clouds, there was nothing there—at least nothing that could be seen.

Angel stepped up behind him and placed a hand on his shoulder. "Do you know how to get in? Is it like the other places?"

He shut his eyes and pulled from the depth of his nightmares the pages, the knowledge from the book his body had consumed what seemed like eons ago. Peter had kept those memories hidden, for they were far too painful to carry in the forefront of his mind. He'd experienced everything his ancestor Luke 23 had. The loss, the blood, and the pain of turning away from his maker; that feeling of extreme isolation made Peter feel alone in a way he never could have imagined before.

"Peter?" Angel's voice insisted on an answer.

"We get in like this." He slammed his hand down on one of the pointed glass crystals that protruded from the thick iron frame. He released a roar as blood spurted from his hand and slid down the fence.

Thunder clapped in the clouds, and thick drops of rain started to fall from the sky.

"Blood!" Argia screamed. "Why is he—"

Kyle placed an arm around her. "It's what he does, the only way in."

"Peter, stop! It's enough," Angel begged.

As much as he hated to, he ignored her and kept pushing, until he heard a clicking, sucking sound. He smiled as more blood gushed from his self-inflicted wound; it knew him, and the door was opening.

Angel tugged at his shirt. "That's not..."

Peter's eyes lifted, and he held his breath. He stood steady even as the skies seemed to open with fire, more powerful thunder than he had ever heard, lightning bolts crashing into the ground around them. He reached for Angel as the Earth shook. *Just open and let us in already,* he thought, staring at the stubborn fence.

"It's not working," Argia mumbled. "It's bad, bad. Peter, we shouldn't do this." She moved her head from side to side, covering her ears as she slid to the ground in a shivering heap.

Kyle reached down to help the small girl. "Get up! It'll be all right. It's always like this. Peter knows what he's doing."

Argia pushed his hand away. "No! The angels!" Her head

moved rapidly from side to side. "They keep warning me. This is not good, not good!"

"We don't have a choice!" Peter yelled, as the last clap of thunder came with fire, throwing sand several feet into the air. The ground separated, and Peter's fist flexed in awe as the most wicked lighthouse he'd ever seen rose from the sand.

The tip of the structure was sharp, covered in a thick, shiny, metallic outer shell, like an arm. With each clap of thunder, it seemed to disappear then reappear, shimmering in reflection of the lightning that rained from the sky. The gate groaned and rocked, and the lighthouse climbed into the sky, inch by inch, sinking the fence lower and lower into the ground.

"And we get across that how?" Kyle stepped back.

Peter grinned, realizing his nightmares had a purpose. He'd seen this place before, and he knew the vivid battle scenes and bloodbaths that flashed through his mind were part of the battle to keep safe whatever was inside. The cracks in the sand, seemed to go on forever, but they were only illusions. Plays on the water and the flashing thunder all worked together to make it appear as though there were deep cracks, when they were really just pathways through the glass-riddled minefield on either side of the dark dips in the ground.

"Follow me," he said. "Stay single file, and whatever you do, don't freak out and sidestep." Peter then took a tentative step on several seemingly stray flat shells and rocks that led from the former fence line to the first fissure in the sand. Sand seeped into the crevice, and thunder and lightning raged above. He held up a hand and watched the rain fall into the crease that looked like a gaping crack, zigzagging toward the lighthouse. Peter's eyes jumped around, searching for other like imperfections in what should have been a calm beach. Through the pelting rain, he spied two similar cracks on the far end of the beach.

"Peter, you're not thinking about walking in that, are you?" Angel asked, her hand grasping his tight-muscled shoulder.

Almost entranced, recalling the nightmares, he became surer with each passing moment, with each step forward. He had a hunch, fueled by his dreams, and he knew he was right and that he was leading them all to safety, no matter how precarious the trail to get there. "Yeah, we are. Trust me. Just don't touch the sand." Peter took a step forward, pressing the ball of his foot within the crevice that was surprisingly firm and smooth under his foot. Nodding to himself and repressing a smile, he walked steadily on the crack, which was only wide enough to put one foot in front of the other.

"Peter! Wait!" Angel patted his back. "Argia is losing it back there."

Peter turned around and almost choked at the sight of Kyle carrying Argia, her foot and hand covered in blood. "What happened?"

"Since you couldn't wait up, and she doesn't wanna do this, she..." Kyle tilted his chin down at Argia, who tightened her hands around his neck. "Man, the girl just lost it and tried to run back to the car. I didn't realize there were shards of glass and some other nasty stuff in the sand, and neither did she."

"I'm sorry, Argia." He waved back at them. "Kyle, thanks for helping her. I know it ain't exactly your style."

Kyle smirked. "Yeah, right. Just keep moving. I'm sick of being in the rain, it's gonna rust my damn shining armor."

CHAPTER 44

Peter's heart was thumping in his chest to the point of pain. After Argia's accident, they'd made quick time along the hidden path to the lighthouse. The crashing waves seemed to rise higher with each passing clap of thunder.

"Do something already!" Kyle yelled. "The girl won't let me go, and she's getting heavy."

"The water's rising!" Angel's finger frantically tapped Peter's shoulder. "The waves are splashing on the path."

There was no door on the structure, at least not a visible one. Peter knew it was there, but it was hidden. After all, the angelic warriors never made it easy. "I'm looking for a clue to get us in." Peter ran his fingers down the jagged walls, comprised of rocks and crystallized glass in various sizes and colors, glowing with each flash of the angry lightning.

"Hurry it up, dude! I don't wanna drown while holding Argia."

Argia's hoarse voice followed. "I'll get down. I'm fine now. I can help Peter."

Peter frowned as the lightning seemed to flash more urgently, like a warning. After a moment, he realized the flashes were coming in a specific rhythm, a pattern, almost like a message of some sort. He forced his mind to put together pieces of the night-mares he'd hidden in the back corners, the bloodbaths that had

243

taken place outside the gates of the place. He recalled his angelic ancestor, Luke 23, running, then waiting. *"One...two...three...four,"* Luke 23 counted in his mind, and then it opened.

"Peter, the angels are talking to me," Argia whispered. Her small hand reached up and pinched his earlobe to pull him down to her.

"It's the lightning, right? Some kind of code?" Peter glanced down at her.

Argia smiled. "Yes. They said listen to the lights."

Peter nodded. "Thank you. Are you okay with this now?"

"Not really. But it's my own fears stopping me. I think the angels already know it's too late to change your mind. The free-will thing and all."

"Yeah, well look, I got this now." Peter counted. One flash. A crystal at the top lit up. Second flash. A crystal below it lit up. After three more, a line of speckled lights ended about three feet from where they stood on the path. "It's over there."

Angel grabbed his arm. "That's in the sand. It'll cut us."

"No it won't. There's a small path, but we have to hold onto the rocks to stay on it. I'll go first, then you, Angel, Argia, and Kyle can pull up the back."

"Hell no, dude!" Kyle wailed. "Why do I always gotta pick up the crap you leave behind? If this all goes to pot, I'll have to save both Angel and Argia."

Peter smiled. "About time you do your job. Remember, you're just along for the ride, half-blood."

"Low, dude, real low. Just get us in there already. I'm soaked and pissed."

"Yeah, well, we all know you've got something against show-ers," Angel joked. "It's no wonder Argia said those things can smell us."

Peter laughed at their banter, then slid his foot onto the sliver of dark rock. He placed his hand on one of the protruding rocks next to his shoulder and one above him for balance. The thundering and lightning urged him on, but the waves pushed water up, clearing away some of the sand to reveal hooks, knives and other sharp, deadly objects.

"Are we there yet, Houdini?" Kyle yelled. "I had one slip, and your girl, Angel, is barely holding on up there."

"Shut up," Peter muttered.

Relief flooded his chest as he reached the end of the ledge. Another sliver of lightning illuminated the sky, and a familiar symbol—three intertwined circles—lit up above him as clash of thunder hit. Bracing himself, Peter slapped his hand over the symbol. Tiny needles slid out of the indentation and siphoned blood from the brand on Peter's palm. Finally, they were in. Peter glanced at Angel, and his chest tightened as regret began to taunt him for what he was about to do.

"Something's happening!" Angel touched Peter's arm for balance.

The rocks moved and shifted, and an oval-shaped crack appeared, morphing into the shape of a door. Slowly, it sank into the ground.

"We have to jump in!" Peter swung his foot forward, then stopped as one last wave washed the sand washed away. The protruding spikes sank, making the ground safe to walk on again. "Never mind. Just follow me."

"To the ends of the Earth!" Kyle called.

"Smartass." Peter shook his head.

Ignoring the frequent urge to punch Kyle in the mouth, he reached back and grasped Angel's hand, then pulled her into the dim hallway. The others followed. Kyle allowed Argia to lean on him as she limped in and steadied herself against the cement wall.

"So...where to now?" Angel gave Peter's hand a squeeze.

He kissed it, not wanting to ever let her go. "I don't know yet."

A groan of movement sounded around them, and the door slid

back up and into place. If not for the beveled glass ceiling that seemed to capture the glow from the lightning flashes in the distant skies, the place would have been in complete darkness.

The wall opposite where they stood started to turn. The floor rumbled slowly, moving them in a circular motion around the middle wall. They tried to reach out to brace themselves, but the floor moved faster with each passing moment.

"Whoa!" Kyle pulled Argia close to him. "What the...?"

"We're sinking, spinning!" Peter suddenly recalled that the place was underground. "Just hold on." The space around them grew darker and darker.

"It's so dark, Peter." Angel's hand went to her forehead. "I'm getting dizzy." Her head dropped against Peter's chest; her arms tightened around his waist for balance.

Peter put his strong arm around her shoulder. "Just close your eyes. It'll stop soon." He hoped it was true, because his own stomach was churning. It wasn't just about the impromptu psychotic carousel ride either; they were in the stronghold, the place where the weapons were stored, along with the answers that would turn around the building war with the Extraho of Obscurum.

Finally, the movement stopped, throwing the dizzy kids into the wall.

Peter's knees buckled, but he held his balance. Angel's grip on his shirt tightened. He felt her shivering. "We're good now...safe." Peter stood and held her close.

All around, the room emitted several clicking sounds and lit up. The cement wall they'd held onto separated in several places, revealing a wall of thick glass as it sank deep into the floor.

Angel released a sigh, steadied herself, and pushed away from Peter. "I'm okay now." She gave a hesitant smile and turned to the wall in front of them.

An audible gasp came from Argia. "This is amazing. Is it glass or what?" She poked her finger out to touch it, but he stopped her.

"Don't! Everything here is booby-trapped. I have to deactivate it." He only hoped he could, because he didn't want to do anything that would keep them from getting inside. "Let me think." Nothing came to mind, so he did what he'd done before to get into hidden places: he slapped his hand against the glass.

Everyone felt a ripple, and a small pin-sized blue light traced his hand. A chill lifted to meet the symbol branded in his palm, and the glass wall shifted.

"It's moving!" Argia uttered.

"Amazing." Angel hopped up and down. "We did it."

Peter nodded as the thick glass barrier rose, sliding into the cement wall above. The room was flooded with light but was completely empty and white.

"Okay, uh...not what I expected." Kyle cleared his throat.

"Never satisfied." Peter snorted and stepped forward, leaving the concrete slab from the hallway to step onto the white floor. The moment his foot touched it, lines of blue lights sprouted from the walls, and strange symbols lit every inch around them. At the far end of the room, a door opened.

Peter turned to take in a full view of the room. He flexed his hand, and the brand reminded him of what he was there to do. He lifted his hand and willed the light to come forth, the only time he'd allowed himself to do so without the threat of a demon near.

"What are you doing?" Angel asked, curious.

"Hopefully, something that'll tell us what these mean," Peter answered.

The tugging and pulling in his stomach indicated the light was seeping out of his hand. This time, it wasn't a weapon but something else. It glowed, widened, and thickened, until Peter could read the etchings on the wall. He saw visions of angels, who stood like giants herding demons with various weapons from the future, past, and present.

"I don't see anything," Kyle said with a frustrated snort. "I'm gonna have a look around while I dry off."

Argia limped behind him. "Wait for me. I'll go with you."

Kyle slowed a bit but didn't turn to answer.

Peter shook his head and let his hand fall. He raked it through his thick curls, sad that no one else had seen what he could.

"I saw it," Angel whispered. "The angels looked like warriors. Is this a warning, Peter?"

He pivoted. "Yeah, but why start listening to them now?"

Angel shook her head. "I don't know. I have this feeling of something looming over me. I can't explain it, but there's just this fear, like something bad is gonna happen if we go through with this. Mostly, like something bad is gonna happen...to me."

"Look, Angel, I know a lot of horrible things have happened. It seems like we'll never get out from under this darkness, but we will. Just hang with me on this, and we'll fight our way out together." His heart clenched at what he wasn't telling her. He wanted her forgiveness for a wrong he couldn't name, but for the time being, all he could do was bend to kiss her.

Angel clung to him, deepening the kiss in desperation, as if seeking more, as if she was seeking a haven, a safe place to bury her fears. Peter tried to give that to her; in that one kiss, he tried to be everything he wanted to be for her. He longed to be her hero, her shelter, her protector, but he knew that in the end, she would be his. Whether she knew and understood it or not, Angel's blood held the answers that would show them how to fight the beasts tearing through the barriers of Hell.

Angel yanked away, breathing heavily, with tears in her eyes. "It's just too much. Part of me wants to stay here forever, to never go back to what I saw out there, to never, ever have to worry about Gavin Steele or the Extraho of Obscurum getting us again." She stepped forward, tracing her hand over Peter's lips. "I don't ever wanna be away from you again, Peter, not ever."

Peter smiled, leaned forward, and hugged her to his chest. It wasn't necessarily to comfort her; it was more because he couldn't bear to lie to her face. "We could, but we have to find answers first, at least look for something to share with the Decretum Venia so they can fight this."

"You don't mean it. I know we'll have to go sometime, but can we just wait a little while?" Her arms tightened around him.

"Yeah, we can. Let's find someplace to sleep, at least for tonight." Peter grasped her hand. He could give her one night, just one, before he revealed the horrible mistake he'd made to save her.

CHAPTER 45

Peter's eyes darted around as they passed through the doorway, leaving the white room behind to step into what resembled a cave. Rock formations curved upward, and stalactites hung down like some sort of ancient interior decorator had put them there. Hues of bronze and gold and sprinkles of silver gave the place almost an otherworldly feel.

"It's beautiful here." Angel walked in a circle around Peter, a wide grin blossoming on her face.

"I know. I've seen it before." Peter's heart raced, and his hands clenched as he tried to relax, knowing it would be his last night of sleep before his heart would be ripped out from the pain he would have to cause the one who held it captive.

Angel grabbed his hand, pulled it to her lips, and kissed it. "Thank you for bringing us here, for trusting me to show me this." She shook her head. "For all those years, my father told me stories of the Decretum Venia and how sacred and special our blood is, but I never imagined we'd have the right to see a place like this."

"We don't have the right." His guilt weighed heavily on him, but Peter pushed it away and pulled her small form into his arms. "Opening these sacred places wasn't the best route to take. They were meant to never be reopened. Before, they were safe and completely unknown, but now Gavin knows about them. He knows there are many, and he won't stop until he's found them...and us."

"He won't find us. We'll find a way to save the Decretum Venia from him."

"It's not just about him. The Order of Dragon are nephilim. *Unlike* us – we were never born from the raping of humans. We were scientifically engineered by the Angels with specific traits of theirs paired with ours. That's why the Order of Dragon's human and demon mixed slaves have no power like ours. The Creator of All didn't give them any. The offspring of the Order of Dragon connected with the demons they've been sending after us through visions and psychic-induced possessions. I'm a beacon, Angel. Like Argia said, they can smell me." Peter released her to wipe his hand down his face. "I'm not supposed to be here. I never shoulda left the orphanage where Pastor Finn hid me and the others, but I was stupid and snuck out every chance I got."

"You didn't know." Angel's pale fingers tugged his chin down. "The time for blaming ourselves is over, right? I pushed you away, the first boy I ever loved, because I didn't want to tell you what they did to me. I didn't think you'd want me after that. I was so...scarred."

"How could you think that?" Peter groaned. "I guess we've both made mistakes, but what I wanna know is, will you love me if I keep making them? I've got no one else, Angel. I will never love anyone else like I love you. I'd die for you, to save you. Would you do the same for me?"

Angel blinked, a bit taken aback. "Why would you ask that?"

"Never mind." Peter ground his teeth together. Trying to prepare her would never work. After they slept, he would show her, and her earlier nightmares would seem like fairytales compared to what he'd reveal.

"O-okay." Angel studied him for a moment, as if she knew there was something he wasn't saying, but she didn't want to push him.

"Let's find someplace to lay our heads before Kyle and Argia find us."

"Agreed," she said. "I don't know about you, but I could use a little shut-eye and a few sweet dreams."

CHAPTER 46

What the place lacked in decoration, it made up for in color and carvings. Peter led Angel down the oblong hallway of rock, stalactites, and beautifully curved, smooth rock.

"Hello!" she called, her voice echoing on the walls.

"Sssh. We don't want Kyle to find us." Peter grinned and led her to one of the darkened curved doorways that stood twenty feet high.

"They didn't believe in doors in this place?" Angel spun slowly around, her eyes stopping at the angels carved on each side of the entrance.

"No. This wasn't meant for sleeping or sticking around for too long. It was supposed to be a hideout where they could get their weapons, heal the sick, and strategize for the next attack." He peered about at some clothing and boxes strewn around.

"The floor doesn't look comfortable. Maybe we should search in some of the other rooms for a better place to sleep." Angel squatted and rubbed her hand on the rock floor, then brushed the excess dust on her jeans.

"This is it. The others went ahead, and you look like you're about to fall down. We need rest if we plan to make it through this." Peter grabbed some of the tattered clothes and shook them out. He rolled them up and squatted to arrange them as a pillow, then lay down. "C'mere. You can lie on me, just for a nap."

Angel smiled. "I can't sleep, but I'll relax for a few minutes."

Peter anxiously waited for her to adjust her head on his chest. His hands sank into the silkiness of her hair. He closed his eyes, finally feeling a bit at peace. "Comfortable?"

"Yes, always when your arms are around me." Angel's hand traced a heart on his chest. "I'm sorry I had a weak moment and wanted to hide here for like...forever."

"You're not the only one who feels that way. We can't give into it. I can't. The repercussions are too bad." Peter rubbed her back; just having her close helped calm his edginess.

"It's just sometimes I feel like this is a nightmare and I'll wake up and see my parents again."

"Oh, it's a nightmare. One we won't wake up from, but we can fight under from. But we'll never be the same as we were before. I'll never be the same." Peter's squeezed his eyelids shut as he willed the dark hue of his mother's comforting form from his mind. His father's memories, he pushed back since they were tainted with images of his watery death.

"Me neither. I was so stupid. I thought I was fierce when I first got away from the killers who murdered my parents—until I met Gavin."

"Gavin's different. A sociopath or something that's controlled by a demon."

"Is he? It seems to me he was pretty bad before the demons came along. My father worked for him. His job was to observe and report what Steele Industries was doing to the Decretum Venia. I think he got too close, that's why Gavin wanted to kill him."

"I think the guy just enjoys killing. It makes him feel powerful. Almost like a god since he has the power to kill at will. I just never thought men like him actually did the killing; I thought they ordered others to do it."

"No, Gavin does the killing. I think he's just picky about it. He prefers killing women. His brother Lucien, he kills kids."

Peter swallowed the ache in his chest at the fear that Angel had been with them long enough for them to hurt her, but now he knew they would've killed her if he hadn't gotten there in time. "They didn't get you."

"No. For some reason Lucien said his need to kill left when he was around me. I felt sorry for him."

"For a murderer? Why would you feel sorry for him?"

Her hand clutched his damp shirt. "I don't know. He just seemed abused and trapped into his brother's nightmare."

"Makes me wonder who's more evil, the demon or the man?" Peter snorted.

"The man." She snuggled close and within a few minutes was snoring softly.

Peter stayed still, holding her to his chest and wishing he could go back in time to when they were in another safe place. He should've stayed there. Now there was no turning back; they could be doomed, but if so, he wasn't going out without a fight.

What am I doing? Peter mentally battled his thoughts. "Killing Gavin Steele wouldn't end this."

Angel shifted, and in a husky voice whispered, "No. This is bigger than him, but killing him will stop a lot." She yawned. "Do you think he's already dead? You said you thought he was after you saved me."

Peter rubbed his eyes with his fists. "I hoped so. But what's happening now proves he's alive. When I came to his beach house to save you, I swore I ripped the demon out of him and sent it back to hell. I didn't stick around to find out."

"Why? Oh, yeah, the place was on fire."

"Yeah, and someone from the Decretum Venia was working

there undercover. He told me to leave and tell the others what was happening."

"So Gavin's alive even though he hasn't been in public in almost a year? Lucien was running the company last I heard on the news."

"I know. Truth is, killing him would mean his death would haunt me for the rest of my life."

"As evil as he is?" Angel shrugged. "I've never killed anyone, but I did want to see him gone forever."

"Yeah, people seem to think that when you murder someone, you move on. Like on television or something. Well, although Hanna didn't exactly die by my hand. I killed her with my actions. I'll never forget her. She's in my dreams, my thoughts—everything. Even though Gavin Steele deserves to be removed from Earth for all the people he's hurt, if I kill him he'll haunt me for the rest of my life."

Angel's fingers gripped Peter's shirt. "He haunts me." She slid her arms around him and hugged him hard. "Gavin isn't human, Peter. I've seen his evil up close. He's got dead eyes, cold and sinister. When he touched me, I felt dirty deep in my soul. I can't explain it but I never want to see him again—unless it's to destroy him."

"I know you will be able to one day. But are you able to deal with what's left behind when you do?"

"I don't know," she sighed, "and I don't care."

They slipped into a reflective silence. Peter couldn't let it rest. He had to know how bad she wanted this, because the next step would change her forever. Not only her, but every child under the age of eighteen born into the Decretum Venia or Order of Grace. If he took this next step and opened the 2nd of the three books left by his ancestors, every last kid would die and be reborn with their engineered angelic DNA in full form.

"Angelica." Peter used her full given name. He did it in rare times when he wanted to get her angry. "You know if you confront him—or it—you may die doing so. He nearly killed you last time."

"I'm willing to chance dying if it means ridding the earth of Gavin and the Order of the Dragon. I'm scared, really scared, but I want that more than anything."

Peter's chest felt heavy. He'd given her a choice. One she didn't realize he'd even given her. Part of him was willing to leave the door to the unknown unlocked and deal with things the way they stood. Right then. Right there. In order to give himself peace.

"Fine. If you're sure, then there's something I've gotta show you."

CHAPTER 47

Loathing seeped from Gavin's gaze as he studied his brother's rigid form across the desk. He held him there by the power emanating from him, now an easy feat. Balaal, his demon lord, struggled within him, piercing his innards with his clawed body, inflicting pain that Gavin now craved with every essence of his being. The beast had once ruled him; Balaal's evil had consumed Gavin's mind even as he was a child in his mother's womb. Gavin had felt it then, cowered from it, until the depth of darkness smothered him and made him whole with it. Now, the twisted, sick, drumming of pain only fed his new addiction.

"Lucien, I will ask you one last time," he barked. "Why did you hide this from me?" Gavin was itching to rip his sheathed claws down Lucien's face, where beads of sweat were forming.

"It was Jack's idea. His demon wants what Balaal has." Lucien loosened his collar. He straightened and adjusted himself, appearing small in the large, dark leather chair.

"Keeping this secret from me is punishable by death, you know." Gavin couldn't stifle his cruel grin, for watching Lucien or any intended victim squirm aroused something in his soul. There was something about their writhing fear, something seductive.

Although his chosen victims were typically women, particularly those who favored his mother, he took a different pleasure in killing men, as it was often more challenging.

"I was trying to handle him myself, brother, to clean up the festering wound within the Order of the Dragon before it spilled over into the powerful position you now hold." Lucien seemed to hold a thought captive before he leaned forward with timid courage and continued, "Killing me will only make his demon master stronger, and it aims to use your intended wife as its host. Do you really want your greatest demon adversary so close, questioning what you've done with Balaal? He may see you as an easy target."

Gavin held no fear when it came to the lower demon that controlled Jack, for he had already found a way to control Balaal, a more highly decorated demon warrior. "He doesn't concern me half as much as my brother who attempted to deceive me."

"Gavin, that's just it. I am your brother, conceived to serve you and your best interests, or else be punished by the demons that meet me at my death. If I die before you, dear brother, there will be no other to protect you, and you will be even more vulnerable to the devices of others, even your intended witch of a fiancée."

Gavin didn't bother to dispute Lucien's words for he was only blindly reciting what they'd been taught since they were children, dumbly falling into the weak role he'd been groomed for. "Then tell me, brother, what is your choice? There must be punishment, Lucien. Surely you realize that in my new form, I'm willing to risk sending you to an early grave, simply for the pleasure it will bring."

Lucien gulped, trembling a bit before regaining control. "What is the other option?"

Gavin grinned, and his mouth almost watered at the thought of torturing his pathetic sibling. "Hell of the mind through ripping of the body. If you survive, you will live to serve me after the Transfero of Lux Lucis is powered with the blood of our enemies. The time is here. The time is now."

"But what of the boy? Jack's lead went nowhere. My men searched based upon that information, and they found no sign of Peter Saints."

"Your men? Pssh!" Gavin belted out a chuckle. "I don't need mere men to search out an angel spawn wrapped in skin. I rule demons now. Our enemies thought they were better than us because their angelic forefathers didn't rape human women the way ours did. Apparently, they took their time and concocted some way to utilize only the best, strongest parts of themselves, to hide that gene within their human hosts. Balaal's awareness of this and more was revealed to me when I merged fully with him, a process that began when Peter Saints walked into our trap and opened the first book of secrets."

"Secrets? I'm confused, brother. Do you not want the Saints boy because his blood must power your Transfero of Lux Lucis?" Lucien scratched the side of his face.

"That was my original thought, until I joined with Balaal and he held me within the hell of his body a prisoner. I listened closely to every insidious thought uttered in his mind, even macabre thoughts of the ways he planned to torture and eat me once he acquired his prize."

"So Balaal's plan was to trick Peter Saints into unearthing some treasure held by the Decretum Venia so the Order of the Dragon can steal it?"

"Steal it?" Gavin chuckled again. "There is no need for that, brother. With each step the boy takes to reveal more and more of the treasure, Balaal and all demons gain strength and knowledge that was once unrightfully hidden from them. All the boy has to do is find the treasure for himself, and it will also be ours."

"And where is he?" Lucien blinked rapidly and composed himself once again.

"He will come to me soon enough, and I will be ready for him. It will be the battle that begins it all."

"What? Armageddon on Earth?" Lucien slouched back in his chair. "That wasn't the plan."

"Not on Earth, brother. Armageddon will be taken to the gates of Heaven, and the blazing fires of Hell will rise on Earth. The angels will bow before me, not Balaal, because he and all demonkind will be mastered by me!"

"You're insane! You're human, while these things have lived since the beginning of time." Lucien shook his head, bracing himself against the desk with trembling hands that betrayed just how uneasy he was in the presence of his powerful and twisted brother. "These are only henchmen for the ultimate master. How will you deal with him?"

"I won't have to. His maker will destroy him for me. I am still part human, favored more than any demon lord. I will be wrapped in the blood of our enemies, my true nature hidden from those Angels that protect the dual plane we call heaven." Gavin forced out his talons. He jerked his head, allowing the painful release of his blended demonic human form. It burst forth, ripping through his shirt and jacket, and his elongated, serpentine tongue swiped across his face. Hunger to rip the doubtful head off his brother's shoulders raced through him.

Fleeing from an untimely decapitation, Lucien jumped up and ran for the door. "Witch! Witch, get in here...now!"

"She can't save you." Gavin's voice echoed around them, nothing like the voice of the weak being he'd been before. Now he held a power he'd only dreamed of. It was captured in the depths of his soul, held prisoner in his core and at his disposal, and there was no devil in Hell as thirsty for evil as he.

CHAPTER 48

With each step Peter took along the hallway, he pushed away the need to hesitate that plagued him. He had to fight through it, and with Angel's gentle pressure on his arm, almost urging him down the cave like innards of the underground structure, turning back at this time wasn't possible.

"Just over here." Peter stood in front of the dead-end of the long hallway that had veered off to the left.

"There's nothing here." Angel pivoted, looking at the stalactites that seemed to resemble an angel diving downward. "Wow! Check out the ceiling."

"Yeah, if you stare it a while, it feels like it's moving." Peter rubbed his hand on his jeaned leg before bringing the puckered brand to his lips and licking it. Closing his eyes, he slammed his hand against the wall. Pricks of needles touched every crease of his hand. He bit back the pain, letting the needles do the work confirming his DNA.

"How'd you know where to go?" Angel pulled his hand into hers and ripped off a piece of her shirt to wrap it.

"Don't bother, things are about to get much worse."

"You can't know that." She entwined their fingers as the wall cracked and revealed stairs leading down into darkness.

"I know because part of me has been here before, a part that was dormant in every male of my family. I didn't even realize it until I took a risk to save you." Peter released her hand. He didn't want to, but he felt like scum holding it, knowing what he was about to ask her to do. She had no idea what fighting Gavin guy would cost them, all of them.

"Strange. There's no echo in here." Her footsteps fell rapidly behind his. It was completely dark, with the exception of a dim flickering light that expelled from each step, as if her footfalls were stirring up a bunch of sleeping fireflies or static electricity. "I know there's more to see at the bottom of the stairs." Peter hastily made his way deeper, the place descended forever it seemed.

"Peter, wait, how'd they do this?"

Peter laughed. "They're angels, they know time from beginning to end. Anything we've known or will ever know. You can't underestimate them—or their bastard enemies."

"Look. Something's lit at the bottom." She tapped his shoulders from a few steps behind.

"I know." Peter hesitated, thinking he should come clean with her. Spill the nasty truth. But he pressed on, jumping down the remaining few steps to stand in front of the glowing stone podium.

Once Angel's foot landed behind him, the stairway in back of them went completely dark, and the light from the dais connected to the wall grew brighter, almost blinding.

Peter lifted his arm to cover the glare in his eyes. Even with its blinding light, none of it seemed to touch beyond the floor where they stood—as if the stairs separated the small floor from another room.

"Unbelievable." Angel ducked her head under his arm.

Peter hesitated. "Look," he groaned, "I have to be honest with you. If we proceed further, there is a price to pay for messing with this."

Confusion marred her expression. "I know. I told you I don't care."

"You should. I should. But I started this and there's only way to finish it, I just want to give you a choice. A real choice based on the facts and not just that I love you." Peter blinked back frustration at his mixed-up feelings. "My love for you consumes me. I need you like air. There's no one for me but you. However, if we do this, I may lose you forever, but we will always be connected in a way that would make what I feel for you now even stronger."

Tears gathered in her eyes. "I love you too but I don't understand."

"If we unleash this, the price could be your life. My price would be causing the death of every child under the age of eighteen who has the blood of the Decretum Venia."

Angel stepped away in shock.

He lunged for her and grabbed her arms. "God, please, Angel forgive me. I meant to give you a choice, but I was scared if you knew the truth you'd hate me. I'm so sorry, so damn sorry."

Her trembling hand pushed against him. "Wait, die? I die? You die...everyone?"

Peter nodded. "But we come back. That's the way it works. The change to our DNA constructed by our angel protectors was developed by one of their best scientists. The catch is, I had to open these books. Treasures that are like portals to the past."

"Why? Why'd you do it?"

"I chose to fight. To live, to see you again."

Angel's hands reached out and tugged his face down to hers for a kiss. "You shouldn't have."

"I had to. You're all I have left." He hit his chest with his fist.

"Let's do it. If this will kill Gavin and stop them, we have to."

Peter held her hand and pressed it to the flat top of the stone, then placed his next to hers. "Don't move, it'll hurt."

The stone cracked at the surface; the light moved, shifted. Up pushed a golden encased book, jewels decorated the top.

"Touch it with me, and brace yourself for more pain than you can imagine." Peter pressed his hand to the jeweled symbol first.

Angel's eyes never left his; she slapped hers down beside his.

The last sound Peter remembered was her blood-curdling scream.

Peter felt the difference in his body immediately. Everything seemed bigger, stronger, and more intense. His hand reached forward, and he felt a large, firmly muscled form that wasn't his own.

"Peter? Where are we?" a deep voice questioned.

"Here." Peter's eyes flew open.

A sooty scent filled the air, and dark clouds hung heavily, as if etched in orange in the moonless sky.

"Get up! They've attacked one of the safe camps the humans were hiding in," called another deep, sure voice from behind.

Peter's gaze landed on the dark-haired angel that grabbed his wrist, a stricken appearance of fear marring the being's pale face draped in ink-black hair. "Angel?"

"What's happened to me? I'm a..." She choked on the words.

"Male angel. Your ancestor had an Irish accent. You're now in his body. How'd you know this was me?" Peter helped Angel's twelve-foot tall male form stand. Devoid of wings, her ancestor still appeared fierce.

Peter knew he occupied his ancestor's form. Luke 23's armor covered a pale, blond form with the strong features that held more muscle and hair. Peter cracked his head to the side, trying to get used to his new body.

"I didn't, but I felt I knew you." Angel's formerly light voice was hidden in the tone of this deep one.

Around her neck, Peter spied the thin gold necklace that activated an invisible layer of armor. Using his last experience reliving his ancestor Luke's nightmares of the thousand-year war between demons and angels, he said, "Touch the necklace."

Hesitantly, her thick male hand touched it. "Whoa! It feels slimy, cold, from the neck down."

"It's armor was built by the angel who designed the DNA strain that started the Decretum Venia and the poison used to bring down the demons. But we need to find out about the weapons. Someone else made those."

"Who?"

"You." Peter turned with Angel as the magnificent angelic male behind him came forward through the dim, fog-lined cracked lands.

"Luke 23 and Michael 2—we need you to go with us to the gates. The demon army has killed many in the front. I believe I have a substance that will weaken them. Michael 2, I have your humans bringing the weapons you designed to the front of the battle lines. I know you said they weren't ready, but we have no choice. Our numbers are diminishing."

Peter spoke up, knowing Angel would be as lost as he in this dimensional slice in a time erased by the Creator Of All. "Use them. Michael 2's not himself at the moment. Go ahead of us, and we'll follow."

"Also, you must know, their dark cloud has grown, consuming all the warriors Michael 2 sent to retrieve Jakaan. We are tasked to save those captured behind the WALL OF ASH."

"Have you designed something for us to break through it yet?"

Peter asked. His eyes sent a quick glance at Angel, stuck in her ancestor Michael's form. Michael's jaw hung slack in shock.

"The poison I sent with Michael's first wave of warriors...was ineffective." The angel's dark skin was so smooth and black it almost had a luminous quality. But his white teeth were revealed as he smiled. "But I'm confident this next one will work. One of the woman from the forces returned to tell me what went wrong."

"How'd she do that?" Peter stepped forward.

"She's a seeker. They didn't see her coming. She was able to become invisible just inside the wall of Ash. They lined the wall with the weaker demons unable to take physical form. They poisoned the minds of the victims and drew them into the middle of the tornado of Ash from the hells of the earth and forced them into the depths of the hellonic realm."

Peter stilled. Those angels captured and taken to hell would be tortured and killed—never to be reborn again, never to go back to their master creator, but to be nothing. Unlike the humans they served, they had no souls. Once destroyed, they were gone.

"I know how you feel, but they knew the consequences and were willing to give their existences to saving their humans. We will get Jaakan back and beg our Creator for forgiveness."

Peter repeated the words his ancestor spoke to him. "We will. Now let's go end this battle so we can win the war." It was as if Luke 23 was in him, driving him here in this period of time that he recorded every word, moment, and nuance.

The angel smiled, his fourteen-foot frame towering over Peter by a few feet. With a nod at Michael 2, he led them forward.

Peter tugged Angel by the arm just as a thundering cry filled the desert-like terrain around them.

"Fight!" the other angel yelled with a wave of his hand. He drew out a long sword. "They've breached our defenses."

Peter's eyes met Angel's. "Do it with all you've got, and prepare yourself. These are some ugly bastards."

Within minutes, demonic forces pressed upon them. Demons of all sizes towered over them, darted beneath them. A slice of a knife at his back whirled Peter around. The demons faced him with teeth bared. The females had hair of snakes that hissed fire. Eyes completely black, devoid of light, and breasts covered in the skulls of men. Their copper snake-shaped bottoms clanked with each twist and counterturn away from Peter's sword.

"You will die at the hand of our master tonight," one hissed.

Peter stepped back and swung hard, burying his blade in the neck of one while a male demon charged forward, his red, bestial face framed by multiple jagged horns. He stabbed his fire-laced sword at Peter's chest, and it ricocheted off the invisible armor created by Michael 2.

"There are too many! Fall back!" one of the angels yelled.

"Take Michael 2 and get to safety!" Peter sliced through the neck of an attacking demoness. He kicked her decapitated head out of the way as he squatted and jabbed upward into a charging male.

"I can't. He's already surrounded!" His voice sounded distant, as though he'd moved away.

"I'll get him. Just go get help." Peter leaped into the air, he was thankful for his huge and powerful form, but he wished the angels of that time had wings. He sliced downward, into the neck of the demon whose back he'd launched on, then pushed harder to sever the head.

He darted his eyes around, searching feverishly for Michael 2 among the chaos. Angel's inexperience might get her hurt, and he had to find her quickly. He belted out a roar of rage as a swarm of demons closed in on him, pressing, stabbing, hitting, and pummeling him from every direction, with great force.

Then, once again, Peter succumbed to darkness.

∼

He woke on the floor near the stone podium, back in his own body and shaken at the attack and brutality forced on Angel. A shriek forced his eyes open.

Angel's body was levitating high in the air. Her hand was pressed to the golden book. Wings sprouted from her back, ripping through her baggy shirt. Tears streamed down her face, and she groaned in pain as the feathered protrusions tore through her flesh. Contorting in a most unnatural fashion, her body was bathed in light from above. The book was thrust against her stomach, then disappeared within her, as if her body had simply swallowed it.

"She accepted it." Peter knew at that moment that Angel had given her life to accept the knowledge of her angelic ancestor. Along with her, all the other kids in the Decretum Venia would perish, only more subtly, as if they were simply going to sleep. The adults would also gain power, though they wouldn't be as strong as their offspring. As for the traitors, they would quickly be revealed.

His mouth opened as he watched. The cuts on her arm spilled a dark substance before the wound closed, the flesh knitting together from some inner light. Each of the hundreds of cuts and marks wiggled with a small light before closing, rendering her skin smooth and clear. The tattered ends of her shirt hung off her body, barely covering her breasts and her back as she fell from above.

Peter jumped under her and braced himself to catch her. Even though she didn't know it yet, her supreme sacrifice had saved them all. He'd loved her forever, but if it was even possible, in that moment, he loved her even more.

CHAPTER 49

Peter held Angel's rocking form against his chest. Her mumbling grew louder with each passing minute. "Michael 1, Michael 2... I'll destroy them. Weapons! The weapons. No, no... My brother couldn't have. No!"

"Angel!" Peter shook her. "Wake up. It's all right. It's all right, baby."

Her eyes flew open, and tears leaked from them as she blinked. "No it's not. God..." Her shaking hand covered her mouth. "Lucien, Peter! He's—"

"Gavin's brother." Peter pulled off his t-shirt and put it over her head to cover her scantily clad form while tugging off the shredded remnants of her blouse.

"No, Michael 2 had a brother, a twin. He took Jakaan, the human, back to Earth. He never returned, but Michael 2 met him in battle with the demons. He turned into one of them!"

"Damn. What does that have to do with Lucien?"

Angel wrapped her long hair into a knotted bun. Peter helped her stand. "It's his descendant. That's why I felt...I don't know, like I knew him, or that he was familiar."

Peter led her up the stairs. "That doesn't mean he's any good. If

270

he and Gavin are related, he's a demon spawn. That's one thing I'm sure of, that hellish evil runs in the family."

"I know, but in a twisted sort of way, he doesn't want to be."

"That won't stop us from destroying him and his brother. They're in this together." Peter grasped her hand.

"I know." Angel's breathing slowed. "I-I can't believe it. You did that, went through all that, died to save me?"

"Yes, like you did just for me. Now we've gotta see what we can do to stop this before things get worse."

Angel took two steps at a time to keep up with Peter. "We can. I know where the weapons are, how they work. All of the Order of Grace descendants are activated, and I know how to communicate with them. Michael 2 created it all."

"I know. He did that and more."

"He was also like a brother to Luke 23, your ancestor. He made a promise that he'd always find you, to seek the place where his blood cries out. He promised to protect you since you'd never been a fighter...but the writer."

Peter's eyes moistened. He felt it, what Luke 23 felt at the time, alone yet honored to have a friendship that went as deep as a blood kinship. "He was the last of his line. All the Lukes before him were killed trying to fight their way into the Wall of Ash. He was the only one not wired to be a fighter. He wrote down everything in the hopes that history wouldn't repeat itself."

Angel tugged on his hand. "And yes, I felt that for you before we fell in love. You fussed about it, but I knew you'd never leave me behind or hurt me. Now I love you more than I thought I'd ever love anyone. You've saved me...and you are worth saving." She stepped up, pulled him down, and kissed him with a desperation and resolution as never before.

Peter lifted her into his arms and pressed her back against the wall; she wrapped her small legs around his. The hunger and acceptance he felt with her drugged him, fed him, and made him feel invisible.

"Uh-humph!" Kyle's angry interruption sounded, followed by a stomp.

Grudgingly, Peter released Angel. "You okay?"

Kyle adjusted a limping Argia in his arms.

"Fine, except when I find my roommate pacing and whispering, only to drop like a sack of potatoes to the floor."

"Sorry, man. I meant to warn you." Peter stepped forward.

Kyle stepped back. "Yeah, about that. What the hell did you do?"

"He'll explain later. I've got something wild to show you." Angel hurried in front of them. Her hands traced along the stone alcove they'd followed. With each curve or twist of her wrist, beads of lights formed on the walls.

"You heard her?" Peter followed, knowing Kyle was too curious not to obey.

Clicking, popping, and creaking thundered through the walls around them. Blue lights at the tips of the stalactites grew and illuminated the dim hallway.

"C'mon. The Command Center is up a level." Angel smacked the wall several times, and the beads of lights moved and gathered at her hand. The wall separated, revealing a stairway that led up.

"What's going on?" Argia stumbled up behind Peter and grabbed his bare arm.

"Do you feel different?" Her eyes had changed, gotten lighter.

She nodded. "Yes. The voices... I can control them better. The demons keep whispering amongst themselves. It's like... I hear them, but they can't see or sense me anymore."

"Good. We'll need that." Peter flicked a glance at Kyle, whose mouth was hanging open.

"Don't look at me, man. I don't feel any different, nothing actually." Kyle frowned. "It doesn't matter. I'm a half-blood, useless, like my father said."

"Man, don't pull this emo crap now. You know we wouldn't be here if not for you. There's a reason you're here." Peter slapped him on the arm. "For starters, you're my friend, and you are of the blood. You couldn't get in here if you weren't."

"I'll take that."

"Now c'mon. The girls are already checkin' stuff out." Peter twisted around and took the steps two by two, with Kyle close behind.

Peter liked Kyle, but he really didn't understand the guy. He was in a better position than all of them. Kyle wouldn't be hunted like them. Now that they'd opened the second book, they would be easily spotted by their enemies, but Argia and Kyle wouldn't.

The stairs opened, and Peter's jaw dropped a bit. The whole place blew his mind. The domed ceiling was black, with lights shifting within it, sparkling like stars. They continued moving until a slightly lighter gray revealed an outline of a world map. Tiny lights beeped and came to life all over the map. The walls were round, shaped like the bottom of a cylinder, but they were also covered with maps of old Earth to present day.

Peter watched with awe, admiration, and great respect as Angel swiped her hand across a portion of the wall. Several symbols appeared, written in the old angelic language of the being that had changed them to become human warriors for their cause.

"Come closer." Angel's Spanish accent hung heavy in her excitement. Her stance was sure and comfortable, no longer broken, the way she was after Gavin tortured her so mercilessly.

"What are you doing?" Peter placed his arm around her waist. When she smiled, he felt forgiven of all he'd done.

"Unlocking the weapons. We'll need them." Angel's fingers flew across the letters and symbols, as though she'd been aware of it all her life. "Here. Look! I can find the Order of Dragon creeps like this."

The white beads of light were replaced with red ones, and they outnumbered the white by about a third.

Kyle stepped up. "How is their army so much larger than ours? What are they doing?"

"Not many of us are needed." Argia placed a tentative hand on Kyle's arm.

Smiling at her briefly, Kyle bent his arm to grasp her hand. "Why not?"

"Because we are stronger," Peter added. He knew it was true. The only mistake he'd made was being impulsive and doubtful of his true purpose in all the craziness. "They're the most involved, but they easily manipulate people to do what they want, get demons to tempt and confuse them," he explained, then placed his palm over the symbol that matched his on the wall.

"How'd you know it was the key to unlocking the weapons?" Angel smiled as he pressed his branded palm down on the curved surface.

"Hanna wouldn't give me this mark for nothing. It meant something to her. She was like Argia and could speak to both sides. When she died, her blood created this brand on me. It was a gift. For a long time, I was angry at her. Now I'm...thankful."

A pulse went through the walled screen. The lights flashed, and the floor shook. Peter stumbled back a bit and reached for Angel, who leaned forward and placed her hand on each side of the drumming symbol resembling the one on Peter's hand.

Then it happened: a slim, gold rope necklace forced itself out of her neck, and then Peter felt a tingling sensation in his own before a thick choker chain rested at the base of his throat.

"What the fu...?" Kyle backed up, his eyes jumping from Peter to Angel.

"I-I don't have one—why not?" Argia asked, her almond-shaped eyes widening as Peter fingered the device at his neck. "Only the warriors had them, the ones who fought the demons. Spies like you didn't need them, because you could get in and out undetected, and could do things with your mind that worked better than the weapons Michael 2 created."

"Speaking of weapons, where is the rest of this heavenly arsenal anyway?" Kyle pivoted around the quiet room that was now lit only by lights in the crevices.

"Within us." Angel smiled. "We can create virtually any weapons we need, quickly and by thought, but they're only to be used against demon kind. Humans won't be harmed, though they will be rendered unconscious."

"What fuels the weapons?" Kyle leaned forward to touch the formfitting ring around Peter's neck.

Peter slapped his hand away. "Inner strength and energy, with a little imagination."

"What now?" Kyle asked.

"We make one call…to Rosa," Peter stated.

The Order of the Dragon was going to the hell they'd crawled out of. *Soon, very soon,* he thought, grinning from ear to ear.

CHAPTER 50

The rush of adrenaline pumped through Peter as he parked under the cover of trees just outside Steele Industries' supposedly secret compound. Some of the others from Decretum Venia were waiting within their cars. It was dusk and the moon was rising.

"They work fast." Kyle slapped Peter's shoulder and pointed to a spot next to an SUV. Rosa climbed out.

"She's here!" Angel hopped excitedly in her seat a bit. "Rosa made it."

Peter tried to hold his jealous irritation in place, because he knew she'd ask about Rob, his competition. Rob wasn't as much of a threat as before, but Peter would have been lying to himself if he didn't admit Angel might have trouble loving him as much after all he'd put her through. "Yeah...and she's comin' over to meet us." Peter got out of the car. When Angel muttered something about where Rob could be, his heart twitched in his chest.

Peter stood taller with each step he took toward the woman who was like a grandmother to him. Rosa's face lit with respect, hope, and love. It floored him how much he needed her approval. He only wished Pastor Finnegan was there. The man was the only father he'd known, and part of him needed him there for this final confrontation with the enemy that had been hunting him his entire life.

"Peter! You've done it—gave life back to the Decretum Venia. The Order of Grace will never be the same."

Peter bent to be smothered in her embrace. "I hope so. I thought I'd screwed up royally, ya know."

Rosa laughed. "Stop it! Pastor Finnegan said you slip into slang when you get riled."

Peter grinned harder. "He talked about me that much?"

"I sure did, son," said the deep baritone, authoritative voice of Pastor Finnegan.

A shiver of hope ran down his back. "I must be hearing things," Peter mumbled.

His gaze landed on the tall figure pivoting from the passenger side of the car. "You! God, I can't believe it's you!" Peter bolted around Rosa to give the man a huge hug. Tears leaked from his eyes, but he didn't care. He only cared about the feeling of safety and security when this man was around.

"It's me, the one and only. Surely you didn't think they'd be able to take out this old dog that easy, did you?" Pastor Finnegan patted Peter's back, then leaned back and reached up to grasp Peter's jaw. "You've grown taller, and you're thicker than when I saw you last." He coughed. "S'cuse me. I'm still recovering from broken ribs."

"Dad..." Peter's voice broke, "can I call you that, Pastor Finn?"

Pastor Finnegan smiled at him, his eyes watering. "I'd be honored...son."

Rosa came up behind them. "About time, you old coot! You should've asked him to call you that years ago. Maybe then we wouldn't be in this mess."

"Hush up, Rosa." Pastor Finnegan grinned. "We can't change

past mistakes. But we can fix them, right?" He reached up and ruffled Peter's curly mane.

"Yeah, we can. So much has happened. Like I told Rosa on the phone, we need to destroy the machine. But they will make it harder for us. Their demon-masters are stronger. Argia said she can hear them clearer now. They're planning something—something big, and it centers on that machine. And, get this. Gavin—he's awake, and alive."

Pastor Finnegan held up a hand. "Gavin Steele—something's wrong with him. The guy, he's—"

"Got a demon in him. I know, I pulled it out and sent it back to hell," Peter spat.

Pastor shook him. "No, son! Listen, Gavin Steel is a demon...a man, something—but definitely NOT human."

Peter frowned. "That doesn't make sense. I pulled the demon out of him."

Angel placed her hand on his back. "Maybe they did something to reconnect them."

Rose snorted. "They did the sacred ceremony. The witch did it. Our spies on the inside reported it to the Elders, the ones that are with us. But now Peter, since you've uncovered this secret, we know the identities of the enemies within the Order of Grace. Their treachery has been revealed."

"What do you mean spies? Sent by the Extraho of Obscurum?" Peter asked.

Rosa nodded. "Yes. Just like us, they've sent their own to spy on us. However, when you changed us by opening this new treasure, we can look at each other and see who is with us. They don't have to be of the blood of Decretum Venia, but their hearts are pure, and souls are loyal."

"This means that those who stir up all the trouble in the Order have been revealed, and are being dealt with," Pastor Finnegan added.

"What about those we sent to spy on the Extraho of Obscurum?" Peter felt sick thinking about the man who'd helped him escape the Extraho of Obscurum's compound at Gavin's house.

Argia giggled. "They'll never find them. They're all like me."

Rosa nodded. "She's right. Argia and I have a similar talent. That's why I worked with her when you brought her to the hideout. I've trained others like her to be our spies. We go undetected by demons and humans. It's been that way for centuries. We'll never be discovered unless we grow ill. Even then it's difficult because we each have an anchor—just like us—who watches out for us."

Argia smiled. "Rosa has been mine."

"Yes, and you two have been up to some interesting things since you left me."

Other kids gathered around them. Gil had gotten a haircut. His once misshapen bush was cropped close to his head.

"You. I never thought I'd see you again, but the other night, I dreamed I fought with you, side by side. It was crazy! Insane!" Gil laughed and reached out to Peter.

Peter balled a fist and tapped down on Gil's. "Are you ready for this?"

Rob's blond head stepped through the crowd, stopping in front of Peter. "Hey. You forever have my gratitude. Thanks for giving me the power to fight those bastards. Now I will become their nightmare, as they were mine."

Diana wrapped her arm around Rob who smiled down at her. Peter wanted to belt out a howl. Rob would no longer be a problem for him. Diana had her hooks in him. The way they looked at each other—they were an item.

Pastor Finnegan cleared his throat. "The people we have on the inside will disarm their security system in about two hours. We only have a small window of time to breach the gates from these locations." He handed maps to everyone. "Study them well.

Peter, you take a group and hit the main mark. That's where the machine is. Everyone else, go to the truck over there, grab some of the explosives, and plant them. Then get out of there to the safe place here. Rosa and her group made it so no one working with the Extraho of Obscurum will be able to pass through her psychic barrier without being blown to pieces."

Peter soaked in the directions Pastor Finnegan rattled out, never feeling better about any other mistake he'd made in his life. This one would save them all, would renew them.

"Are you ready?" Angel grinned at him.

Peter's heart stopped at the awakening power within her. "Yeah, let's roll out!"

CHAPTER 51

Peter led Angel and the others through the dense shrubbery and trees that bordered the back of the compound. They had committed the map to memory and burned it, and Angel had explained to the others how to initiate their weapons to use against any demons that might attack.

Peter patted one of the guns Pastor Finn handed him in case they had to fight off any guards, even though their informant had mentioned that the security system on the building that housed the Transfero of Lux Lucis machine was mainly computerized.

Angel crouched beside him. "There it is, Steele Industries. You want me to go through first?"

Peter narrowed his eyes, noting the guards at the front entrance and the shadow figures of the demons standing behind them. Almost mimicking the movement of the guards protecting the abomination, the demon's fire-licked eyes searched as if they expected someone.

"Yeah, what's the plan?" Kyle asked, gun in hand.

"I'll go with her. I got a feelin' they're waiting for me anyway," Peter answered. "Cover me and Angel."

"If you go out there, Peter, I can't hide you from the demons. They'll know you," Argia warned. "But if I go first—"

"No." Peter threw the word over his shoulder as he squeezed through the opening in the fence. "For once, just listen to me and stay here," he whispered. He stood tall and kept his hand on the gun in the pocket of his jeans.

The guards turned their gazes on him, then stood there in shock for a moment before they pulled up their guns.

Peter stood his ground as the door to the facility opened. He gulped, stumbling back when Gavin Steele a tall, blond, ruthless figure, stepped out of the door. A posse of smoke-shadowed demons flooded out behind him. Peter swiped his hand on his neck, and the golden rope popped out. Instantly, his lower body was covered in a transparent shield. He sliced his hand down, and a glowing sword extended from his fist.

"I see you've been playing with your new toys. Well, so have I."

Gavin flicked his wrist and the demons of ash turned to flesh within the blink of an eye. Their once-ashen bodies were covered in spots of flesh, copper pieced-together armor topped by their beastly heads flanked in multiple horns. The fire in their eyes died into a depth of dark emptiness that reached into a person's soul.

Power drummed inside Peter as though it was hungry for the age-old fight. He grinned. "I killed you before, I'll do it again, Balaal," Peter spat.

Gavin wiggled his finger. "It's not Balaal you need to be afraid of, boy." A growl rose from deep in his chest, and with it, his dark, tailored suit ripped. With a jerk of his head, flesh tore, teeth grew, horns ripped through. He threw his back. An agonizing roar sounded in the air at his transformation from man, to demon-man.

Peter raised his sword high, narrowed his eyes, and searched for the demon within Gavin, but all he saw was the white skin of a man that covered the body of what appeared to be the warrior demon Balaal, with three horns on each side of his patchy blond head. His hands were now clawed and pale, equipped with red-tipped talons, and his teeth were jagged and pointed. Blue eyes stared at Peter, eyes full of madness, evil, and an insatiable hunger for pain, blood, and death.

"Kill it!" Angel charged. She held a glowing sword above her head. She snapped back, and beams of light whipped out and wrapped around Gavin with sharp, cutting tips.

"No!" Peter yelled.

In an instant, droves of lesser demons flooded from the entrance, breaking the door right off its hinges as they pushed through. Some were made of flesh, others of ash, but they were all crazed, hostile, and bent on destruction.

Angrily, Peter cut, punched, and kicked his way to Gavin and Angel. So many monsters poured out of the building that the crowd forced Peter and the others backward, farther from the entrance. Demons crowded Peter's path. Roars and yells hung in the air as he sliced down one demon, only to be jumped from behind by another.

"Argia! Do something!" Peter yelled.

Argia screamed. The demons stirred into a frenzy as if her voice drove them insane.

His eyes narrowed as he ducked a clawed attack. The demon's eyes blazed as its red claw ripped again and again through the air. Peter ducked, dodged, then kicked the thing in the knee. He braced himself for a return blow as smaller demons seized him from behind.

Violent scratches came at him in unending succession, but even the sharpest of their claws had little chance of grazing his flesh, thanks to the protective shield. Unfortunately, he felt his protection weakening against the onslaught. With a roar, Peter whipped his arm through the air, creating another shield to protect his face and head.

Peter went berserk against the throng of beasts biting at him and jabbing with their knife-like fingers. His branded hand throbbed. A blast of light burst forth, disintegrating a multitude of the ash demons and burning the flesh-covered ones clear through. Some wobbled as half their bodies completely disappeared. Peter spun around, cutting them through with his sword.

With the way clear, Kyle's frightened eyes met his. He pointed his gun, shooting consecutively at the demons behind Peter.

Ducking, Peter yelled, "Get to the safe place! I can finish them."

"Not without you, dude." Kyle pulled another gun from his belt. "Angel's surrounded."

"The others..." Peter punched and stabbed at a demon charging from the side. He flexed his fists and sharp needles of light poured out, landing in the eye of one demon and the neck of the other.

"The others are going after the missing kids." Kyle finished them off with several shots through their eyes.

"Get out of here! I'll get them," Peter ordered.

"But Argia." A flash of remorse flittered over Kyle's face.

"I'll make sure she's safe. Warn the others!" Peter punched through his shield, making it disappear as he pierced it with a glowing knife he threw at the demon charging behind Kyle.

"I trust you! Don't let her die." Kyle ran, gunshots ringing in his wake.

Peter sprinted, stopping here and there to cut down an ash demon. He ran past Gil, who was fighting demons with a vengeful roar Peter didn't believe possible.

Gil signaled him. "Angel's close to the door! But the big demon is fighting her. Argia and I can handle these weaker ones. Go!"

Peter cleared through the break in ash demons, sparing them in order to save Angel. Sliding to a stop, Peter's eyes landed on her back. She was surrounded by thick red demons and facing off with a female demon whose snake-covered head spit fire with each hiss of her sharp snake-like tail.

Peter assailed them from behind. Pulling every ounce of strength from his chest, he raised his branded hand and screamed, "Die!"

The fighting behind him seemed to intensify and, without seeing it, Peter knew some of the others had arrived and picked up the fight. It gave him strength, hope.

Gavin stepped through the crowd of demons surrounding Angel and Peter. Angel glanced at Peter and lifted her sword higher with each step from Gavin, whose demented demon-human form's wicked stare stilled his demon-slaves.

"Peter Saints." Gavin laughed in a sickening hissing deep voice. "That's not all I have for you. I've got to thank you, though, for ripping Balaal out of me and giving me the power to control him."

Peter stepped forward, anger throbbing in his chest. "I don't care if you control him. I will destroy you."

"Strong words for a boy whose father I killed. Whom I manipulated into making me the most powerful being between earth and hell." Gavin's eyes trailed Angel, who was geared for attack. "And your friend, Angelica Ramirez, daughter to one of my former employers and confidants. I had the pleasure of slicing his heart in pieces as an appetizer at one of our Order of Dragon ceremonies. Tasty." Gavin's long pointed tongue slithered out to lick his pale chin and jaw. "But his daughter will taste even better. Balaal sampled her blood and it was spicy. Sweet."

"Die!" Peter surged forward, slicing down Gavin's bared chest. Dark reddish black blood seeped from the cut.

Gavin laughed. "Is that all you've got, boy? Perhaps I should show you what I've learned since we last parted."

The ground shook, rose, separated, and moved with such force that Peter stumbled backward to catch his balance. Thunder and an unnatural pounding tickled the ground beneath their feet. The land cracked in a circle behind Gavin, encircling the building within it, and dark, thick smoke forced its way through.

"What the...?" Peter mumbled.

"I don't know, but I have to stop him!" Angel shrieked in what seemed like pain, her hands fisted, her sword dropped, and piercing snakes of light poured from her body where her scars had been.

Gavin raised his hands higher. He roared, and the dark smoke poured upward to the sky that lit with rapid thunder. Spears of light from Angel rose and, in unison, stabbing through Gavin's middle.

Gavin yelled, "You're too late!" In a flash the thick, gray mass gained momentum and spun within the cracked earth like a tornado of gray murky cloud that held cracks of light within it.

"No! God No." Peter's mouth dropped in shock as he gazed upon the monstrosity that was the Wall of Ash. He couldn't believe Gavin was able to summon it from the very bowels of Hell, separating them from destroying the machine.

Gavin lunged forward and grabbed Angel. "Mine." He grinned like a greedy kid at a preschool toy box. He twisted her around and dragged her backward, toward the cyclone of darkness, so powerful that it ripped her hair out of its braids.

Furious, Peter attacked, waving his hand and forming a longer sword. He raised his hand and forced out a wave of blinding light.

Gavin staggered, loosening his hold on Angel, who fell to the side, only to be attacked by ash demons.

Peter dodged past her and ripped through the air, aiming his blade at Gavin's neck.

Gavin's hand jutted up; he held the sword a bay. "Yes!" Gavin's eyes lit up, as if he hungered for the fight itself, as if the combat and the threat of pain and death pleased him.

Peter smiled back, fed by the power within him, and made a fist with spiked brass knuckles, then landed a punch.

Gavin wore a shocked expression for a moment, but recovered quickly and grabbed Peter by the neck. His other hand pried at the thick gold necklace with determined precision.

Peter kicked, stabbed, and wrestled against the foul one's hold. Blood seeped from Gavin's wounds, but the demon-man refused to stop his determined attack on the band around Peter's neck. A wicked smile of teeth and tongue bloomed on Gavin's face as Peter's blood dripped on his fingers and Gavin ripped the gold band from Peter's neck.

Pain drummed through Peter's body. His protection was gone. He pushed forward with every ounce of will and power within him. Light flooded his vision, poured from him, and he landed punch after punch on Gavin's face and torso with his spiked fists.

Gavin smiled with each blow, as if he enjoyed it, and he retaliated by clawing Peter's face. Peter stumbled again. Every wound Gavin inflicted with his sharp fingers generated pain Peter felt to his bones, to his very soul.

Next, Gavin grabbed him around the neck, twisted him around, and forced him back toward the thundering tornado of the Wall of Ash.

"Get off!" Peter reached behind him and pulled at Gavin's horned head. He ran his hands down the man-beast's face and found his eyes. "Ugh!" Peter pushed into the soft tissue, forcing a grunt from Gavin.

Gavin jarred him and dove backward, into the darkness. "Your blood! It will fuel my machine, Peter Saints!"

There was no air. Peter was suffocating, choking on the thickness of death. Blinded by the darkness, Gavin's arm secured around his neck. There was a bump, then a hit, a scratch, a bite, and burning pain. Miniature demonites swam in the darkness, their glowing, fiery eyes staring at him, their dark, tadpole-shaped bodies racing through the murky depths to feed on Peter.

Peter struggled. His hands frantically searched for Gavin's eyes again. His chest heaved with exertion, but he mustered all his strength to press harder and harder at the fleshy orbs. Gavin's muffled yell gave him satisfaction and urged him on.

Suddenly, flashes of light forced their way through the darkness, scattering the demon slugs from their onslaught on Peter's body. Sharp strings of energy surrounded Peter, pulled at him, wrapped around him, and yanked at him.

Peter kicked back, pulled his head forward, and butted back against Gavin. Leveraging himself against Gavin's startled frame, Peter lunged forward as the ropes of light cocooned him, yanking him out of the cloud of darkness.

The ground came fast, and Peter hit face-first.

Angel's arms wrapped around his waist. "We've gotta go! Rosa gave the order to get to the safe place. I-I couldn't leave you."

"Thanks," he croaked.

Angel pivoted and yelled at Argia while helping Peter stand. "Do it now!"

Rosa and Argia stood, holding hands, eyes intense and expressions fierce, with an invisible force around them. They brandished wicked swords that pulsated with flying blades, easily downing the demons that attempted to crowd them. Thunder clapped around them, and thick clouds gathered. There was no rain, but the clouds grew thicker and reshaped, collecting above the two.

In unison, they sang louder than humanly possible. The glass-breaking pitch would have sent Peter to his knees had Angel not placed his hands over his ears. The ground trembled and quaked. A thick, transparent wall was constructed from beads of light that seemed to form out of thin air. The wall thickened, connected, and absorbed the thunder that raged from the sky.

"They're blocking them in, trapping them in a dimension between Heaven and Hell," Angel yelled.

The stray demons that weren't behind the wall disintegrated into thin air, shattered by the powerful voices of Argia and Rosa.

Men with guns stormed the area, but froze at the sight of Argia and Rose, whose skin glowed. Blood dripped from their ears, mouths, and eyes, falling to the ground in crimson droplets that landed like rocks.

"Now!" Angel's arms directed the straggling members of their group toward the trees.

Peter smiled and forced himself to ignore the soreness of his many injuries. He grabbed her hand and ran, not looking back. He practically dragged her with him, never stopping. His mind raced, his chest hurt, and his soul was weakened, but he wasn't defeated. *I'm alive. I lived, and I'll be back...to finish this.*

CHAPTER 52

Peter held Angel close, her back to his chest; he never wanted to let her go. His love for her was boundless, but now he was consumed by her, in absolute awe of her. She'd saved him, and he would never doubt her love for him again. She'd risked her own life to save him from the hell Gavin had threatened to drag him into.

A massive, thick cloud of thundering gray death darkened the skies, now encased within a transparent wall created by Rosa and Argia. Their wall of protection wouldn't last. He'd seen the same tactic before, in his nightmares of times past, a battle in another time. It would buy them some time, but it was not a permanent solution.

"I can't pull the demon out of the man," Peter mumbled. "He will get out."

"I don't know what's worse. Gavin seems more evil." Angel tangled her fingers through his.

"There's gotta be some way to bring the bastard down permanently," Kyle spat, holding his arm around Argia's shoulder as he rubbed absently on her arm.

"They are stronger," Argia whispered. "They won't stop till

they find you, Peter. I'm sorry, but you've made their master angry. He's trapped for now, but they'll help him find a way out."

"How can Gavin be their master? I don't understand. What did I do?" Peter asked.

Angel sighed. "I think when you saved me and weakened that demon in Gavin, the Order of the Dragon did something to bring him back. When they did, he imprisoned Balaal, and now he's somehow feeding off the demon's power."

"The Wall of Ash is hell on Earth." Peter fought back a shiver as he recalled his time within it. "I just made it past the surface, and it was awful. None of us can go in there and live through it."

"Maybe the Decretum Venia will have an answer," Kyle suggested. "They're stronger now, able to reunite since the enemies and spies were flushed out with Angel's discovery."

"I hope they can. If they don't, I will." Peter tried to be positive, but he had a sinking feeling that the only way to save them all was for him to finish it, and his bet was that things would get much worse before they got better.

THE END

A NOTE FROM THE AUTHOR

Thank you for reading Deviant Storm, book 2. If you have enjoyed it, please consider leaving a review. You can visit my Author page:

www.amazon.com/LM.-Preston/e/B002R7KUCC/

To stay updated on upcoming books, sales and new releases follow me:

Email: lm.preston@yahoo.com
Web: www.lmpreston.com
Blog: http://lmpreston.blogspot.com/
Goodreads:http://www.goodreads.com/author/show/3348681.L_M_
P
reston
Facebook: https://www.facebook.com/THE-PACK-by-LM-Preston-127604857259681/
Google+: https://plus.google.com/+LMPreston
Twitter: https://twitter.com/LM_Preston
Instagram: https://www.instagram.com/lm_preston/

A Note From The Author

DISCOVER THE NEXT IN THE SERIES
Fierce Tides,
Purgatory Reign Series book 3

Coming November 2017

For more information and updates on the series please visit
www.lmpreston.com

OTHER BOOKS BY LM. PRESTON

The Pack by LM Preston–

Teen, blind, vigilante on a mission to save the missing kids on mars.
Shamira is considered an outcast by most, but little do they know that
she is on a mission. Kids on Mars are disappearing, but Shamira decides
to use the criminals' most unlikely weapons against them—the very kids
who they have captured. In order to succeed, she is forced to trust
another, something she is afraid to do. However, Valens, her connection
to the underworld of her enemy, proves to be a useful ally. Time is
slipping, and so is her control on the power that resides within her. But
in order to save her brother's life, she is willing to risk it all.

Bandits by LM Preston –

Daniel's father has gotten himself killed and left another mess for Daniel
to clean up. To save his world from destruction, he must fight off his
father's killers while discovering a way to save his world. He wants to go
it alone, but his cousin and his best friend's sister, Jade insists on tagging
along. Jade is off limits to him, but she insist on changing his mind. He
hasn't decided if loving her is worth the beating he'll get from her
brother in order to have her. Retrieving the treasure is his only choice.
But in order to get it, Daniel must choose to either walk in his father's
footsteps or to re-invent himself into the one to save his world.

Wastelands – Bandits Series, by LM Preston – Daniel's doing the
unthinkable. He's planning to break into a prison to prove to his dead
father that he has changed, only problem is – he hasn't.

Flutter Of Luv by LM Preston–

Dawn, the neighborhood tomboy, is happy to be her best friend's shadow. Acceptance comes from playing football after school with the guys on the block while hiding safely behind her glasses, braces, and boyish ways. But Tony moves in, becomes the star running back on her school's football team, and changes her world and her view of herself forever.

Explorer X-Beta by LM Preston –

Barely escaping their captors, Aadi and Eirena are determined to save their dying friend. After their final confrontation with the species that tortured them, they've changed— unfortunately, not for the better. The changes caused by a terrible experiment force Aadi to accept the possibility that he may never be fit to go home, and that holding onto his sanity, or leading his friends to safety will end in failure and may rip his friendship with Eirena apart, forever. Time is slipping away and the possibility of losing his friend is not an option, but the foe that awaits them may be worse than the one they left.

ABOUT THE AUTHOR

LM. Preston is an avid reader. She loved to create poetry and short stories as a young girl. With a thirst for knowledge she attended college and worked in the IT field as a Techie and Educator for over sixteen years. She started writing science fiction under the encouragement of her husband who was a Sci-Fi buff and her four kids. Her first published novel, Explorer X - Alpha was the beginning of her obsessive desire to write and create stories of young people who overcome unbelievable odds. She loves to write while on the porch, watching her kids play, or when she is traveling, which is another passion that encouraged her writing.

For more information, please visit
www.lmpreston.com

THE PURGATORY REIGN SERIES